DELIGHTING HER HIGHLAND DEVIL

Time to Love a Highlander Series
Book Seven

by Maeve Greyson

ARE YOU SIGNED UP FOR DRAGONBLADE'S BLOG?

You'll get the latest news and information on exclusive giveaways, exclusive excerpts, coming releases, sales, free books, cover reveals and more.

Check out our complete list of authors, too!

No spam, no junk. That's a promise!

Sign Up Here

www.dragonbladepublishing.com

Dearest Reader;

Thank you for your support of a small press. At Dragonblade Publishing, we strive to bring you the highest quality Historical Romance from some of the best authors in the business. Without your support, there is no 'us', so we sincerely hope you adore these stories and find some new favorite authors along the way.

Happy Reading!

CEO, Dragonblade Publishing

Additional Dragonblade books by Author Maeve Greyson

Once Upon a Scot Series
A Scot of Her Own (Book 1)
A Scot to Have and to Hold (Book 2)
A Scot To Love and Protect (Book 3)

Time to Love a Highlander Series
Loving Her Highland Thief (Book 1)
Taming Her Highland Legend (Book 2)
Winning Her Highland Warrior (Book 3)
Capturing Her Highland Keeper (Book 4)
Saving Her Highland Traitor (Book 5)
Loving Her Lonely Highlander (Book 6)
Delighting Her Highland Devil (Book 7)

Highland Heroes Series
The Guardian
The Warrior
The Judge
The Dreamer
The Bard
The Ghost
A Yuletide Yearning (Novella)
Love's Charity (Novella)

Also from Maeve Greyson
Guardian of Midnight Manor

CHAPTER ONE

On the road to the Devil's Pulpit
Finnich Glen, Scotland
June 21, 2023

"I DEMOLISHED ANOTHER laptop." Jovianna Jacobs clutched the steering wheel, bracing herself for what would surely be an acerbic response from her mother, the remarkable woman who always insisted Jovianna address her by her first name.

Amaranth Jacobs didn't say a word. She simply drew in a deep breath and released it with a heavy sigh. But her fingers tapped a rapid-fire warning on the armrest of the car door. More was to come. Her reaction was building. She cleared her throat and appeared overly interested in the scenery flying by the passenger-side window. *"Another* one, Jovianna?"

"Go on and say it. Get it over with so we can enjoy our outing."

Jovianna's mother chuckled and shook her head. "You are so like your father. Absent-minded to a fault." She tucked a silvery strand of her thick, shoulder-length hair behind her ear. "I'm sure you realize that's the third laptop you've ruined in the past six months."

"I am aware."

"The board will not be pleased, and I'm not sure if I can sway them this time. You understand that?"

It was Jovianna's turn to unleash a heavy sigh. The dreaded board. Those who could either nurture or end her career as a professor of history specializirlg in Scottish culture at the University of Glasgow. The powerful dozen who had been more than kind and generous with her in the past. Of course, it didn't hurt that her mother was one of them and a well-respected alumnus who not only brought the university fame but also a fair share of donations because of her discoveries in archeology.

"What happened this time?" Amaranth asked with a subtle lift of her perfect brows.

"Mr. Walkersby couldn't seem to get the presentation to show on the overhead." Jovianna needed to keep the explanation dry, simple, and without emotion. Nothing but the facts. When her esteemed parent heard the entire story, she might very well wet herself from laughing.

"Mr. Walkersby?" Her somehow ageless elder frowned as though trying to place the name, then brightened with a wicked gleam in her eyes. "That quite handsome young man recently hired on as an assistant professor? The one with all those delightfully climbable muscles?"

"Amaranth."

"What?"

"Samual Walkersby is five years younger than I am. What would Father think if he looked down from heaven and saw you drooling like some kind of—"

"Careful, young lady," her mother warned, "and your father would be glad I was living life to the fullest and enjoying my time left here on earth. You know that as well as I do." She shook off the scolding with a twitch of a shoulder. "Now. What happened with the fine young Mr. Walkersby and the ill-fated laptop? Come now, tell Mummy."

Tell Mummy, indeed. Jovianna ignored the seldom-used endearment from her earliest childhood years and squinted to read the signage in the distance. The Devil's Pulpit. Not much farther. Thank goodness. They were almost there. At least while exploring the physically challenging gorge, *Mummy* would be too preoccupied with her footing to tease Jovianna overly much.

"Mr. Walkersby is a lover of coffee and always shows up at the lecture hall with a rather large cup." Jovianna didn't add that he also brought her the loveliest chai teas as well. That fact was not pertinent to the incident. "Unfortunately, he placed it on the stand beside the laptop."

"I believe the techs have successfully dried out a laptop or two," Amaranth said. "The physics department refuses to ban beverages from their labs. Are you certain it's completely destroyed?"

"Oh yes. Without a doubt." Jovianna cringed, bracing herself even more. "While trying to help him open the presentation, I knocked the coffee into his lap." She clenched the steering wheel so tightly that her knuckles popped. "And while trying to make amends by using my shirttail to wipe off his trousers, my bracelet snagged on his belt buckle and became quite caught."

Amaranth snickered and hissed like a teakettle about to boil over. "And then?" she asked while failing to regain her composure.

"He thought standing might make it easier for us to disengage, but when I backed up, my bum tipped the stand, dumped the laptop, and then I accidentally stepped on it." Jovianna shook her head. "They are quite wobbly when you stand on the keyboard. So much so that I stumbled and stomped the screen too." She risked a glance at her mother. "Destroyed. Utterly shattered."

Red-faced and her shoulders shaking, her mother exploded in a fit of laughter. "Oh dear, Jovianna. My poor, sweet fumbler. You are so like your father."

"Yes. You said that earlier." In fact, Amaranth always said that. Jovianna didn't understand why. She couldn't ever remember her father being as clumsy as she was.

She parked the car and was relieved to discover only one other vehicle was present. It seemed familiar, but she shook away the feeling as silly. It had been a very trying day. She wouldn't trust her instincts about anything at this point. But thankfully, there was only that one car. At least they would have the lovely gorge mainly to themselves and be able to enjoy the magical glen as if it were their own private sanctuary.

Amaranth patted her arm. "We'll work it all out with the board, sweetie. Don't you worry." Love and pride beamed from her. "Besides, if they try to let you go, I'm sure your students will rally behind you with another protest like they did the last time you were in danger of losing tenure. That was quite the impressive bonfire they lit that day."

Jovianna couldn't help but smile at the memory of a solid fifty or more of her students chanting around the raging inferno they started with the remains of the antique podium she had accidentally splintered to bits when she fell on top of it while trying to fix its wobbly leg.

That incident had been a near expulsion for her because the decrepit wooden stand had been a gift to the university from Dr. Grisham, beloved past president of the college, upon his retirement. "That laptop won't be much of a fire starter," she said while exiting the car.

"Probably not." Her mother shot a quizzical look at something behind Jovianna. "Isn't that your inimitable Mr. Walkersby?"

"Hello!" The familiar voice came from behind the only other car in the area.

Jovianna locked eyes with her mother, willing the woman to keep quiet about the laptop.

Amaranth's brows shot to her hairline as if she took that as a dare. She smiled the dangerous smile that always made Jovianna clench her teeth. "Why, Jovianna," she said in a loud voice while waving. "Look! It's Mr. Walkersby."

Before turning, Jovianna mouthed, *Behave,* then faced the handsome assistant professor. With a forced smile, she tried not to dwell on how impressively firm his lap had felt while she cleaned up the spilled coffee. "Samual? You didn't say you were coming to the Devil's Pulpit today."

"I wanted to surprise you." He flashed a nervously polite smile at her mother. "It's good to see you again, Dr. Jacobs. I didn't realize you would be joining Jovianna today."

"Obviously." Amaranth's gaze slid from the picnic hamper in the crook of his muscular arm to the bottles of wine in a cloth tote, then back to his face. "And do call me Amaranth. After all, Jovianna is Dr. Jacobs too. Less confusion that way."

His pale green eyes widened as if he suddenly realized the thoughtlessness of his words. "Forgive me, Dr.—I mean— Amaranth. I didn't mean to be rude. I simply meant that—"

She silenced him by lifting her hand. "Stop while you're ahead, Samual. No need to dig that hole any deeper. I know what you meant."

He lifted the basket and cast a pleading look at Jovianna. "I brought enough for three."

Poor Samual. Jovianna almost felt sorry for him. Almost. After all, his discomfort was his own fault. Several times now, and for a multitude of reasons, she had gently but firmly declined his suggestions that they get together during off-hours. They worked too closely at the university. Mixing pleasure with business was all well and good until something went wrong and made the workplace uncomfortable for everyone.

She relieved him of the wine, took it over to his car, and placed it back inside. "A picnic for three before we descend into the gorge sounds lovely. But I think water is a better pairing with lunch. The way down can be tricky." A glance at the increasing dreariness of the sky made her frown. "And if a storm blows in while we're walking the gorge, we'll need our wits about us. Flash flooding, you know."

"Too true." Samual scowled at the picnic basket as though he despised the thing. "Trouble is, I didn't think to bring any water."

"No worries," Amaranth called out as she popped open the back of Jovianna's Land Rover. "Jovianna always brings a case or two when we take our little outings. Staying hydrated is very important. My girl never forgets the lessons she learned on the digs."

"I didn't realize your historical studies included archeology. How interesting." Samual offered Jovianna his best smile in an awkwardly endearing sort of way.

"They don't, actually." Jovianna joined her mother at the back of her vehicle and added extra cans of water to her backpack. "But when your childhood is spent traveling the world with your parents as they unearth history, you pick up a few things." She held out a refillable bottle. "You can use this one if you like."

"Thank you." He took it from her and slid it into the over-sized pocket of his baggy shorts. "I already found the perfect spot. Shall we eat before we explore?"

Amaranth smiled, then nudged her shoulder against Jovianna's and lowered her voice. "Shall I feign an attack of old age so you can see about getting caught in his belt buckle again?"

"Stop it," Jovianna hissed before turning to Samual and waving him on. "You go ahead and set up. Amaranth and I have a few things to gather. Be there in a sec."

As soon as he got well out of earshot, she turned back to her feisty parent. "For the love of all things peaceful and good, will you please behave yourself? You know I adore our outings. Don't make this one memorable for all the wrong reasons. Please?"

Her mother shrugged, then held up both hands as though surrendering. "I simply thought you might like a lovely summer tumble with such a fine specimen." She leaned to one side and eyed Samual as he bent over to unload the basket. "Excellent hips. I'm sure his thrusting power would not disappoint."

"He is five years younger than me," Jovianna said.

"Your father was five younger years than me." Amaranth quietly chuckled. "That was a good thing, he always said. An older man would never have had the stamina I required."

"I think I just vomited a little." Jovianna handed the lighter backpack to her mother.

"How do you think you got here, Jovianna?" Amaranth swung the bag up onto her shoulders with the smoothness and agility of someone half her age. "Come now, sweetie. I would never say anything improper in front of one of your colleagues." Her smile somehow became a little more mischievous. "Now, I'm not saying I won't make him or you uncomfortable for the sheer pleasure of it, but you know I won't say anything inappropriate that he could use against either of us."

"I know." Jovianna slung her pack over her shoulder and locked up her vehicle, finding some small comfort in knowing that her mother would never do anything that would endanger their reputations or their careers. Amaranth loved to tease, but she prized their lifetimes of work and study for the treasure that it was. Jovianna nudged her mother as she fell in step beside her. "I agree he is a fine specimen, but work romances can be so very messy."

Amaranth nodded. "Indeed. Remember Viola, Meredith, and Herbert? Lost three excellent educators over that brouhaha."

Samual rose and gave a theatrical bow as they approached. "If you'll be seated, dear ladies, it would be my honor to serve you."

"My, my," Amaranth said as she swung her bag to the ground.

"Ever the considerate gentleman," Jovianna added, deciding a little flattery wouldn't hurt. After all, he had laid out quite an impressive spread of cheeses, fruits, and touchingly fancy crackers and biscuits. She felt sure that once the eligible females of Glasgow discovered him, he would soon forget all about her. He merely needed a little more time to settle in and get to know the area. "You did bring enough for three. My goodness, Samual. If we enjoy all this, we'll be napping rather than trekking through the gorge."

The man looked so pleased he almost glowed. "Nothing is

too good for the esteemed Jacobs ladies."

"The biscuits are divine," Amaranth said as she nibbled one while circling the rest of the plates. "I shall recommend you for immediate tenure, young man."

"I vote we eat just enough to hold us through the gorge, then come back and enjoy our fill to renew ourselves," Jovianna said. She knew if they ate too much of the richness spread before them, they wouldn't be fit to explore anything. Her napping comment had not been a joke. "What say you both? Save the lion's share for after we've walked a bit?"

"We can enjoy some cheeses and bits of apple," Amaranth said with an authoritative nod at the rest. "The high carbohydrates and sugary treats will serve us better later." She turned to Samual. "Do you not agree with Jovianna?"

"Absolutely." His tone of adoration almost made Jovianna choke on the cracker she'd just swallowed. "Whatever Jovianna decides is always fine by me," he added with a warm smile.

Amaranth circled the blanket covered in food again, nudging Jovianna as she passed. "God bless him, he has it bad," she said barely loud enough to be heard.

"Beg pardon?" Samual looked up from filling a small plate.

"She always says a blessing before she eats," Jovianna said. *"God bless the ham and don't let the cheese go bad.* I think she picked it up from a Scot. Didn't you, *Mother?"*

"Oh yes," Amaranth said while dutifully crossing herself. "A very virtuous colleague I once worked with on a dig in the Hebrides instilled the trait within me."

"Here you are." Samual held out a plate to Amaranth, then tipped a quick nod at Jovianna. "And yours is coming."

"Served me first," Amaranth said under her breath. "Wise young man, indeed."

"You promised to behave," Jovianna whispered.

"Did not." Eyes flashing with wicked merriment, Amaranth sauntered off while sampling the offerings Samual had put on her plate.

"I'm really looking forward to seeing the Devil's Pulpit," Samual said as he handed Jovianna her treats. "Never been here before."

"Finnich Glen is gorgeous." Jovianna selected a dark orange chunk of cheese, hoping it was her favorite cheddar. It was. "This is one of Amaranth's and my favorite spots to visit."

"Might I ask you something?" He glanced over at Amaranth, then leaned in close. "Have you always called your mother by her name?"

Jovianna smiled, noting that even though her mother appeared to be casually admiring the gorge and ignoring them, the sly old minx still stayed well within earshot. "When I was a surly bratling of about thirteen and thought both my parents were idiots, I decided to call them by their names to distance them and hurt their feelings. Much to my angst and displeasure, they both embraced the idea with gusto. Totally deflated my plan to torment them. After a while, I tired of the plan and reverted to *Mother* and *Father*." A self-deprecating laugh escaped her as she recalled that day. "Father couldn't have cared less what I called him as long as we continued our robust discussions during tea. Mother decided she enjoyed being called by her name. Said it not only made her feel younger but would make it easier to pretend she didn't know me whenever I was impossibly rude."

"I shall strive to remember her example if ever I become a parent." Samual finished the last of his apple while casting an admiring glance at Amaranth. "Quite the lady, your mother."

"That she is." Pride and love filled Jovianna. "I would truly be lost without her."

Amaranth returned, hoisted her backpack onto her shoulders, and gave them both a curt nod. "Let's go before the weather turns. A little rain won't be a bother, but if it pours, our day will be over before it's good and started."

"I've got the ropes," Jovianna said as she settled her gear in place. "Shall we show him Jacob's Ladder or take him down our favorite way?"

Amaranth turned to Samual. "Have you ever rappelled?"

"No." He eyed her as though suddenly regretting his decision to join them.

Pity for him moved Jovianna to take the lead and head for the precarious footpath of ancient stone steps that descended into the gorge. "Come on, then. We'll use Jacob's Ladder, and you can hold the rope there if it's still in place. But mind your footing. The rocks are wicked steep and will try to throw you. That's why some call them the Devil's Steps."

"Bloody hell," Samual said halfway down. "They get worse the farther we go."

Jovianna couldn't help but smile. She might be clumsy as a newborn colt in the classroom or out in public, but put her in the wild and she became as surefooted as a mountain goat. She filled her lungs with the primordial scents of damp earth, lush vegetation, and the indescribable ancientness of the area. Ages of legend and folklore wrapped around her like an exciting bedtime story. The whooshing gurgle of the rushing water urged her to hurry to come and play. Emerald moss and tangled snarls of vines and saplings welcomed her back, promising to hide her from the world and all of its problems.

"The water really is crimson," Samual said, his voice filled with awe.

"It's the red sandstone." Jovianna scooped up a handful of the crystal wetness and let it trickle through her fingers. "See? Not a river of blood, as rumored."

"Shame on you, Jovianna," Amaranth scolded. "Ruining the legend for the boy." She pulled a pair of telescoping hiking poles from her pack, extended them to the desired length, then twisted their handles to lock them in place. "I brought an extra pair, Samual. Would you like to use them? The shallows can be quite slippery."

"No, thank you," he replied, but didn't sound too sure.

"That means she likes you," Jovianna teased as she centered a headlamp on her forehead, tightened the strap, then clicked on the light. "She doesn't mind if I take a dousing."

"You two take this place quite seriously." Samual wiped his hands on the seat of his pants while eyeing their headlamps, walking sticks, and fingerless gloves with grips on the palms. "I thought we'd just wade around a bit and admire the rock formations. Is where we are headed that treacherous?"

"It can be." Jovianna resettled her poles and pondered suggesting that perhaps he should return to their picnic site and wait for them to return. She didn't want to hurt his pride but also didn't relish the idea of having to call for a rescue squad to helicopter him out of the gorge should he get hurt. "Did you happen to bring your biking helmet?"

"You're not wearing helmets." He looked from her to her mother. And whether it was the poor lighting or reflections off the water, he seemed red in the face, as if taken with fever. "Do you think I'll need one?"

"Helmets are where I toss caution to the wind," Jovianna said. "I simply don't like them." A light peppering of rain across the water gave her an idea. She pointed a walking stick at the staircase. "Looks like the rain's come early. You should save our picnic for us. Get it under cover." She fished her keys out of a side pocket of her backpack and tossed them to him. "You can put them in the Rover, if you like."

He looked both relieved and deflated as he caught the keys and started backing toward the steps. "I believe I will. Don't wait for me. I'd hate to be the reason you didn't get in the full walk you wished."

"Mind the steps, young man," Amaranth said. "This light rain makes them even more treacherous."

"Thank you, I will." Samual started up the already muddy walkway, then turned back and gave them both an embarrassed smile. "I'll have your treats waiting. Don't be too long."

"We'll be back before you know it." Jovianna offered him an understanding nod before turning away and moving farther down the stream. Poor Samual. No more worries about advances from that one. Not after emasculating him with Finnich Glen.

"We should be ashamed," Amaranth said as she caught up with her. "Poor boy."

"I know, but it's not like I invited him out here and then turned on him. I just didn't want him hurt." Jovianna used her poles to tap out the rocks under the moving water. The rain pelted down harder, as if scolding her to go back to the cars and apologize. Adjusting her headlamp to the highest setting, she tipped her face skyward. "Should we go on or not?"

Her mother glanced upward, squinting at the tiny patch of sky visible through the thick foliage meeting across the top of the gorge. "Hard to say. It doesn't look that dark. With any luck, it will blow over. I'd love to at least get to the Devil's Pulpit and take a picture to post on my birthday. I want folks to understand that age is just a number. Your mindset is what matters."

"Onward, then." Jovianna led the way. Her mother feared nothing, and it made Jovianna proud and determined to be just like her. The rain fell harder, sluicing down through the leaves. A soft rumbling of thunder in the distance gave Jovianna pause. Fearless was one thing, foolhardy quite another. She eyed the rising water and increase in bubbling froth as it dumped into the deeper pools and created swirling eddies. The Devil's Pulpit, the rocky outcropping that legends named as the place where Satan himself addressed his followers in the crimson-hued water, was still a little way ahead.

She turned and waited for her mother to make eye contact. Speaking was useless over the roar of the drumming rain and the swift water. Amaranth locked eyes with her, then gave a determined nod. The beam of her headlamp bobbed up and down with her decision to keep going.

As they worked their way through a narrow passage where the gorge's rock walls almost met across the water, they kept to the staggered ledges the current had left behind as it wore away the stone. As the route opened into the part of the gorge that was a shallow tumbling of water across a bed of colorful gravel, the strap of Jovianna's headlamp snapped, and it flew off her forehead as though shot like an arrow.

"Bloody hell!" Jovianna lunged for it, her hiking poles flapping from their straps around her wrists like awkward bracelets. She missed snagging it, and the headlamp rushed onward, caught in the fast current. Buoyancy had been a selling point to the expensive thing, and she wasn't about to lose it. She shed the walking sticks and backpack and wedged them in a tangle of saplings growing out of reach of the water. The thump of Amaranth's hiking pole across her rump made Jovianna turn and face her.

"Leave it! We should turn back." Her mother's eyes flashed with a rare emotion: worry. Jovianna's fearless parent was concerned about their situation.

An excellent swimmer, and knowing she could handle the familiar terrain, Jovianna motioned for her mother to start back without her. "I paid a bundle for that bloody thing. I'll not lose it the first time out!" She pointed up ahead where the headlamp had wedged in a rock shelf beneath the surface. Its brilliant LED light shone through the shadows. "I can reach it," she shouted. "The water's not that deep there. You go back."

"I will not leave you here alone!"

"Stay right here on the shoal. All right?" She waited for her mother to agree, knowing by the protectiveness flashing in her eyes that she wouldn't.

Amaranth took her backpack and poles and wedged them alongside Jovianna's. She waved Jovianna onward. "Let's go."

Jovianna disagreed, but they didn't have time to argue. A flash flood was imminent. She needed to retrieve the headlamp so they could backtrack and climb out of the gorge before the narrow passageway they had squeezed through became too treacherous.

With a glance and a nod at her determined mother, Jovianna kept close to the wall on the left. She sidled along the stone shelf that extended from the edge of the shoal like a long, thin arm. A shiver raced across her as the rushing stream shoved against her thighs. Even though it was June, the water was chilly enough to make her thankful she had packed extra clothes in her bag. If the ledge held out a little farther, she might reach the headlamp without a swim after all.

"Give me your hand," Amaranth shouted. "I'll hold you so you don't fall."

"I may have to jump in." Her mother wasn't a strong swimmer and didn't need to risk it. "I'll be fine," Jovianna shouted back with a reassuring smile.

"Do it!" Amaranth edged closer and caught hold of Jovianna's sleeve.

Jovianna glared at her but didn't jerk away for fear of making her mother fall. The stubborn woman needed to listen. Jovianna was both taller and weighed more than her petite parent. Amaranth needed to remember her physics. But arguing was futile. Jovianna relinquished her hand to her mother's surprisingly firm grip, then crouched while stretching to reach the high-tech headlamp that was also a waterproof camera and had cost her a month's rent.

As she looped a finger through the hook holding the strap, a gut-clenching surge of nausea hit her as hard as if someone punched her in the stomach. She threw herself back against the rocks and sucked in deep breaths and blew them out. Maybe that cheese had been bad. Bile churned upward, burning the back of her throat. She turned her head toward her mother and mouthed, *So sick.*

Amaranth clamped her free hand across her mouth and sagged back against the rock wall as though she was ill too.

They had to get out of there while they could still manage it. Jovianna hated to leave the light behind, but the gorge was challenging enough when the weather was good and they were healthy. Flash flooding and food poisoning could be a lethal combination.

She pushed up from her crouched position but fell back

against the rocks. Swirling black spots filled her vision as she turned away from her mother and vomited. A dizzying pressure squeezed her skull as though trying to crush it. The spots merged into blinding blackness. Muffled roaring filled her ears. She hit the water and found herself at the mercy of the current as it slammed her against the rocks.

Funny thing about sandstone ledges—not nearly soft as sandy beaches. Her head hit hard. The water swallowed her. And the blackness turned very cold.

CHAPTER TWO

The Devil's Pulpit
Finnich Glen, Scotland
June 21, 1760

TOBIAS RISK CROUCHED beside the Devil's Pulpit and rinsed the blood from his cheek. How dare that wee bastard try to shoot him in the face. All because he had stopped their coach to relieve them of their purses.

The cool water eased the sting of the wound that was naught but a mere grazing. The lad who had fired the shot best thank the Almighty that he'd been in a decent mood. Elsewise he would've returned fire and sent the youngling and his sire to meet their Maker.

Instead, as punishment for such insolence, he'd relieved them of their horses and carriage as well as their coin. The gentleman and his son might not agree that being abandoned on the roadside tied and gagged was a kindly act. But their family would. Their wise driver had seemed happy enough with being bound and left alive, too.

The memory of the pair's indignance made him huff with amusement and revive the stinging throb in his cheek. He splashed more of the water's coolness across it. The encounter had resulted in a fine foursome of horses and a newer carriage, as well as a fair bit of silver. Not a bad day's take at all. The annoyance of a wee scrape was worth it.

A strange rumbling from farther upstream, beyond the narrow pass, made him rise and draw his pistol. As a torrent of water gushed through the space between the stone walls of the gorge, he leaped to the top of the pulpit stone. What the devil could have caused such a sudden surge in the stream?

Something tumbled toward him through the waters. A flash of white. A rippling of color. A body. Nay, two bodies. He shoved his weapon back into his belt, jumped into the shallows to intercept them, then backed up as the waves strangely receded and left the pair draped across the stone ledge as if placed before him like an offering. Women. Clothed as men. Nay, not clothed as any men he had ever seen, but wearing strange, clingy breeks and tight bodices that glistened like the skin of an eel.

"Fitch! Cade! Down here now!" As he waited for his men, he eased closer and crouched between the women. He lifted the tangle of wet hair away from the face of the larger one. What a shame. Quite the beauty, with full lips, high cheekbones, and a delicate profile regal enough for any portrait. Blood oozed from a gash on her forehead. It crossed through a purplish knot running along her hairline. An ugly red scrape outlined her jaw. He eyed her chest, covered in the strange fabric. No sign of breathing. Poor lass. Already gone. Perhaps someone killed her and dumped her in the gorge to hide the evidence.

"Get away from her!" The smaller woman sprang upon him, surprising him enough to knock him off balance and send him sprawling back on his arse. She crouched over the lifeless beauty, pressed an ear to her chest, then rolled her onto her side. "Cough it up, sweetie. Your heart still beats strong. You must breathe deeper. Time to get those lungs cleared." She thumped the lass hard between the shoulder blades again and again. "Do it, Jovianna! Don't you dare disobey me. I can hear the water in there—now force it out! Now!"

Jovianna. Odd name for a woman. Tobias rose and offered a rare prayer for the still lass—even though the older one trying to get her to breathe sounded like an English. She also behaved as if she might be the dying one's mother. Only a mother would weep and rage while trying to save her child. Or a sister, perhaps. But the owner of a maid wouldn't care.

"Jovianna Lillian Jacobs—breathe! Do it now!" The old one sobbed, hitting and shaking the lass harder. "Listen to your mother! Do as I say!"

Tobias could stand it no longer. He took hold of the elder by the shoulders and lifted her away. "'Tis God's will, woman. Let her go in peace."

Baring her teeth like a cornered animal, she slapped him away, dropped to her knees, and started pummeling her daughter's back again.

"Who are they?" asked Fitch Macaslan, Tobias's trusted second-in-command. He frowned down at the women. "And what the devil are they wearing?"

Before Tobias could answer, Cade Maccolman, the oldest of their small brigade, eased around and knelt beside the mother. "I saw a man save a drowned lad once by holding him so his head hung down around his knees. The water gushed right out. Would ye like me to try that, mistress?"

"I am willing to try anything," the woman said, tears streaming down her face. "She is my only child, and I fear if I do CPR, I might stop her heart."

Tobias strode forward. "Tell me what to do, Cade. Ye dinna need to split open yer chest wound again."

The old Highlander scowled as if Tobias had just accused him of being half a man.

"Do ye want to tell Mrs. Gibb that ye ruined her fine stitching and started it bleeding yet again?" Tobias pushed around him and took hold of the nearly dead lass around the waist. He lifted her like linen folded across his forearms.

"Not like that," Cade said with an impatient growl. "Hitch her arse up higher so yer fists shove her belly up under her ribs. Wait!" He halted Tobias with a hand on his shoulder and turned to the mother. "She's not got a bairn coming, does she?"

"No. Now just do it." The woman stood there wringing her hands, her gaze locked on her daughter.

Tobias adjusted his hold until the lass's fine, round arse hit him mid-chest and her long legs draped down his front. The rest of her hung over his arm, limp as could be. For good measure, he jostled her up and down, hoping to shove the water back out the way it had come in.

A violent gurgling rewarded his efforts. Then she vomited. Hard. All over his boots. The poor muscles of her middle clenched against his arms as though holding on for dear life.

"Jovianna!" The mother alternately sobbed and laughed, patting her poor, heaving daughter's back all the while.

"Put me down," the beauty said in a rasping croak while batting at his knees. "Please."

He swept an arm behind her legs and righted her in his arms. "There now, lass. All will be better now."

She squinted her eyes shut in a tortured grimace as she clutched her head. "Bloody, bloody hell." She cringed as if the sound of her own voice pained her.

"Bring her over here," her mother said. She patted a moss-covered stone that, over the years, the waters of the glen had shaped into a perfect bench.

He reached it in two long strides and placed the lass upon it as gently as he could. "Donnor!" He cupped his hands around his mouth and bellowed in the direction he knew the rest of his men waited. "Blankets, and be quick about it."

"How many?" Donnor called back.

"At least two." Tobias eyed the lass where she lay curled on her side, hugging her head. "Or more. Whatever ye can find." They might have to make a litter to carry her up out of the gorge.

"What?" The mother bent closer to her daughter's face, nodded, then turned to him. "Jovianna asks that you not shout. I'm sure she has a concussion."

"How else can I help her? If I dinna shout, my men willna ken what we need to ease her troubles." Damnable English. Even their women had little sense.

A sudden leeriness fell across the older one as she gave him a long, slow up-and-down look as if seeing him for the first time. "Of course you must shout. Forgive me. I am an overwrought mother concerned about her daughter." She offered him a polite dip of her head and a smile. "I am Amaranth Jacobs and will forever be indebted to all of you for saving her life."

"And I am Jovianna," the lass whispered without opening her eyes or letting go of her head. "I appreciate your help too."

"And you are?" Mistress Amaranth moved closer and held out her hand as if she thought him a merchant and wished to honor a pledge by shaking hands.

"*Diabhal Dubh-Chridhe,*" he said out of habit, knowing they wouldn't understand Gaelic and think it merely his name. And it was the name he used whenever he and his men robbed wealthy travelers. These two were English and could not be trusted. At least not yet. He did not take Mistress Amaranth's hand.

"Black-Hearted Devil?" Mistress Jovianna repeated in another rasping croak while barely cracking open an eye. "Your mother actually named you that?"

Fitch snorted, and Cade barked out a laugh.

Tobias shot them a hard glare before turning back to the women. "Ye are English yet ye understand Gaelic?" It remained to be seen if they would report him for using the forbidden language, even though they both had just sworn their gratitude. But, of course, they were English and probably had no sense of honor or keeping their word.

"Only know bits and pieces of it," Mistress Jovianna whispered, then flinched and closed her eyes tighter.

He offered Mistress Amaranth a curt nod and aimed another at her ailing daughter. "No, ladies," he said with the sourness the

English always brought out in him. "My mother did not christen me with that name."

Donnor approached with an armload of blankets.

"Blankets until we decide what to do with ye," Tobias said. The longer he studied them, the more his irritation grew. He did not need the burden of a pair of women that could be a danger to those he protected.

"Thank you." Subdued and suddenly acting as though struggling with grief, Mistress Amaranth quietly took the blankets. She folded one under her daughter's head, then spread another across her. Without another word, she wrapped the last one around herself, sat on the stone beside Mistress Jovianna, and stared at the ground.

"What's wrong?" the injured one asked in a loud whisper. She barely opened her eyes and frowned at her mother. "Amaranth? *Mother?*"

"Look at them," the old woman said. She locked eyes with him and didn't attempt to speak quietly. "Their dress. Flintlock pistols. The weave and stitch of these blankets."

The young lass forced her eyes open wider, revealing their beguiling sapphire blueness for the first time since her return to the living. She aimed a confused frown at him. "Why are you dressed like eighteenth-century pirates?"

"Highwaymen, mistress." Tobias moved a step closer. "And this *is* the eighteenth century. The twenty-first day of June, year of our Lord 1760, to be exact." The blow to the lass's head must have addled her. "And I feel certain yer mother just realized that the two of ye have fallen into the clutches of some of the most uncivilized Highlanders that Scotland ever begat." He politely touched the brim of his hat. "But I assure ye, we could never be as ruthless as the English."

"1760," the lass repeated. Her voice cracked with emotion. "June 1760?"

"Aye." He lifted his tricorn and raked back his long black hair that had slipped its tie. "And now that I have enlightened ye about yer mother's fears, would ye mind telling us how the two of ye happened to be here?"

"Can that not wait until we are warm and dry and my daughter is better?" Mistress Amaranth glared at him while scooting in front of her daughter as if to shield her.

His men shuffled in place, clearly uncomfortable with his brusque treatment of the women. It could not be helped. Too much was at risk.

He shook his head. "Nay, Mistress Amaranth. It canna wait. For ye see, I dinna ken what to do with ye until I hear yer tale. I willna risk the lives of many for the needs of two."

"I promise we're not dangerous," Mistress Jovianna said, while weakly pushing herself upright. One eye squinted shut and still holding her head, she swatted her mother's help away. "Just because we are English doesn't mean we're as awful as those you've dealt with." She attempted a tremulous smile but failed. Instead, she lurched forward and heaved out more water, retching hard and long.

Tobias flinched for the poor lass even though he had yet to decide if she and her mother were some sort of trap.

After several deep, shuddering breaths, Mistress Jovianna swiped the back of her hand across her mouth and eased back down onto the ledge. "Sorry. I guess I swallowed half the waters of Finnich Glen."

Regrettably, he still needed to know more about them before offering them further aid. He eased a step closer and fixed his scowl on Mistress Amaranth rather than her ailing daughter. "Ye may not be dangerous at the moment, but forgive me if I require a bit more information. Again, I ask—how do ye happen to be here in bonny Scotland instead of England? And are not only dressed strangely but appear to be alone and unprotected."

Without opening her eyes, Mistress Jovianna took hold of her mother's forearm and squeezed. A sure sign she was trying to silence the old woman. Mistress Amaranth lowered her gaze, placed her hand on top of her daughter's, and remained silent.

Tobias's apprehension churned harder. Too many depended on him and were already at risk because of England's determination to break the Scots. Their homes, their means of survival—hellfire, their very *lives* were his responsibility. These two and their silence left him no choice.

"Fine, then," he said, and turned to his men. "We are done here."

"What about them?" Fitch asked.

"Aye." Cade stepped forward, his concern focused on the mother. "Ye dinna mean to leave them here?"

Tobias gave an unconcerned shrug. "What choice have they left me? Ye ken as well as I what is at risk here."

"They are helpless women," Fitch said.

"They are English." Tobias stared the man down. "Need I remind ye of the *helpless* English widow who led the soldiers to yer father and his men after she won their trust with food and shelter?"

Fitch bowed his head and turned aside, but old Cade stepped forward. "This is different, and ye know it."

"We are no safer now than we were right after Culloden when the Butcher hunted us like animals. Our survival depends on our wits and the ability to beat them at their own cruel game." Tobias tossed a glance over at the women. His conscience would have yet another thing to damn him for if he left them here wounded and helpless because they refused to give him a reason to save them. But he had no choice. He had learned to live with a damning conscience long ago. This would be no different.

Mistress Amaranth turned and stared at her daughter while fisting her hands in her lap. With trembling fingers, she smoothed the wounded lass's wet tresses away from her forehead. Her daughter's eyes barely opened and met hers. Somehow, the two communicated without saying a word.

The old woman rose, her chin lifted as she stepped forward as though ready to fight. "We are on the run. Again."

"Again?" Tobias asked while watching for evidence of lies.

"We left London because my husband owed someone money and couldn't pay." She stared at him without blinking, defiance in her eyes. "And when he died, they came after my daughter and me." She spoke clearly and stood in front of her daughter in a protective stance. So far, everything about the woman seemed truthful.

"Who are these people chasing after ye?" Tobias kept his tone grim and uncompromising.

"The Earl of Tenbury is the leader," she said. "He and his associates are quite adept at fleecing the hopeful fools turned away from White's. They are happy to escort their unsuspecting prey to more questionable gaming hells."

Tobias knew of White's. His useless brother had lusted after acceptance into the exclusive gentlemen's club ever since receiving his earldom by groveling his way up King George II's arse. And if Mistress Amaranth's husband had tried to enter the place, the man must have thought his place in society warranted it. "Yer husband frequented such dens?"

"Yes." Mistress Amaranth's jaw tightened. "My husband was one of their fools." She squared her shoulders and restored herself with a deep breath. "So, we left London and found sanctuary with my distant cousin in Glasgow. He was our only living relative, and we thought ourselves safe. Until Tenbury's men found us again."

"Who is this cousin?" Tobias wanted to believe her. So far, everything she said made sense. Perhaps too much sense. Almost like a well-constructed tale.

"Samual Walkersby. A merchant of cotton, linens, and silk." Sorrow filled her voice as she bowed her head. "They killed him on the way here. Shot him in the back." She turned and looked at Mistress Jovianna, who was once more trying her best to rise from the stone bench. The old woman's gaze then shifted to the narrow passage the water had carried them through. "We tried to take refuge in the gorge."

"But the treacherous gorge spat ye out at the feet of a wicked

Scot," Tobias said. His focus shifted to Mistress Jovianna.

Pale and looking ready to heave yet again, the lass weakly stumbled to her mother's side. "See?" she said, barely hiding her contempt for him. "The English treated us like rubbish too. Now, will you give us refuge? At least until we're whole again and can take care of ourselves?"

Not entirely convinced but feeling somewhat better about taking them in, he nodded. "Aye, mistress. We will offer ye what safety we can." He gave her a dark smile. "Bear in mind, though, we are who some might consider hardened criminals ripe for deportation for enslavement on the plantations either in the colonies or the Indies."

She glared at him for a long moment, then threw up a hand. "Well, you appear to be our only choice right now. So beggars can't be choosy about their saviors, now can they?"

Apparently, the blow to the lovely lady's head had not diminished her wit nor curbed her tongue. Again, he touched the brim of his hat and offered a polite nod. "Tobias Risk at yer service, mistress."

She visibly gagged while swaying from side to side. "Sorry. That was not directed at you. My world is still spinning a bit."

"Lie back down, Mistress Jovianna. We'll fashion a litter to haul ye up from the gorge." He turned to his men. "Fitch, tell Pag and Silas what we need. Donnor, stand watch up above, ye ken? Cade, have ye any whisky left in yer wee flask? The ladies might appreciate a sip to warm them."

Cade pulled out his prized flask. The round, hand-sized container of silver sported more than a few dents and had once belonged to his father. After hefting it in his hand, he offered it to Mistress Amaranth with a kindly smile. "I didna ken how much was left, but there should be enough there to warm ye and yer daughter."

"Thank you." She offered it to Mistress Jovianna first. "I know you're not supposed to drink with a head injury, but it's the best way to knock the chill, since you're soaked."

The lovely lass pushed it away, making Tobias decide to get involved. He knelt beside her. "Ye should listen to yer mother, mistress. A wee sip would do ye a world of good."

"Maybe so, but it will burn as hot coming back out as it did going down." Her squinty, one-eyed glare dared him to argue.

"It will numb the pain," he coaxed her.

"Thank you, Mr. Risk, but I'll still pass." She offered him a smile that he could tell she didn't mean and clutched the blanket tighter around her.

"Ye may call me Tobias." He rose, shucked his coat, and tucked it around her.

"Thank you, Tobias. You may call me Jovianna."

"That wouldna be proper, mistress. At least not until we know one another better."

"Whatever makes you comfortable," she said, while lightly touching the gash on her forehead.

He would not be comfortable around either woman until time told whether or not their tale was true. Mistress Jovianna was especially dangerous. Not only because of her beauty but also her spirit. Even though she found herself in a helpless situation, she remained steadfast and calm. He admired that about her but couldn't allow his admiration to make him careless. After all, they had yet to explain their strange clothing.

"Did yer cousin have ye dress that way?" he asked.

"What?" She closed her eyes and tucked into a tighter ball beneath her coverings.

"Yer manner of dress. The strange trews and shiny, tight tunics. Did yer cousin advise ye to wear such things to escape Glasgow?" As soon as the words left his mouth, he knew himself to be a fool. If that hadn't been the reason for what they wore, they might now claim it to disguise the truth.

"Easier to ride across rough country without fighting skirts," she said without opening her eyes.

"Please let her rest," Mistress Amaranth said. "I'm sure getting her out of here will be an ordeal. She needs to save her strength."

"As ye wish, mistress." He touched the brim of his hat and moved a few strides away while motioning for Fitch and Cade to follow. "Yer thoughts?" he asked as soon as they were out of earshot of the women.

"I dinna think them dangerous," Fitch said, then glared at him. "And aye, I remember well what happened to my father. But that doesna mean every English woman is a heartless whore." He glanced back at the ladies again. "These two seem…different."

"Cade?" Tobias eyed the old Highlander. The man had been through more than any of them, and bore the scars and horrific memories to prove it. One of the few who had survived Culloden, he shied away from cities and towns out of fear of arrest even fourteen years later.

"Ye ken how I feel about the English," the man said.

"Aye." Tobias waited, knowing it sometimes took Cade a while to put his thoughts into words.

Cade stared at the women, squinting as though sighting a gun. His nostrils flared. "I smell their fear, but I dinna think it is us who stirs it." After a thoughtful nod, he shifted his focus back to Tobias. "I believe them to be running from something. Whether or not it is the earl's men, I canna say. But I will point out that they headed northward, away from England."

"If they started at Glasgow," Tobias said.

"Where else would they start from?" Cade frowned. "Chances are we would have come across them had they been coming from Edinburgh or Stirling."

Cade was right about that. Tobias recalled that their most recent benefactors who had supplied them with the fine horses and carriage had been traveling from Stirling. Travelers from Edinburgh would use the same route. It was why they watched that road. "See what's taking them so long with that litter. Daylight burns swiftly, and I dinna relish climbing out of the gorge in the darkness."

Both men departed, leaving him to observe the mysterious

Englishwomen alone. He meandered closer, noting that Mistress Jovianna appeared to have started shivering. So much so that her mother had added her blanket to the rest piled across her daughter.

"She needs the warmth of a fire or some sort of shelter," Mistress Amaranth said. "And soon."

He agreed. What little color had been restored after she expelled the water had now drained from the young woman's cheeks. "Are ye strong enough to climb up the embankment unassisted?" he asked Mistress Amaranth.

"Of course. Why?" The woman eyed him as though he'd sprouted a second head.

He didn't bother to explain. Just strode forward, scooped her daughter up into his arms, and settled her against his chest like cradling a child. She moaned but didn't open her eyes or speak. That concerned him even more. "Tuck the blankets and my coat tighter around her."

Her mother hurried to do so without question.

Tobias took the lead up the side of the gorge, finding an incline that wasn't too fierce to manage. If Mistress Amaranth had issue, he felt sure she would call out. He concentrated on jostling the poor lass in his arms as little as possible. Even still, she groaned or hitched in a breath with his every footfall. The farther he trudged, the tighter she held on, fisting her hands in his shirt. "Just a little farther, lass. A little farther and we'll build ye a fine, warm fire and set ye a pallet right beside it."

"Thank you," she whispered against his throat, her soft breath tickling his flesh.

He swallowed hard and tried to move faster. The softness of her in his arms, her clinging trust, the gratitude in her whisper— all of it affected him in a way difficult to ignore. "No need to thank me, mistress," he said softly. "Just get better, aye? Ye've been a brave lass. Dinna give up now, aye?"

She didn't answer, just curled tighter against him.

Donnor and Pag met him just as he crested the summit.

The only thing that kept him from bellowing at them about their tardiness with the litter was that he knew it would hurt the lady's head. So he poured his irritation into his glare. "Build a fire and a shelter for them in case it rains. Make haste, aye?"

Dread filled the men's faces as they nodded and hurried away.

Mistress Amaranth rushed around him and directed him to a downed tree with a good-sized trunk. "Sit here and hold her until they get the fire going. Your body heat will help her."

He eyed the spot and debated her request.

"Please!" The woman tugged on him, trying to steer him that way. "You've done this much to help us. All I'm asking is that you keep her warm until the fire is going. Please." She hurried over to the trunk and cushioned where she wished him to sit with a folded blanket. Her pleading look twisted his insides. It was more than obvious that the woman feared that he didn't have a heart and might yet abandon them.

He would prove her wrong. Settling down on the log, he gently repositioned the lass against his chest and pulled the blankets closer around her. Her shivering had stopped, but she still shifted with every breath. A good sign that the lovely but troublesome Englishwoman still lived. And he was glad. He still didn't fully trust her, but he didn't want her to die. He wanted her to heal so he could get to know her better. Get to know her well enough to call her Jovianna.

CHAPTER THREE

JOVIANNA DIDN'T KNOW which nauseated her more: her pounding head or the realization that they had somehow landed in the eighteenth century—1760, to be exact. So, she kept her eyes shut and curled tighter against the warmth of the man who couldn't decide if he trusted them because they were English. But he had helped her. Still helped her, in fact. He patiently held her close to keep her warm until the others got the fire going.

She understood his leeriness and why he despised the English. The last fourteen years of his time would have been some of the worst in Scotland's history. Unfortunately, more was to come. The Highland Clearances. Potato famine. She tried to remember the rest, but another wave of nausea throttled her, making her swallow hard to keep from vomiting on him a second time.

Tobias Risk fit the Gaelic moniker *Diabhal Dubh-Chridhe,* the Black-Hearted Devil, the name he had given them at first. Well, he sort of fit it. She hadn't decided if his heart was black or not. Time would tell. But he did have a seductively devilish look about him. Hair darker than the blackest coal. Pale blue eyes that flashed with a fiery iciness and an unyielding gaze that burned right through you. She had no doubt he could spot a lie in an instant. Thank goodness Amaranth was a gifted storyteller able to convince any audience that up was really down.

His heart beat strong and steady beneath her cheek and hadn't even increased in rate when he carried her out of the gorge. Taller than her five foot eleven by a good head and shoulders, the man towered over her. An unusual situation she rarely encountered. And those shoulders—broad and well muscled, with a brawniness that highlighted his tapered waist and made his swaggering gait even more impressive. She felt sure he also possessed what Amaranth would describe as delightfully climbable abs.

Every time she shuddered, he adjusted his hold as though trying to find a way to ease her misery. That made her smile. No. Tobias Risk was not a black-hearted devil. He was a wounded bear of a man trying to survive. Survive. How the bloody hell were she and Amaranth going to survive in 1760? The thought made her groan.

"Just a wee bit longer, lass. I ken ye're cold and miserable. But with the rain starting, the fire will take some coaxing."

"Thank you for helping us," she whispered, fighting a sudden rising panic and the threat of tears. "I know you didn't want to."

"It's not that I didna wish to help ye," he said, then went quiet for so long that she thought the conversation over. "Scotland's war has never ended, as some would suppose. But the difference now is we fight for our lives and our homes instead of which king sits upon the throne."

She understood that at an academic level but knew it wasn't the same. She also knew it wasn't only the English to blame for the clearances. Many of the chieftains who had not had their lands seized had turned on their own people, sold them out and replaced them with sheep to cover higher taxes and maintain the lavish lifestyles to which they were accustomed. But she was only aware of this because she had read it in a book. Tobias and his kin had lived it. Were living it.

"I'm sorry," she whispered. "I understand that Amaranth and

I are an annoyance you don't need."

"Ye call yer mother *Amaranth*?"

"That's her name." She tucked in closer, thankful that the man emitted the heat of a well-stoked furnace. The cool, misting rain coming down soaked everything to the bone, making the June day unseasonably chilly.

"Aye, I ken that's her name," he continued, apparently unwilling to let it go. "But she is yer mother."

A heavy sigh escaped her. "When I was a young, obnoxious brat who thought I knew everything, I started calling my mother and father by their first names because I wanted to hurt their feelings. Make them think I had outgrown them and didn't even think of them as parents. Rather than rant and rave as I had hoped they would, they both ignored it. Went on as though nothing had changed and thoroughly deflated my attempt at tormenting them. So, I went back to calling them *Mother* and *Father*. Father didn't care what I called him as long as we continued our talks about books or history. Mother insisted I continue calling her by her first name because it not only made her feel younger but also made it easier for her to pretend I wasn't her daughter whenever I behaved badly."

His rumbling chuckle vibrated through her head, making it hurt worse. She clutched it with both hands, silently damning whatever rock had hit her hard enough to send her back through time and leave her so incapacitated.

"Sorry, lass. I didna mean to shake ye." He shifted positions again and tucked the damp blankets closer around her. "Yer parents shouldha reddened yer arse for ye for being so disrespectful."

"I suppose so. But then Amaranth wouldn't have a way to feel younger, now would she?" She barely opened her eyes and tried to look around without moving her throbbing head. Vision still blurry, all she could make out was Tobias's linen shirt and the scar emerging from the folds of his neckcloth. She pulled in a deep breath and was mildly surprised at his scent. She had always assumed the past reeked, for lack of a better word. But he didn't stink. He smelled of the wide-open land. Rain. Wood smoke. And the salty, not unpleasant musk of an active man. He startled her when he rose and started walking.

"The lads built ye a bit of cover next to the fire to keep the rain off ye." He dropped to one knee and eased her down onto a pallet inside a makeshift shelter of leafy branches woven together. As he shifted aside, the heat of the fire greeted her, but it was nothing compared to his warmth.

"Thank you. This is very nice." She offered him a smile. "Not as warm as you, but I'm sure your arms were about to go numb from holding me."

"My arms are fine, lass. Dinna fash yerself." He didn't return her smile, but his gaze didn't seem as flinty as before. With a polite nod and touch of his hat, he rose and walked away.

Amaranth scooted into the roomy lean-to and joined her on the pallet. "How are you?" She held up two fingers. "Your vision—clear or blurry?"

"I can tell you're holding up two fingers, but they're still a little fuzzy around the edges." Jovianna adjusted the folded blanket serving as a pillow. "And my brain is pounding against my skull with every heartbeat." She blinked hard, trying not to give in to tears. "What are we going to do?" she whispered.

Amaranth scrubbed her face with both hands, then raked them back through her wet hair. "I have no idea, sweetie. I'm still trying to wrap my head around what happened." She leaned forward, peered out of the shelter, then drew back inside. "I always believed the concept of time travel possible. Even fantasized about it while on digs. But I never in my wildest dreams thought I would ever experience it."

"Do you think if we traveled back upstream and found the spot where we both got ill, it would reverse and send us back home?" Jovianna shuddered at the thought. Depending on how much rainfall this time had experienced, attempting to go upstream could be deadly.

"I don't know, sweetie." Amaranth resettled into a cross-legged position and propped her elbows on her knees. She stared out of the shelter, her expression a pained scowl. "I guess we should be thankful we didn't land in the middle of the Jacobite uprising."

"We hit the Highland Clearances," Jovianna said, trying to find a position where her head didn't throb as badly. "That's still not good."

"I suppose so." Amaranth turned and stared at her.

Jovianna recognized that look. It meant trouble. "What?"

"The way I see it, we have two choices." Amaranth picked up a stick and started idly plucking away its leaves.

"And those choices are?" Jovianna asked.

"Convince the men to leave us here with a bit of food and try getting upstream as soon as you're up to it, even though we don't know if we can recreate the phenomenon. After all, how many times have we tramped through this gorge and never landed in another century?"

"Or?" Jovianna already knew the answer. She didn't want to hear it, but there was no stopping her mother.

Amaranth shrugged. "Assimilate into this time and survive."

"You realize we can't teach here?" Jovianna said. "Women didn't work at the university until 1908."

"Teaching at the University of Glasgow isn't the only profession in existence."

"You're too old to be a prostitute, and I'd rather not pursue that line of work, thank you." Jovianna pushed up to a sitting position, mimicking her mother's cross-legged pose. Palpating her facial bones for any breaks, she kept her eyes closed and struggled to maintain her balance. "How else would you suggest we earn a living?"

"Maids. Nannies. Pub wenches. Basket weaving."

Jovianna opened her eyes and scowled at her mother. "Since when do you know how to weave a basket?"

"Have you forgotten the dig in Turkey? You were only seven

at the time, but the woman you befriended at the market taught us both."

With a roll of her eyes, Jovianna returned to massaging her temples and brow bone. Amaranth needed to be serious. "I can't think straight right now. Not with this pain."

"Mistress Jovianna."

Jovianna popped to attention and immediately regretted it, squinting until the ache in her head settled back to a dull, nauseating roar. "Yes, Mr. Risk?"

"Tobias, remember?" He crouched in front of the shelter with a steaming cup in his hand and held it out to her. "Mrs. Gibb prepares this herbal mix for me, and I drink it when needed. Headaches sometimes trouble me. Willow bark, butterbur, and other ingredients she refuses to tell me about are in it, and it works a fair amount of the time."

"I'm going to help gather more wood for the fire," Amaranth said. She crawled out from under the lean-to before either Jovianna or Tobias could respond.

"Thank you." Jovianna accepted the cup and hazarded a sip. The bitter concoction numbed her lips with a strange stinging. She swallowed hard to keep it down. "Powerful stuff there."

A hint of a smile twitched at the corner of Tobias's mouth. "Ah well, I dinna ken what all she puts in there. But it does help with the pain most times."

"I didn't even notice anyone boiling any water." She waved him in and patted the pallet beside her. "Since Amaranth has decided to gather wood, you might as well sit in here out of the rain."

He paused, staring at the spot as if debating whether or not it would be siding with the enemy.

"But if you don't want to, I understand." She took another sip and shuddered. "Bloody hell, this stuff is awful."

"Perhaps I could sit for a bit." He angled around and sat beside her. With his legs bent and arms wrapped around his knees, his height forced him to sit hunched over. "'Tis no wonder ye failed to notice us working at the fire. Yer nest here is like a wee burrow. We procured an enclosed carriage that wouldha kept ye drier, but ye needed to be close to a fire."

"I do indeed. And when you say procured...?" She left the question open-ended.

"Highwaymen. Remember, mistress?"

"You didn't kill them, did you?"

His jaw tightened as he stared straight ahead and squinted at the crackling fire that hissed as the raindrops hit the flames. "No, lass. I only kill when forced." He turned and nodded at the cup in her hands. "Finish yer tonic. It canna help ye whilst sitting in that cup."

For the first time, she noticed the angry red scrape across his cheek just below his right eye. "You're hurt."

"'Tis but a grazing. I rinsed it in the stream."

"But the bacteria. It needs to be cleaned with an antiseptic."

He frowned at her. "I dinna ken those words, but they sound like something a healer would say. Are ye one?"

She shook her head, then groaned and pressed the heel of her hand to her temple. "No. I am not a healer. I've got enough wits about me to take care of myself. That's all." As she took another sip of the bitter tea, she made a mental note to be more careful about her choice of words. She found that challenge daunting. "Would you and your men consider leaving us here with a day or two of food when you move on? Just enough so we can make it once I'm better."

His hard, cutting stare filled her with a pang of unreasonable guilt for breathing some of his air. "The Highlands are no place for a woman alone, mistress. Have ye not learned that lesson yet? Especially when ye claim to be on the run from men who already killed yer cousin."

"I know, but..."

"But what?" The rumble of his deep voice was a low warning growl.

"Amaranth and I don't want to be any trouble to you." She

wasn't sure what else to say, since it was obvious that Amaranth's Plan A was now not an option. "I can't help but think that the lot of you would be on your way home right now, if not for us."

"We would. But plans change. We are used to that."

He sounded angry, and she hated that. Whether it was because he had saved her life or changed his plans to help her, she wanted him to like her and not resent her. Which, in a way, was odd. Normally, she tried not to worry about what people thought about her. She'd learned long ago that did little good. As clumsy as she was most of the time, if she worried about looking like a fool, she'd end up never stepping out her front door.

The silence became uncomfortable. She leaned closer and eyed his wound, desperate to restore the fragile peace between them. "If Cade has any whisky left, I could clean your wound for you. Of course, it'll sting like the dickens, but it might help stave off any infection."

One of his dark brows ratcheted higher. "Ye would help a dreaded Scot?"

"That dreaded Scot helped a bloody Sassenach. Perhaps we two could set an example." He smiled, and it made her laugh. She pointed at him. "You smiled!" Then she touched her head. "And my head didn't hurt as bad, even though I laughed."

His smile shifted to a wry grin. "I have been known to smile on occasion." He nodded at the cup. "I told ye the remedy works." He leaned closer, his expression shifting to a smug look as though he wished to drive the point home. "Best drink the rest of it as I also told ye, aye?"

"Yes, sir." She choked the rest of it down, then turned aside and spat out the clumpy dredges. "My tongue is numb."

"It'll pass." He exited the shelter, then turned back and pointed at the pallet. "Rest ye now, aye? Silas will bring yer supper soon as the broth thickens enough to suit him. This place is safe enough, I reckon. We willna leave it till morning."

She crawled out after him, then carefully rose to her feet, her arms extended for balance. The remedy had not only eased her pain down to a bearable level but also settled her stomach.

"Did I not just tell ye to rest?" Tobias glared at her, his jaw back to its hard line of earlier.

"I need a moment of privacy in the bushes." She was about to pee in her water-resistant leggings, defeating the purpose of remaining as dry as possible, even though she was already soaked to the skin. The magical combination of unknown elements in the herbal tea appeared to possess the properties of a very strong diuretic, making the urgency increase with every passing second.

"She shouldn't go alone," Amaranth said, appearing at her side as if by magic.

"She either goes alone or not at all." Tobias jutted out his chin as though daring them to challenge him.

"So you mean to say we are your prisoners?" Amaranth tried to stand toe to toe with him even though her barely five-foot frame made her efforts laughable.

Jovianna waved them both out of her way. "You two argue this one out while I'm gone, all right?"

"Pag! Make sure the lady's privacy is respected. Guard the area till she finishes." Tobias returned Amaranth's stern glare and offered a polite nod. "I wouldna call ye *prisoners*, madam. More like guests we dinna wish to lose, ye ken?"

Too far out of range to hear the rest—and at this point, not really caring—Jovianna hurried to the nearest cluster of bushes in front of a large boulder and scuttled in between the hedging and the rock. The stone provided the perfect place to prop her rump to preserve her balance as she relieved herself. A sigh escaped her. Much better. At least that problem had been easily solved. She wrestled the damp leggings back up in place, wishing she had opted for the next size up. Just as she stepped out from behind the screen of leaves, Donnor thundered into the camp and dismounted before his horse came to a full stop.

"Riders coming. Looks like sheriff's men," he said.

"They wear the coats?" Tobias asked.

Donnor nodded. "Same as the ones we saw at the pub in

Edinburgh."

Tobias jerked a thumb at the shelter. "Under the blankets, ladies. Cover yer strange clothes, ye ken?" Without waiting for their response, he turned to Cade. "The carriage and its horses?"

Cade smiled. "Tucked away till morning. I feared we might have company."

As she and Amaranth crawled into the shelter, Jovianna nudged her mother to the back. "I need to be in the front. My Scottish accent sounds more convincing than yours."

"With any luck, speaking will not be required." Amaranth shimmied beneath the blankets and pulled them up around her neck.

Jovianna had just covered herself and hidden her head wound with a tangle of hair as the three men, all wearing the same style of coats dyed a deep reddish brown, rode into the camp with their flintlock rifles ready.

"Who be the leader here?" asked the man in the front.

"I am." Tobias stepped forward with a fierce expression.

"We came upon a gentleman, his son, and their driver who had been robbed this side of Stirling." The man urged his horse to walk forward while looking all around the camp. When he came up even with the shelter, he leaned over and squinted at it.

Jovianna made it a point to keep her eyes open to the barest slits.

"Pity for them." Tobias edged closer to the shelter, and Jovianna noticed his hand now rested on his pistol. "I've heard that highwaymen riddle the roads between here and Edinburgh. By whose authority do ye ride into my camp and insinuate that me and my kin had anything to do with it?"

The man snorted, then spat on the ground at Tobias's feet. "I made no insinuations. And the sheriff principal of Edinburgh grants us the authority to question anyone we find along these roads." He pointed his gun at the lean-to. "Have whoever is in there to come out. I would speak with them."

"My wife and her mother are not well," Tobias said. "Leave

them be."

"Guns at the ready, lads," the man told the other two, then dismounted. He strode to the front of the shelter and squatted in front of it.

Jovianna moaned and faked her best shiver. Amaranth joined in, shivering too, as she huddled against Jovianna's back.

"Woman," the sheriff called out in a booming voice. "What ails ye?"

"Fever," Jovianna said in her weakest whisper.

The man leaned closer and tilted his ear her way. "Eh?"

She coughed the wettest cough she could and sprayed the man with spittle. "Fever," she rasped again.

"Fever?"

"Aye," she answered, then groaned again and added a loud, wheezing exhale.

The sheriff wiped his face on his sleeve and backed away. "How long they been like this?"

"It took them yesterday, causing us to make camp here, since they could travel no farther." Tobias nodded at Cade to his left and then Donnor, Fitch, Pag, and Silas to his right. "All of us are feeling poorly now. No telling which of us will fall with it next."

"If they been here since yesterday, they had nothing to do with robbing those two near Stirling," said the second sheriff from his horse. He cast a leery glance all around and backed his mount farther away. "Remember that fever that took down the whole of Airth?"

"Aye," said the third sheriff, edging his mount away as well. "I say we keep looking for the Devil of the Highlands and his men. Leave these poor folk in peace."

The leader offered Tobias a curt nod. "God be with ye and heal yer family. Forgive us for the intrusion."

Tobias accepted the apology with a slight dip of his chin.

The trio left at a hard gallop as though wishing to outrun the illness they believed they had just encountered.

Jovianna raked the hair out of her face and pushed up to a

sitting position. "You don't think they'll be back, do you?" she asked Tobias. No matter how polite those men had been when they left, she didn't trust them. All three had possessed a feral, bloodthirsty look.

Tobias crouched beside her, his gaze locked on the direction the men had taken. "No. Yer convincing them ye had a fever frightened them well enough, I reckon." He cast a side-eyed scowl her way. "Ye missed a fine opportunity, mistress. There is a fair price on my head and on the heads of my men."

She shot back the same hard glare she reserved for students disrupting her lectures. "You have been nothing but kind to my mother and me. You've behaved like a complete ass some of that time, but you've still been kind and helped us. I daresay it would be bad form indeed for me to repay that kindness by turning you over to the authorities."

He not only smiled but shook with a rumbling laugh, then pulled off his tricorn, held it to his chest, and bowed his dark head. "I beg yer forgiveness for behaving like an arse at times."

"Ye never apologize to us for being an arse," Fitch said from behind him.

Tobias released a long-suffering groan, raked back his hair, then placed his hat on his head and pulled it forward, cocking it low over his brow. "I shall never hear the end of this from them."

"May I help with the meal?" Jovianna crawled out of the shelter, thankful that the special mixture of herbs had made her feel so much better. "It doesn't seem proper that I should sit and do nothing."

"I do the meals," Silas said. The wizened old man waved her away without bothering to glance up from the pots he nestled down into the coals. "And I dinna need help from anyone."

Tobias pointed at the shelter. "Ye should rest while the herbs keep yer head from pounding."

"And we need to clean that gash on your forehead," Amaranth said from behind her. "If Mr. Maccolman will once again allow us to use his whisky."

"Cade, mistress." The old Highlander pulled the flask from an inner pocket of his waistcoat and held it out. Wide streaks of silver ran through his light brown hair and reddish-blond beard, but a youthful flirtatiousness twinkled in his eyes. "And I am happy to be of service to ye any way ye need."

Jovianna ducked her head to hide her smile. Cade appeared quite taken with her mother and didn't care who noticed it.

Amaranth accepted the flask from him and rested her hand on his forearm a little longer than necessary as she gave him a grateful nod.

Taking a seat on a nearby stump, Jovianna folded her hands in her lap and tried to reason away the mixed emotions that the sight of a man interested in her mother, and her mother's interest returned, stirred within her.

"Cade is a good man," Tobias whispered from behind her, so close, his warm breath brushed her cheek.

"I am sure he is." *But he's not my father,* she wanted to shout while at the same time choking on the guilt of not wanting her mother to enjoy another relationship ever again. Father had been gone over a year now, and Jovianna knew he would want Amaranth happy. In fact, those had been his dying words just before the injuries from the car accident stole him away. "I'm sure he is," she repeated, flinching as her voice cracked.

As her mother turned away from Cade and started toward her, her steps slowed. She cocked her head the slightest bit and frowned. "Sweetie? Are you having a downturn? Should you lie down while I clean the cut?"

Ashamed of herself for being so selfish, Jovianna waved her mother forward. "I'll lie down once you're finished." She sat straighter and swept back her wet hair. "Come now. Let's not drag this out and give me longer to dread it."

Tobias came from behind and tipped her head back, steadying her against him. "Close yer eyes and breathe, lass. 'Twill burn like a fiend, but I'll hold ye." He loomed over her, offering a faint half-smile. "The scar shouldna be so bad as to ruin yer chances for a match."

"I am not looking for a match. I just want it to heal." She jerked and hissed through clenched teeth as the whisky set her flesh on fire.

"So, ye already have a betrothed? Or a husband somewhere who shouldha been here to protect ye from the earl's men?"

"She has no one," Amaranth said as she dabbed another stinging slosh of whisky across the cut. "She is too picky. I fear I shall never have any grandchildren."

Jovianna pushed them both away and rose to her feet. "That is quite enough," she said. "Of both whisky and gossip, thank you very much." She fanned her forehead as she marched across the camp, putting as much space as possible between herself, her mother, and Tobias. Donnor, Fitch, and Cade hurried to get clear of her path. Even Silas spared her an interested stare as he added some dried, leafy bits to a pot.

Pag hurried over to her, holding out a cup. "Water to slake yer thirst till time for more of the devil's brew?"

She accepted the drink and shot a disgruntled look back at her mother and Tobias. Now was not the time for Amaranth's teasing about her lack of a love life. She sipped the cool, sweet water and turned back to Pag, the youngest of the group, who appeared to be barely out of his teens. Maybe. She was a terrible guesser of ages. "Thank you, Pag. I assume by *devil's brew* you mean Tobias's headache remedy?"

"Aye." The red-haired lad grinned. "Mrs. Gibb once said she'd rather deal with Old Scratch himself than Tobias when his head is aching. 'Twas her that named the healing mix the Devil's brew."

"Pag!" Tobias had moved closer without making a sound. "Is it not yer turn to stand guard?"

"Aye, sir. Right away." Pag trotted off, pausing only long enough to turn and give her a sweet smile and a polite bob of his head.

Tobias stepped in front of her, blocking her view of the departing young lad. After a moment, he faced her. "Dinna encourage him, ye ken?"

"He offered me a cup of water, and I thanked him." She took another sip, trying to quench the sour burning that had started behind her breastbone. Pressing a hand to her chest, she glared up at him. "I do not prey upon men and don't appreciate your insinuating such."

"Good." His gaze dipped to the hand she held against her chest. "The herbs can make yer innards simmer a bit, but an oatcake helps. I'll fetch it."

Bewildered, she watched him stride over to one of the horses and start rummaging through a leather pouch lashed to the saddle. "What a strange man. Angry for no reason one minute and kind and helpful the next."

"Not strange at all," Amaranth said from beside her. She offered a smug grin while turning Cade's flask in her hands. "He is marking his territory, dear."

"He's what?"

Amaranth shook her head and walked away, calling back over her shoulder, "Think about it, sweetie. You'll figure it out."

CHAPTER FOUR

W ITH HIS BACK propped against a stump near the shelter and his gaze locked on the eastern horizon, Tobias soaked in every sound, every movement around the camp. Leaves rustled in the gentle breeze whispering through the darkness. The waters dancing around the Devil's Pulpit gurgled and splashed below. Even though Donnor and Pag walked the perimeter of the camp, watching for any sign of danger, Tobias would not allow himself to sleep. Not after the visit from the Edinburgh sheriffs. At least it would be dawn soon and they could be shed of the place.

A shuffling from inside the women's lean-to caught his attention. Labored huffing and quiet groans of unrest. The pounding ache must have returned to Mistress Jovianna's head. He knew the pain, having experienced several such injuries himself. Without a sound, he rose and checked the covered pot of water squatting deep in the banked coals. Silas knew to keep hot water at the ready. None of them enjoyed Tobias's leadership when his headaches ran unchecked because of the lack of Mrs. Gibb's herbs.

He found a cup, added three pinches of the mixture from the pouch he always kept inside his waistcoat, then ladled in hot, steaming water. After swirling the brew for a moment or so, he stepped over to the shelter and crouched beside the pallet. Even though she lay on her side, facing the back of the shelter, he could tell she was awake by her tensed shifting. "Mistress Jovianna?"

She rolled to her back and draped an arm over her eyes. "I didn't think the headache would be as bad when it returned."

"It could verra well be bad for days." He wouldn't lie to the lass. She needed to be prepared. "Ease up and drink, mistress. I mixed this dose stronger."

The glow of the firelight lit up her pained scowl as she turned onto her side and propped up on her elbow. She accepted the cup without argument, took a hearty gulp, then released a very unladylike belch. Her eyes flared wide and rounded with embarrassment. "Pardon me. I didn't mean to do that."

He sat on the pallet beside her and offered a teasing smile. "It will be our secret, aye?"

She took another sip, a shorter one this time. "I'm sorry if I woke you." She moved to a sitting position and cupped the drink between her hands. "The throbbing in my head made it impossible to be still."

"Ye didna wake me." Without thinking, he chucked a finger under her chin and angled her face toward the firelight. The wound on her forehead concerned him. "The swelling is down, but the edges of the cut have turned a fearsome red." He pressed the backs of his fingers to her cheek and then her throat. "Ye dinna seem feverish, though."

She arched a brow with an expression of gentle reproach. "For someone who hates me, you appear to be trying very hard to take good care of me."

"I never said I hated ye."

"You hate the English."

"Aye, I do." He nudged the cup back toward her mouth. "Drink or ye will never feel better." A disgruntled huff escaped him. Surely she didn't think he hated her? "And I never said I hated ye."

She wrinkled her nose at him, making it impossible not to

devour her every mannerism and imprint them in his memories, preserving her in his mind forever.

"I know you never *said* you hated me," she said. "But I am English, and you hate them."

"If I recall, I mentioned not trusting either yerself or yer mother. A perfectly natural response, considering yer manner of dress, the fact that ye are English, and are two women traveling unprotected." He nodded at the half-empty cup, then gave her another pointed look. "But I never mentioned hating either of ye."

After another sip, she smiled down into her cup. "I'm glad you don't hate me, because I like you."

Her words filled his heart with a warm lightness, lifting it with a subtle stirring he hadn't felt in a very long time. "Ye like me even though I'm an arse at times?"

Her soft laugh reminded him of the musical waters in the gorge below. With a smile, she lifted her cup as though toasting him. "Yes. I like you even though you are an ass at times." Before setting the rim of the cup to her lips, she paused. "You are a kind man, and I am thankful you were the one to find us."

He forced himself to look away, breaking the dangerous pull between them. Time to speak of other things. Things of a safer nature. "It is my hope that we can leave here at dawn. Do ye think ye will be fit to travel?"

"I will be fit." Her tone had changed. Grown quieter. Almost fearful. She stared down at the cup again, but her smile was gone this time.

"What troubles ye, lass?"

"The unknown, I guess." She twitched a halfhearted shrug. "My world, everything I once knew and called my own, is forever lost to me now." A shuddering sniff escaped her, making her duck her head. "Sorry. Being silly, I know. I should be grateful to be alive and in the company of such honorable men."

"Loss can be hard, whether it be a person, a home, or a precious memento that reminds ye of better days." He squinted up at the gentle lightening of the sky silhouetting the treetops. "All we can do is push forward and hold tight to our memories." He looked at her just in time to catch a teardrop escaping the corner of her eye and rolling down her cheek.

She swiped it away with an angry flick of her hand.

"There is no shame in weeping, lass," he said. "It cleanses the soul and soothes the heart."

She pressed her hand to her mouth and failed to stifle a pitiful sob. "I hate crying. It makes my head hurt worse and gives me a snotty nose."

He pulled a square of linen from inside his waistcoat and held it out. "'Tis clean, mistress, if ye wish to wipe yer eyes and nose."

"Thank you." She snatched it from him, dabbed her eyes and the end of her nose, then started crying harder as she stared at it crumpled in her hand.

Unable to stop himself, he slipped his arm around her and held her, shushing and rocking as though she were a greetin' bairn. He glanced back, deeper into the shelter. How the devil could the poor lass's mother sleep through all this?

"I didna mean to make it worse," he said softly. "Should I not have offered my handkerchief?"

Mistress Jovianna's muffled, high-pitched "no" came from his chest where she had buried her face.

He awkwardly stroked her hair and debated nudging her damnable mother with the toe of his boot to see if the woman was dead. While his grandmam had told him weeping was good for the soul, she had failed to advise him on the proper care and treatment of an overwrought maid. But the longer he held Mistress Jovianna, the more natural it seemed to cradle her in his arms and hold her while she cried. Her shuddering sighs seemed to be lessening, so perhaps he was doing something right.

She shifted and looked up at him with her cheek still resting on his chest. "Sorry, again. It's just that..." Her face already glistened with wetness, but her eyes overflowed with more tears. "It's just I've had a bloody awful couple of days."

"I know, lass," he said quietly. "All ye can do is survive them one at a time, then cast them aside and grow stronger to spite them." With startling clarity, he realized he spoke to himself as much as to her. "Dinna dwell on the bad or it will overpower ye. There's good to be found in every day, even though some days, looking for it is hard and finding it even harder."

With another trembling smile, she reached up and hesitantly touched his face with a tenderness that almost made him groan. "You are as wise as you are kind."

"I dinna ken about the wise part," he said in a gruff tone meant to hide the loneliness she stirred within him. Her mouth was so close as she lay in his arms. But to kiss her would be the greatest folly. He knew that, but yearned for it just the same. With a strength he never realized he possessed, he tipped his head away from her touch and offered a polite smile. "I only know what I know."

She patted his chest and awkwardly pulled away, filling him with an irrational disappointment. With his handkerchief clutched to her chest, she sat straighter and finished her tea. Then she lifted her face to the east with a sudden serene beauty that took his breath. She gazed at the horizon with a wistful look.

"A new day to find some good," she whispered.

"Aye, lass. I think ye will find good in this day when we arrive at Risk Manor."

The vibrant reds and golds reflecting off the clouds cast an almost magical light across the camp. The in-between time when night handed the world to the day and whispered of promises to come.

"Risk Manor." She pulled her attention away from the rising sun and settled it on him. "Tell me about your home so I can look forward to seeing it."

He searched for the words to describe the place of his birth— a once impressive estate now badly in need of repair, a mere shadow of its former grandeur. Years of heartache, hatred, and war had taken their toll. "It is the place where I watch over those

I have sworn to protect. My kin. My clan. Those who tend the Risk crofts and call them home."

"You are their chief, then? Clan Risk's laird?"

He clenched his teeth and pulled in a deep breath before answering. "No, mistress. That would be my younger brother, Jamison Risk, the Earl of Grampian."

"I see." Jovianna leaned forward and tapped her cup upside down to dump out the wet herbs.

"So, ye willna ask, then?" He knew she wondered why the younger son rather than the older was the laird.

She set the cup on the ground beside her and gave him her full attention. "I thought it rude to ask. Such things can sometimes be complicated."

He snorted. "Aye, lass, that they can."

"I'm sorry."

"Dinna be." He had hardened himself to the pain of being stripped of his birthright years ago. "I am still able to care for the people, and Risk Manor is my home."

"Titles don't make the man," she said. "Actions do." Her tone revealed more than her words. Loyalty rang in her voice.

He studied her for a long moment in the morning light. The fierce sincerity in her eyes touched his heart. "Ye are a rare woman, Mistress Jovianna."

"Not really." She combed her fingers through her long hair, flinching as she worked out snarls and tangles. "Ouch! I may have to cut this mess."

"Dinna cut it," he said before he could stop himself. Her silky tresses shone a rich, burnished bronze shot with strands of gold and copper. 'Twould be a sorry shame indeed to lose such beauty. "Mrs. Gibb can help ye with extra combs and ribbons."

She flinched again as though that idea nettled her as badly as the tangles. "How will your people react to your bringing a pair of Englishwomen into their midst?"

"I am seriously considering leaving the one who plays dead here." He waited for Mistress Amaranth to react. "Does yer mother often eavesdrop?"

Mistress Jovianna turned and poked her mother's shoulder. "How long have you been awake?"

The woman snorted and flopped over to face them. "I was merely being polite and not interrupting."

"Bollocks to that," Mistress Jovianna said. "Do you take us for a pair of fools?"

"Out of my way." The elder pushed out between them, hopped to her feet, then straightened her clothes. "You may carry on now. After I freshen up a bit, I shall see if Cade needs any help packing up the camp. I am very good at packing." She stomped away with the haughtiness of a queen.

"I'm so sorry about her." Mistress Jovianna rose from the shelter and stretched. Her obscenely tight clothing outlined every muscle, every delicious curve of her long, lithe form.

He hardened to the point of almost splitting the seams of his trews.

"I guess I should go wash my face too," she said, "while my head is feeling better. Thank you." She gave a shy twitch of her shoulder. "For everything, Tobias."

Painfully aware of his bulging trews, he turned away as he stood, acting as if he was merely retrieving his hat from the ground. Rather than place it on his head, he held it in front of his roaring man parts like a shield. "Ye are quite welcome, Mistress Jovianna."

"I really wish you would call me Jovianna. It's what friends do."

Friends? The word made his heart sink in a way it had no right to. Rather than belabor the feeling, he offered her a concerned tip of his head. "Then, as a friend, might I tell ye that yer clothing will cause issue at Risk Manor?" He wouldn't mention the fact that it was already causing him issues right now. "Did ye bring nothing with ye that we might find upstream, where ye fell into the gorge—Jovianna?"

Her face lit up at his use of her name. Such an odd thing to please a woman. Wee lasses usually longed for the day they would be respectfully addressed as *Mistress*. With his hat still held in front of his crotch, he turned and eyed that direction. "Where exactly did ye tumble into the gorge?"

"That way." She suddenly appeared uneasy. "But we didn't carry anything with us. It was faster to travel with nothing but the clothes on our backs."

"I understand, but that doesna solve our current dilemma."

"What about the carriage you procured? Did it have trunks that might have clothing?" She rubbed the center of her chest, drawing undue attention to her firm breasts that bobbled with a tempting jiggle every time she ran her knuckles up and down her breastbone. "The heartburn from the herbs is back."

"Silas! An oatcake for the lady." Tobias didn't dare don his hat and fetch it for her. Not yet. The woman had fairly undone him. "Fitch."

The yawning man looked up from adding more wood to the glowing coals to renew the fire. "Aye?"

"Have Donnor and Pag check the coach for any sort of clothing our guests might change into, ye ken?"

Fitch's gaze slid to Jovianna. His eyebrows shot higher as he nodded. "Aye, seems like I remember a few trunks strapped to the back. I'll have them fetch it."

Strange how a new day, the realization that Jovianna and her mother did indeed appear to be in dire straits, and weren't spies or a trap, made all the men more aware of their revealing clothing. That and the fact that Jovianna's health was better. None of them would lust after an injured woman. But now Tobias wondered if he'd ever be able to wear his hat on his head again until they found her some decent clothing.

Silas handed her an oatcake and a steaming cup. "Tea, mistress. Always keep some on hand, no matter how short our trips from the manor house might be."

"Thank you, Silas." She breathed in the steam as if enjoying a rare perfume, took a sip, then smiled. "Very nice. And I'm sure the caffeine will help my head too."

"Nay, mistress." Silas shook his head. "It is tea. I swear it."

Tobias noted that once again she became uneasy. "What is *caffeine*, Jovianna?"

She stared at him, frowning but chewing her lip as well.

"Jovianna?" Now that he had started using her first name unadorned, he couldn't seem to stop.

"Caffeine is a part of the tea. Like the part of an herb that makes you feel better." Her fretful air shifted to one of almost pleading. "It's the caffeine in the tea that wakes you up and gets you moving." She took another sip and turned away, as though trying to escape the conversation. Nibbling on her oatcake, she meandered closer to the ledge overlooking the gorge and stared down into it with an unreadable expression.

A sound that reminded him of the high-pitched chattering of a squirrel made him turn. Mistress Amaranth, the liveliest elder he had ever seen, flitted around Cade, instructing him in the proper rolling and tying of a blanket. Tobias huffed out an amused snort. That old Highlander had packed up more camps than the number of sleek, silvery hairs on Mistress Amaranth's head. And yet the ancient warrior stood there, docile as a well-trained hound, nodding as though he had never rolled a blanket in all his years.

Tobias had never seen Cade behave this way with a woman. He tried to eye Mistress Amaranth as the old Highlander might see her. She was a comely matron. Tiny as could be, but it was easy to see that Jovianna had gotten her beauty from her. They had the same eyes and slant of their mouths when they smiled. As he watched the older woman dart around the camp like a whirlwind, it struck him—Mistress Amaranth overflowed with a liveliness and vigor too tempting for Cade to resist. All that she was drew Cade Maccolman to her like a bee to sweet clover. Much like the inescapable pull nagging at him with Jovianna. That observation brought him up short.

"There are the lads," Fitch said from behind him. "I dinna ken where they hid the thing, but apparently it wasna far from camp."

The coach rattled into the edge of the clearing, and Tobias was pleased to see an assortment of trunks and boxes strapped on the back. The former owner must have been en route to a place they intended to stay for the rest of the warmer months. The gentleman had relinquished several pouches of silver. The man must have been a laird who wintered in Edinburgh or Stirling but spent the milder months overseeing his lands. With any luck, things for the women of his household were in the baggage.

Tobias went to fetch Jovianna from the overlook.

She jerked and caught her breath. "Heaven's sake, I didn't hear you walk up."

"Forgive me, mistress." He directed her attention to the carriage. "There are a number of boxes and trunks to go through."

She drew a deep breath as though composing herself, then nodded. "Very good. Hopefully, there will be things to help make Amaranth and me more presentable."

As she started toward the vehicle, he stopped her with a light touch on her arm. "What is it, lass? What troubles ye?" Her uneasiness worried him. Did she fear the earl and his men would find them again?

She shook her head. "Ghosts from the past that I need to leave there." She forced a smile and hooked her arm through his. "Come. You said you wanted to leave bright and early. We're wasting daylight, as my father used to say."

They made their way over to the pile of trunks and boxes the men had unloaded. Quietly, so only she could hear, he asked, "So ye have forgiven the man for yer circumstances?"

As she crouched in front of the largest trunk and fumbled with the latches, a sadness shadowed her thoughtful smile. "My father made mistakes, but we all do. He was a good man." She rattled the large brass closures, grunting as she pried and pulled at them. With an angry growl, she rolled back on her heels and shook her head. "They must be locked."

"Nay, lass. Like this." Tobias reached around her, adjusted

the latches until they aligned with their bases, then flipped all three open. He hoisted the heavy lid upward and secured the hinges so it wouldn't slam shut on her. "Common latches. Have ye never owned a trunk like this?"

"No." She bit out the word as though he had insulted her, then hurried to lean forward and paw through the contents. "Nothing here but bolts of cloth. Silk. Linen. I think this one is a very light wool."

"Mrs. Gibb will be delighted. All the women will be." Tobias crouched beside her and unloaded the thick folds of cloth, stacking them on his knee. "What about deeper? I see ribbons and lace. Buttons and threads. Are there any garments at all?"

"No. This one has everything to make what we need but nothing already made." She took the bolts of cloth, repacked them, and closed the lid. "Maybe the next one will have something."

"This one has shoes," Fitch said, tipping the box on its side so they could see.

"Stockings and combs here," Donnor said while handing the small, round container down. "Ye can make use of those if we find anything else."

"Clothes!" Amaranth clapped her hands, then patted Cade's arm. "Cade said this fancier trunk would be the one we needed. Well done, my fine man."

Cade's entire face flushed a bright red at the praise.

Amaranth held up a white shift, a petticoat with pale blue stripes, a dark blue skirt, and a matching jacket. "I think these will come the closest to fitting you, Jovianna. There are several stomachers that match. Pick whichever you like best." With an evil grin, she bent and snatched up one last item and waved it in the air. "And don't forget your stays."

Tobias shook his head at the shameless woman, then pointed at the horses across the clearing. "The men and I will wait over there and give ye yer privacy. Call out when the two of ye are decent, aye?"

"That will be just fine," Mistress Amaranth said as she dove back into the trunk. "Jovianna and I will be ready before you know it."

He very much doubted that. Experience had proven that women never dressed in haste. "Aye, then. On wi' ye. Fast as ye can, ladies."

Jovianna gave him a look as if begging him not to go.

"What is it, lass?"

"Nothing." She forced a smile that didn't reach her eyes, then joined her mother at the trunk.

Concern chewed at him as he herded the men over to the horses and made sure they all kept their backs to the women. "Something is troubling Mistress Jovianna."

"I did not find a body," Fitch said, as they stood shoulder to shoulder. "Rode quite the ways. Thought if I found their cousin, and we gave the man a proper burial, it might grant them some ease." Leeriness echoed in his tone. "But I found nothing. No horses. No sign of blood. But most importantly, no tracks. A group of men would be hard-pressed to travel through here without leaving any sign at all."

"Agreed." Tobias ground his teeth and stared off into the distance. "So, they lied."

"It would seem so." Fitch resettled his footing, shifting as though uncomfortable with the distasteful report. "I am sorry."

"And what is that supposed to mean?" Tobias asked.

"We see how ye've taken to Mistress Jovianna." Fitch gave him a hard, side-eyed glare. "Daren't ye deny it. We're not fools."

"I dinna believe them to be a threat," Cade interrupted.

"And that is because ye are taken with Mistress Amaranth," Fitch said. "Ye dinna wish them to be a threat."

"Amaranth's husband is dead." Cade moved closer, as though ready to defend not only her honor but his own. "And she repeated the same story of how they came to be here and didn't change a single detail. The rains couldha washed away tracks and blood. Ye ken that as well as I."

"Aye, but it didna rain hard enough to wash away a body," Tobias said.

"Maybe the murderers took it to prove the man's death and make a claim on any inheritance Amaranth might have been owed." Cade's hands closed into white-knuckled fists.

"Why would a woman's distant cousin leave her an inheritance?" Tobias wanted it to be true as badly as Cade, but the reasoning was weak.

"She said he was her only living relative." Cade glared at Fitch, daring the man to argue.

Tobias scrubbed the stubble of his day-old beard, wanting to believe the women but worried about doing so.

"They threw them sheriffs off," Silas said. The balding man waggled a scraggly brow. "Had them three convinced they better turn tail and run before the fever got hold of them."

"Well, those ladies sure didna have any weapons," Pag said. "With them tight clothes of theirs that showed all their wares, we wouldha seen them."

"Dinna be eyeing the women," Tobias said. "'Tis rude."

"Ye would have to be blind to not notice their—"

Tobias cut the lad off by grabbing him up by the chest. "Finish that sentence at yer own risk."

"I meant no disrespect." Pag held up his hands, his feet dangling a foot above the ground.

"Neither did I," Fitch said. "I merely reported what I found. Or rather, what I failed to find. Ye needed to know, Tobias."

Tobias let the boy drop. Turning to Fitch, he leveled a hard glare on the man he trusted more than any in the world. "Do ye feel they are a danger to us and our cause?"

Fitch gave a slow tilt of his head, like a perplexed dog eying a poisoned bone. "I dinna ken. They said nothing to those sheriffs. Of course, we outnumbered those men, and perhaps they feared what we might do if they raised the alarm and the men fell to us." His scowl deepened, knotting his brows tighter together. "But they dinna strike me as a danger to us. Even the old one that chatters nonstop and flits around like a wee bird has moments where she looks sorely troubled and afraid of something." He shrugged. "I believe there is a story to them they have yet to share."

"I say we watch them close," Cade said. "And ye ken as well as I that when we reach the manor house, Mrs. Gibb and the maids will report anything amiss. Those hens dinna miss a thing."

"I agree there is more to them," Tobias said. He blew out a heavy sigh and tried to rub away the weariness burning his eyes. "And if we canna discover what troubles them, I feel certain that Mrs. Gibb and her army of maids will know Mistress Amaranth's and Jovianna's life history before a sennight has passed."

CHAPTER FIVE

A YELP ESCAPED Jovianna as her mother yanked the stays tighter. "I need to breathe, *Mother*."

"That jacket looks to be about a size too small for you. If we don't squeeze you in wherever we can, we will never get you into it. And I fear the skirt will hit you mid-shin, but it can't be helped." Amaranth came around to the front and adjusted the frilly neckline of the shift. "This is quite fancy for this era. The owner must have been well off." She stepped back and eyed the length of the white linen gown that shielded the outer clothes from sweat and body oils. She made a face and shook her head. "Your father cursed you with his height."

Jovianna tried to reach the ties of the stays to loosen them but failed. "I must breathe. Either loosen them or I'm going to find a knife and cut them off." She meant it, too. Appearing respectable enough to be accepted was one thing. Being tortured for it was quite another. She glanced at her trekking shirt, leggings, panties, and sports bra in a pile on the ground. "Should we hide our clothes for when we return?"

Her mother didn't answer. Instead, she gathered the folds of the striped petticoat and held it ready to slip over Jovianna's head. "Slip this on and I'll loosen the corset."

Jovianna backed up a step. "You did not answer my question about our clothes." Whenever her mother avoided answering anything, Jovianna knew she would not like the response.

"We are not going back," Amaranth said, her mouth set in a hard line. "I see no sense in endangering our lives by trying to re-create a phenomenon that nearly killed you the first time." Her eyes misted over with rare tears. "I almost lost you, Jovianna. I will not risk that again."

Jovianna had expected that response. Didn't much care for it, but understood it. She wasn't all that keen on almost drowning again to try something that might not even work either. After all, as her mother had said before, how many times had they trekked the gorge before without triggering whatever had sent them to this time? But to leave everything behind? The thought made her shudder.

"Do you really think we can live here? Safely?" She leaned forward, allowed her mother to slide the petticoat over her head, then shook it down in place. That was her greatest fear. If anyone ever found out the truth, they would surely execute them for being witches.

Her mother loosened the stays, then held out the skirt but still didn't answer.

A heavy sigh escaped Jovianna as she snatched the garment and shook it out. She stepped into the dark blue skirt of light-weight wool and worked it up to her waist, shoving the layers of petticoat and shift down inside it. "This waistband will never fasten." Whoever the clothing originally belonged to had not only been a great deal shorter but also smaller around. "You should wear this one. Are there none any larger?"

"Everything is smaller." Amaranth handed her a pair of stockings and their matching ribbons. "And yes, we can survive here. We know how we should look. What we should say. Our education will aid us in fitting in and looking like we belong."

"Hand me another ribbon to feed through this buttonhole so I can extend this waistband to fasten it." Jovianna pulled the opening around to the front and waited with both ends of the band in her hands. Amaranth handed her a thin blue strand that perfectly matched the skirt. Jovianna folded it in half, fed it through the buttonhole, then looped it around the button and tied everything securely with a double bow.

As she slid the skirt around and placed the fastening at the back, she glanced up at her mother. "Our story about how we ended up here is what concerns me. What if they search for our *distant cousin's* body? Does an Earl of Tenbury even exist? I don't recall ever reading or hearing that name."

"Tenbury Wells is a market town and parish in the north-western extremity of Worcestershire. I always thought the name sounded regal, so I decided to put it to good use." Amaranth held out a pair of shoes. "Here. These should fit well enough. The leather is so soft they shouldn't be uncomfortable even if they are snug."

"Bloody hell." Jovianna swallowed hard against a returning wave of nausea and held a hand to her forehead, which had already started throbbing again. "They're going to discover us for certain. You know I have never been a convincing liar."

"I know." Amaranth held a garment up in each hand and eyed them. "Quite handy when you were a child but a dreadful bother now that you're an adult." She lifted the gown on the right and then the one on the left. "Light blue or deep green for me? What do you think? And by the way, if you could convince yourself that you're merely crafting a story and not actually lying, that might make it easier for you. After all, look how creative you are with music. You can't read a single note but play the violin like a virtuoso and sing like an angel."

After snatching up the shoes, stockings, and ribbons, Jovianna went to the stump to don them. She wished she could be as positive about their situation as her mother. And she supposed it could have turned out a great deal worse than it had. She paused in the tying of the ribbon to secure her stockings to steal a glance at Tobias. True to his word, he and his men stood with their backs to them, providing as much privacy as could be had, considering the area. Tobias was a good man. Kind. So very interesting. And if she hadn't tumbled back into this century, she never would have had the pleasure of meeting him.

"Damn, damn, damn," she said as she tied the ribbons snugly.

"Who or what are you damning?" Amaranth asked. "Are the stays still too tight?"

"No. My heart is." She might as well tell her mother. The woman had the uncanny ability to see right through her, anyway. "I do not like lying to Tobias. Not when he appears genuinely concerned about our welfare. It is not fair to him."

Her mother rewarded her with a knowing smile. "I believe he is genuinely concerned about you in a number of ways."

"I don't believe you're right about that." Jovianna remembered how he had shied from her touch when he had a splendid opportunity to kiss her. Not that he should have kissed her. After all, they had just met. Even so, she had been sorely tempted herself. Hadn't he been? Surely his hesitation was because of her heritage. At least, she hoped that was the reason.

She shook away the silliness of her turmoil. "He is concerned because I'm English and all the strangeness that is us. He fears we might be a danger to his people."

"It sounds as though his brother could be trying to clear the people from the lands for the profit of raising sheep for the wool industry." Amaranth shimmied off her twenty-first-century attire and donned a shift so long that it hit the ground and bunched around her feet. "Dear me, this will never do. Perhaps one of the others is shorter."

"So, were you eavesdropping the entire time this morning?" Jovianna slipped on the soft doeskin shoes with short, sturdy heels. They were snug at the toes but not unbearable. "You have no shame at all, do you?"

"You are my daughter, and it is my right to protect you any way I see fit. If that means listening in on conversations, then so be it." Amaranth pulled on another shift and smiled as the hem hit her at the ankles. "Much better. Now, what do you think, dark green or the light blue?"

"Green. The light blue will wash you out." Jovianna stood and tugged at her ill-fitting clothing. With any luck, she wouldn't split any seams or shock anyone with her daring display of ankle and shin. "I look like I had a sudden growth spurt while wearing these clothes."

"They're not that bad," Amaranth said.

"You are lying." Jovianna gathered up their discarded clothes. "I suppose I should bury these? The labels and underthings could be a problem. If I toss them on the fire, they'll simply melt and raise an unexplainable stench."

"Agreed. But you better hurry. I'm sure the males are getting restless." Amaranth turned. "Finish my laces first? I like the one-piece gown better for me, I think. None of the skirts were short enough."

"Yours fits much better than mine. You're lovely." Jovianna buried their clothes in a shallow hole, then eyed the bundle of combs still in the box with the rest of the shoes. "And now for our hair. Hand me a comb. I'll do yours and you can do mine."

"Cade! We are decent," Amaranth called out. "Nothing left to do but our hair."

Jovianna braced herself, knowing her appearance might be more decent than her modern clothes, but it still left a lot to be desired. She pulled an ivory comb free of the bundle and started running it through Amaranth's thick, silvery hair as the men ambled over to them.

"Ye look quite…" Tobias's praise stalled out as his gaze swept down to her hemline. The man had the audacity to curl his upper lip and frown as though he smelled a stink. "Ye are…" he started again, and failed a second time.

"Ridiculous," she finished for him. "Yes. I know. As Amaranth said, I am cursed with my father's height. But hopefully, your people will find me more respectable than they would have in the other clothes."

"Ye dinna look ridiculous." He circled her, eyeing her as though she was a prime bit of livestock for sale. "Ye are quite…" He paused a third time, his sleek, dark brows angling into a befuddled frown as he searched for the proper words.

"She is lovely," Cade said, as though chastising an impudent child. "Dammit, man. What the devil is wrong with ye?"

Jovianna couldn't help but laugh as she secured her mother's hair into a respectable bun. "Leave him alone. He was trying to be nice but still not lie. I know what I look like." She pulled a darker set of combs from the bundle and handed them to Amaranth. "Shall I sit on the stump so you can reach better?"

"Good idea." Amaranth took her position behind the stump.

"I did not wish to offend the lady," Tobias said, finally finding his tongue. He scowled at his grinning men. "Stow the trunks and get ready to ride, ye ken? The women are nearly ready, and there ye stand like a lazy gaggle of geese."

Jovianna bit her lip to keep from smiling, then flinched as Amaranth tugged through a particularly knotted length of hair. "Bloody hell! Are you trying to pull me bald?"

"Heaven help me. You're as tender-headed as you were as a child. Stop being such a baby. Rats could nest in these snarls. I know your head is sore, but they have to go."

"Then cut them out." Jovianna reached back and grabbed the hank of hair her mother was currently attacking.

"No," Tobias said. "Give me the comb."

"Give you the comb?" Jovianna repeated.

"Aye." With an unyielding glare, he waited for her mother to place it in his hand.

"There you are, sir." Amaranth handed it over with a knowing smirk. "I'll help pack the carriage while you unsnarl the lady's tangled mop. Best of luck to you. She screeches at the slightest pull, as though you're trying to kill her."

Jovianna silently cursed her mother as the woman sashayed over to help the men. She squared her shoulders, took a deep breath, and blew it out. "Go ahead. I'm ready."

"'Tis not an execution, lass."

"If you are as ruthless as Amaranth, it will be." She fisted her hands in her lap and cringed in readiness.

He leaned so close that his warm breath tickled her nape as he lifted her hair. "The trick is to start at the ends and untangle the snarls with a gentle touch as ye work yer way higher. That way, ye dinna get kicked."

"Get kicked?" She frowned as the tortoiseshell comb made a quiet rasping sound with every pass through her hair. "Are you comparing me to a horse?"

He didn't answer for several strokes. "A lively filly with a shining mane and braided tail is a beauty admired by all."

"If I were standing, I would kick you," she said.

"Why? Did I pull?"

"No, but no woman wants to be compared to a horse."

"Ah, but that's where ye err, lass. 'Tis truly a compliment." The deep baritone of his voice was as moving as a lover's touch. "A wise man treasures his horse. Cherishes it, even, and does everything he can to ensure it's kept safe and content."

She found herself relaxing. The steady rasp of the comb along with the rhythmic stroke of his hands mesmerized her. "And are you a wise man?"

"About horses? Aye." He combed her hair back from her face, taking extra care when he passed across her bruised knot. "Yer hair shines like the finest silk." A soft, rumbling chuckle escaped him. "Much lovelier than any horse I have ever brushed, I assure ye."

"Thank you—I think." His attentions soothed away her earlier worries, somehow making them seem more manageable and not nearly so daunting.

The combing stopped, and she immediately missed it.

"All the tangles are gone," he said. "Do you wish it in a simple braid?" He handed her the comb and started plaiting it before she could answer. "Have ye a ribbon ready?"

"No." She frowned as Amaranth handed the small, round box

that held the ribbons, lace, and pins up to Pag to secure on the carriage. "And they're lashing down the box containing them."

"Dinna fash about it. I can use one of my leather ties." With a gentle tugging, Tobias secured the end, then draped it over the front of her shoulder. "Good enough?"

"Very good." She smoothed her fingers down the perfect evenness of the weave, then stood and faced him. "Thank you for rescuing me from Amaranth."

"My pleasure, lass." His gaze shifted to the coach and the others. "It appears we are ready." He gallantly offered his arm. "To the carriage, aye?"

She took his arm, smiling up at him as they crossed the clearing.

Amaranth already sat inside the coach, and Pag held open the door.

Jovianna came to a standstill and eyed the thing, none too sure about climbing into the close quarters even with the leather window covers rolled up and secured out of the way. Her stomach churned a low warning, and every instinct shouted for her to turn tail and run.

"Jovianna, really? Still?" Amaranth waved her forward. "Come on, sweetie. The only way you will ever overcome your claustrophobia is by desensitization. You know that."

"My knowing and my ability to do it are two very different things." Jovianna gave Tobias a nervous smile. "Sorry. I've been afraid of small spaces ever since I was a child. I was in a tunnel that collapsed and was trapped for a few hours."

He stepped closer, peered inside the coach, then stepped back. "'Tis built for four. The two of ye should have plenty of room. And all the windows are open."

She pulled in a deep breath, smoothed her already sweating palms across her skirts, then climbed onto the step. "I will do my best. Who will drive?"

With a proud grin, Pag bobbed his head. "That would be me, mistress, and dinna fash yerself. I'll keep the pace steady and smooth as I can."

"If I ask you to stop, will you stop?" She would endure it for as long as she could because Amaranth and Tobias both thought her silly. She could tell by the way they acted. "Promise?"

Pag held a hand over his heart and gave her a solemn dip of his chin. "I swear it, mistress. Anything ye need, ye just ask, and I shall see it done."

Tobias huffed a growling snort and glared at the lad. "Into the driver's seat with ye, then, aye? I wish to reach the manor before nightfall."

Jovianna held her breath, stepped inside, then plopped onto the seat that would have her facing the front during the journey. Her toes bumped the base of the seat that faced her. How in heaven's name could four people possibly travel in this thing without stomping each other to death? "Scoot over," she told Amaranth. "You're on my side."

Amaranth rolled her eyes, then scooted as far over on her side of the coach as she could. "Breathe, Jovianna. We'll be just fine. Every window is wide open. Lots of sunshine and fresh air. There is nothing at all to fear."

Unless they tipped over, got wedged in a ditch, and the walls collapsed and crushed them. Jovianna didn't voice those concerns, just clenched the window frame so tightly that her knuckles popped.

Tobias closed the door with a hard thud and latched it. The carriage took off with a lurch that made Jovianna clench every muscle. Her stomach cramped and her bowels threatened to embarrass her.

"Concentrate on the loveliness of the land," her mother said as they careened along with a nauseating sway. She shifted her bum from side to side like a nesting hen. "The cushions could use a bit more padding, but this ride is not bad at all."

Bile rose hot and high in the back of Jovianna's throat, and her mouth filled with a dangerously sour taste. She stuck her head out the window and bellowed, "Stop the coach!"

Pag immediately halted.

She fought with the latch, shoved the door open, and leaped to the ground. Propping her bum against the sturdy wooden wheel, she bent over and concentrated on breathing. Her mouth watered so violently that it was a wonder she didn't drown in her own spit.

Pag came up beside her. "Saints' bones, mistress. Was my driving that bad?"

"No, Pag," she said between deep breaths. "I don't do well inside carriages."

"Then ride up top with me," he said. "Plenty of room on the driver's bench."

Up top. In the wide-open air. Nothing around her, and if the coach tipped, she could jump to safety. "A fine idea," she said, feeling better already. "I wish we had thought of that earlier."

"Are ye not well enough to travel?" Tobias called out. He urged his mount back to them.

"Pag thought of something we should have done to begin with," she said, finding herself looking forward to the prospect. She caught hold of the rails, hoisted herself up onto the first foothold, then smiled over her shoulder at Tobias. "I'm going to ride up here with him."

His concerned frown shifted to a thunderous scowl. "Get down."

Still holding tight to the rail, she turned and shook her head at him. "If I get back inside, I'm sure to get sick. Up top, I think I'll be fine and won't cause any more delays. You said you wanted to reach the manor before nightfall."

He walked his horse closer. "Get. Down."

"I either ride up top with Pag or I walk." She wasn't about to get back inside that carriage.

Tobias's eyes narrowed and his squared jaw locked to a hard, determined slant. Without taking his glare from hers, he rode forward, yanked her off the side of the coach, and plopped her onto the saddle in front of him. "Get moving!" he shouted back in a growling roar, then urged his horse into a hard gallop.

Jovianna held tight to his shirt in one hand while clamping her other arm around his waist. "Are you trying to kill me?" She bounced mercilessly, and the front lip of the saddle jabbed into her thigh and bum. "What is wrong with you?"

"What is wrong with me?" He pulled his horse to a hard stop. "I willna have ye riding beside Pag. Nor will I have ye walking. Therefore, my stubborn wee mistress, this is yer only other choice." Lightning flashed in his pale eyes that somehow seemed a fiercer blue with his unreasonable anger. He glared at her with his teeth bared, as though daring her to argue.

She adjusted her position and almost slipped off.

He caught her and crushed her against his chest, tipping her face up, her mouth a mere whisper from his.

She tightened her hold around his waist. "What would be wrong with my riding beside Pag? It's not like we wouldn't be in plain view and easily chaperoned if that's your worry, which is utterly ridiculous. He is little more than a boy."

"That *boy* would gladly claim ye as his own if ye allowed it."

"Well, you have my word I won't be allowing it. Now, let me down so I can get back up on top of that coach."

He stared at her, not blinking. His nostrils flared the slightest bit. "No."

"I do not understand you. You act jealous, yet this morning you had a perfectly good chance to kiss me and didn't take it. What do you want from me?"

An agonized growl escaped him. Then he crushed her mouth with his. With his fingers buried in the hair at the back of her head, he held her locked in place, kissing her with a fierceness that seared through her, melding her into his embrace. He forced her lips open wider, delving in as though proving he had every right to claim her. She found herself kissing him back, tightening her arms around him.

Just when she thought she would surely melt into a puddle of pure submission, he lifted his head and glared down at her. "That is why I willna let ye ride beside the boy. Understand?"

"Yes," she whispered, her mouth still throbbing. She didn't really *understand* but sensed that now was not the time to have that conversation. Was the kiss an example of what Pag would do if given half a chance, or was Tobias telling her she was off-limits to everyone but him? She hoped the latter was the reason but wasn't experienced in this sort of thing and didn't want to botch it. "Uhm, but I still can't ride inside the coach."

He gave her a disgruntled glare, then tipped his head as if unable to believe she still didn't comprehend his intentions. "Ye will ride with me. The entire way, ye ken?"

"Can I shift a bit and straddle the horse?" She shot a glance down at her right thigh. "The hard ridge of your saddle bites my bum with every gallop."

The corner of his mouth crooked upward the slightest bit, and devilment flashed in his eyes. "Does it indeed?"

The aching spark his kiss had started roared into unbridled wanting. She wrapped an arm around his shoulders and hitched herself up higher in his lap. She couldn't help but smile as she noted an even harder ridge there. "Yes. Indeed, it does."

Lifting her as easily as if she was a child, he resettled her astraddle the horse, wrapped an arm around her waist, and yanked her back against him. "Better, lass?" The warmth of his breath caressed her ear and sent a delicious shiver through her.

"Yes. Thank you." She swallowed hard and ran her tongue across her lips. They had a lovely, bruised feeling that she couldn't recall ever having before. Her ego felt much better as well. He had kissed her like he meant it. Like he liked her even though she was English.

She lifted her face to the warm sunshine and smiled. A contentedness buoyed her as she filled her lungs with the sweet, fresh air scented with pine and the fragrances of the flourishing summer countryside.

Her mother was right about the gorgeous scenery. The jagged crags and rolling hills were painted with deft strokes of green and dusky blues beneath the brilliance of the bright azure sky. Dense woodlands were shaded a multitude of the richest greens. Thick carpets of white and yellow wildflowers swayed alongside the dirt road. The lands surrounding Loch Lomond and what in the twenty-first century would be known as the Loch Lomond and Trossachs National Park seemed even more vibrant and breathtaking in the eighteenth century. Somehow, everything was more alive. Perhaps it was because there were fewer distractions. No cell phones or internet. No blaring radios, hum of farm machinery, or vehicles roaring on the roadway. Nothing but the rugged, unapologizing beauty of Scotland. A serenity that demanded you acknowledge it alone.

Even though it seemed almost sacrilege to speak, she needed to know more about this man who both confused and thrilled her. "This trip. Your *procurement* of goods and, I assume, coin. Was it a success? Will it be enough to protect your people?"

He exhaled a heavy sigh that shifted him against her. "I believe we now have enough to cover this season's rents." His thighs flexed behind hers as he urged the horse to a faster clip. "And with any luck, a bit to spare for what is needed this winter. Last year's harvest was not what it shouldha been. It's my hope this year's is adequate, if not more."

"Have you tried potatoes yet?" According to everything she knew, the crop was introduced by 1760 and did quite well. At least until the blight in a little over eighty years that would cause the terrible famine. "But don't depend solely on them for a food source. To do so will be deadly." She bit her lip and silently damned herself. She should not have said that.

"A few of our crofters planted potatoes for the first time this year, and the plants appear to be doing well." He slowed the horse, apparently to make hearing each other easier. "What is this deadliness you warn of?"

"It will not come in our lifetime." She wished she had kept her mouth shut. But in for a penny, in for a pound. Hopefully, he was a typical superstitious Scot and believed in the sight. "In a little over eighty years, a blight will come and take out the crop, causing widespread famine throughout Scotland and Ireland. Many will die."

He brought the horse to a standstill, and his arm slid out from around her waist. "And how do you know this?"

She clamped on tight to the lip of the saddle, wondering if he was about to shove her off and ride away. "Amaranth and I have the sight," she said quietly. "Another reason we ran from Glasgow." She made a mental note to mention this slight embellishment to her mother, wondering if her parent would be proud of her attempt at telling a convincing lie.

"Ye are witches." The way he said it didn't sound like an accusation but more like a statement of fact.

"No. White ladies," she said, remembering her thesis on French and Celtic mythology and folklore. "Sometimes, we know things." She bowed her head, hoping she wasn't digging her own grave. "But not always. Unfortunately, neither of us has control over the visions." When he didn't answer, she risked a glance back at him. "Should I get down from the horse now?"

"Why have ye stopped?" Fitch shouted from behind them.

The clatter of the coach creaked to a halt, and an eerie silence hung heavy in the air. Cade and Silas rode up, then came to a halt beside them.

"Is someone approaching? Did ye spy something?" Cade rode forward a bit and scanned the countryside with a leery scowl.

When Tobias still hadn't answered, Jovianna made the decision for him, cursing herself for being a prattling fool and not keeping her thoughts to herself. Holding tight to the saddle, she tried to swing her leg over and slide off gracefully, but got tangled in her skirts and started to fall. "Shite!"

"Are ye trying to break yer neck?" Tobias caught her before she hit the ground and gently lowered her the rest of the way. His eyes narrowed to a hard glare as if he were willing her to hear his thoughts. "Off to the bushes with ye. Next time give me a moment longer to help ye down."

She understood completely. Or, at least, thought she did. She was to keep her mouth shut and not repeat the white lady lie to anyone. Without a word, she darted into the edge of the woods, took cover behind a large tree, and leaned back against it. Heart pounding, she closed her eyes and prayed for the wisdom to filter her words before they tumbled out of her foolish mouth, doubting very much if that miracle would ever happen.

CHAPTER SIX

"A RE YOU UNWELL?" Amaranth stepped from around the tree without a sound.

"No! I am an idiot." Jovianna pressed a hand to her chest to calm her pounding heart. "And don't sneak up on me. I am a proper mess as it is. My nerves are pure rubbish."

Her mother grinned. "I don't doubt it. I saw that kiss."

"The kiss is not the issue here." Jovianna pushed away from the gnarled trunk and sat on one of its large, knobby roots. "Without thinking, I blethered on about the potato famine and not depending solely on that vegetable as a food source."

"Oh, dear."

"Exactly." Lifting her head from her hands, she fixed a frustrated glare on her mother. "And to explain how I came about that knowledge, I told Tobias that you and I are white ladies and receive visions about the future from time to time."

"Jovianna," said her mother in an appropriately scolding tone. She sidled a few steps to one side and looked back at the road where they'd left the men. "I realize the great Scotland witch hunt was back in 1597, but the 1700s had a few executions too. You know that."

"I told you I was a poor liar." Jovianna hiked up her skirts and started relieving herself.

"What are you doing?" Amaranth asked.

"What does it look like I'm doing?" After drying with a bit of spongy moss, Jovianna sorted her clothes back in place and stood. "That's why he stopped the horse." She shook her head with a frustrated jerk. "Not because I needed to pee, but because I shocked him so badly with the white lady lie. I don't think he wanted to tell anyone. So he just kept me from falling off the horse when I tried to get down and told me to go use the bushes."

"Well, there is that, then." Amaranth stepped around the cluster of tree roots, lifted her skirts, widened her stance, and peed standing up.

"How do you not pee on your feet?" Jovianna asked.

"Years of perfecting the art in the field." Her mother sorted herself and craned her neck, watching the men in the distance.

Jovianna peered around the tree. Tobias had dismounted, as had the others. They milled around in a restless cluster in the middle of the road. She could only imagine what they were discussing. Drat it all. He was such a kind, interesting man, and she had completely tossed every possibility with him away. "So, do we run for it while they're distracted?"

"And where exactly do you suggest we run to?" Amaranth assumed that superior look of disbelief that Jovianna hated.

"At the moment, I have no idea," Jovianna said. "But right off the top of my head, I would say that anywhere but here would do."

"No. We are ill-supplied to survive, and the nearest town where we might find work would take us days, if not weeks to reach on foot." Amaranth waved her forward. "Come. We need to play this out and see if we can make it work. Just keep me apprised of everything you say to Tobias, so I don't contradict your statements with whatever I say to Cade. Is the potato famine the only thing you predicted?"

"Yes." Jovianna felt like a child about to be made to apologize to the parish priest for stealing the communion biscuits. "Thank heavens the Jacobite uprising and Culloden are behind us."

"Yes. Thank heavens for that." Amaranth looped her arm through Jovianna's and tugged, forcing her daughter to walk alongside her. "I know you have always excelled in your studies and music and struggled with, shall we say, *people skills*, but you must try to do better. Especially with Tobias, since he is their leader. You can be just as brilliant at interacting with others as you are with books and musical instruments. Our survival depends on it. Understand?"

"Yes, Mum." Jovianna blew out a heavy sigh, feeling as deflated and beaten as a worn-out party balloon.

"You haven't called me *Mum* in years." Amaranth gave her a quick hug.

"It seemed fitting." Jovianna braced herself as they reached the roadway. Tobias turned and settled a hard gaze on her. At least, it felt like a hard gaze. It was hard to tell with his black tricorn cocked so low over his brow. Bowing her head, she fell in step behind Amaranth on her way back to the coach.

"Jovianna."

The way he said her name made it impossible to ignore him. She swallowed hard and faced him. "Yes?"

"Where are ye going?"

"I thought I would ride the rest of the way on the coach." She cast a glance up at the driver's seat, doubting he would have any issues with her sitting beside Pag now.

"What did I tell ye earlier?" He moved toward her with the slow, fluid grace of a panther on the hunt.

She made a halfhearted flick of her thumb in the carriage's direction. "I thought maybe you might have changed your mind."

"I have not." He reached her side and offered his arm, fixing her with a piercing stare that both thrilled and frightened her.

"Very well, then." She accepted it and fell in step beside him as they returned to his horse.

"Mount up and head on," he told the others. "I shall guard

the back the remainder of the trip."

The men obeyed, and the carriage rattled onward. Tobias stood beside his mount, watching them until they were quite a bit out ahead. Then he turned and settled a worried gaze on her. "Ye must never repeat what ye told me to anyone else, ye ken?"

"I know." Jovianna nodded. "I'm sorry." And she was. More than he would ever know.

"Dinna be sorry." With a gentleness that made her heart hurt, he lifted her up onto the horse's back. "Ye said yer gifts were another reason ye had to leave Glasgow. Ye dinna wish to stir such a danger again, do ye?"

"No." She stared down at the worn leather of the saddle, its edges burnished a dark brown from years of use. "I have always had a problem with keeping my thoughts to myself, and when we talked of crops and rents, I was worried about your people and just wanted to help."

"I know that, lass." He launched himself up behind her, settled in place, and nudged the mount into motion. "And I am grateful." He tightened his hold around her waist. "But also worried for yer safety."

They rode along in silence for what seemed like forever. Silence was safest. Jovianna rubbed her forehead, willing it to stop throbbing. The magical effects of the devil's brew had finally worn off, but long gone was the convenience of a quick stop for a nice, hot cup of tea and an aspirin.

"Yer pain has returned?"

She forced herself to sit straighter and lowered her hand to her lap. "No. Just checking the size of the knot."

He pressed his mouth close to her ear and whispered, "It pleases me to discover that ye canna lie worth a damn."

A heavy sigh escaped her. "That I do not." She shielded her eyes with her hands, hoping if she blocked the sunlight, the pain would stay to the level of a dull roar.

"If ye can bear it, we will be there soon, lass. Within the hour." He urged the horse into a gallop and thundered past the coach and the other men. "Mrs. Gibb might even have a better remedy for ye," he shouted over the clattering hooves.

She bounced back against his chest and clutched her head. "I'm going to vomit all over your horse if you don't slow down."

He immediately curtailed the beast's gait to a slow, steady walk. "Do ye think ye might be able to lie on the bench inside the coach?"

When she opened her eyes, a wave of dizziness and sparkly orbs of light clouding her vision convinced her to try. "I hope so, because upright on a horse is becoming unbearable."

He halted the animal, dismounted, and gently pulled her down into his arms, cradling her like a babe against his chest. "Keep yer eyes closed, lass. I'll carry ye there and get ye inside without ye seeing a bit of it."

With her hands over her eyes, she nuzzled closer, pressing into the curve of his neck and shoulder. "You are a good man, Tobias Risk, and I am grateful for you."

"I am not a good man," he said quietly as he walked back to the coach. "Ye'd best learn that part of me died long ago."

Before she could argue, he called out to Pag and Amaranth. "Open the door and spread more blankets across the seat to make it softer. She's feeling poorly and canna go any farther without lying down."

"That concussion is going to plague her for a while," Amaranth said. The carriage squeaked as she hurried to make the bench as bearable as possible.

Jovianna curled into a tighter ball, trying to block out the memory of the small enclosure. She had to do this. With her head pounding and her stomach churning, even riding beside Pag was no longer an option.

"Come on, sweetie," Amaranth said. "I've got it ready. Open your eyes and scuttle in."

"No." Tobias almost barked out the word. "I will lift her in and place her on the bench so she doesna have to open her eyes."

"You'll never fit through that door," Amaranth argued.

"Woman, never tell me that which I can or canna do." Tobias repositioned Jovianna in his arms and held her tighter. "Dinna listen to her, Jovianna." His voice had softened, become almost tender. "Are ye ready, lass?"

"I'm ready," she whispered, determined not to succumb to a panic attack. A sudden lurch upward made her swallow hard, then she found herself gently lowered onto a soft pile of blankets. She curled to her side and kept her hands clamped over her eyes.

"There ye are." He touched her cheek, then kissed her temple.

"Thank you," she whispered past the knot of unreasonable emotions trying to choke her. "You are a good man. I will never think otherwise."

"Never say never, lass." The coach shook and creaked, then the warmth of his powerful presence was gone.

The door closed with a quiet thud, the latch rattled, and then the dreadful box on wheels lurched into motion.

"That man is falling in love with you," Amaranth said.

Jovianna shifted, pressed her face into the rolled blanket beneath her head, and held it against her eyes. The dark pressure seemed to lessen the pain. "He's a good man."

"You keep saying that. Do you not have feelings for him?"

A heavy sigh escaped Jovianna as she debated denying everything she thought and felt about Tobias.

"You know you can't lie to your mother," Amaranth said.

"I am aware." Jovianna scooted back deeper into the blankets and cushions. The bench of the seat seemed inclined to toss her onto the floor. "How can I possibly care about a man I just met?"

"Well…" Her mother's voice took on the scholarly tone that warned an educational lecture was imminent. "He resuscitated you after you had drowned, carried you out of the gorge, then tended to your pain with his personal mixture of herbs. He also stayed awake all night and, when your headache returned, tended to you again and soothed you not only with his presence but with another dose of herbs that Cade told me were scarce and were the only thing known to ease Tobias's own headaches." She paused for the span of a breath. "Humans by nature, especially females, are prone to respond to such behavior with feelings of gratitude, tenderness, and even love. And since the dawn of time, primal instincts have guided females to the males who will father strong, healthy children and protect them. Tobias is a fine specimen of a man and has also exhibited a protective nature. It doesn't matter how short of a time you have known him. You could very well love him on sight, as I did your father. We married after knowing each other only three weeks, and experienced forty joyous years together until that damn accident."

"You make it all sound so scientific." But Jovianna smiled, finding comfort in the explanation she already knew, but her wise mother confirmed.

"Everything is science, sweetie." Amaranth laughed. "You know that."

"I concur, but I also know that everything could change once we arrive at his home. A man's family and his people can easily change his mind and his heart. We are English, and even though we speak the same language, we're still strangers in a land made hostile by our own kind." A dip in the road bounced her hard and made her hiss.

"Pag! Do better!" Amaranth shouted.

"Sorry, mistress," filtered down to them over the noisy, creaking rattle of the coach.

Before her mother could start in again, Jovianna lifted a hand to stave off any more words. "Shush, please. I need to concentrate on not puking or having a panic attack."

"You may not have to concentrate long." Amaranth sounded thoughtful. "There's a whitewashed cottage up ahead. Probably one of Tobias's crofters."

Jovianna tensed, waiting for the coach to stop. But they didn't. Curiosity nagged at her, but she didn't dare uncover her eyes and look. "Are we passing it?"

"It would seem so." Her mother made a few humming sounds.

"What are you *hmm*'ing about?" Jovianna risked easing the blanket away from her eyes, but sunlight stabbed a spike of pain through her skull and increased the nauseating churn in her stomach. "Bloody hell." She groaned and shoved her face back into the blanket. "Well? What do you see?"

"A farm, and those working in the fields appear to be pleased with Tobias's return. They've removed their hats and are waving. Waving their gardening implements, too."

"Gardening implements?" Jovianna envisioned tiny rakes and spades like she used in her windowsill garden.

"Hoes, dear. Scythes. You know the sort. And it looks like a few children are now running behind the carriage, following us in."

The sound of barking confirmed that one or more dogs had also joined the parade.

Panic and dread battled for control over Jovianna. Then she remembered. "Do not say a word to Cade about the potato famine or us being white ladies. Tobias doesn't want anyone else to know."

Amaranth didn't answer. A very pregnant silence filled the coach.

Jovianna blew out a heavy sigh. "How on earth did you already have time to tell him about both?"

"I was trying to validate your story, and you'll be relieved to know that Cade seemed very accepting of our ability to predict the future."

"My next prediction is that they're going to serve a pair of roasted English witches as the main course for tonight's supper," Jovianna said.

"There is no recorded evidence that people ever ate any of the witches burned at the stake."

Jovianna found that less than reassuring but didn't have time to argue the point, since the coach lurched to a stop. "What's happening?" she whispered.

"Breathe, sweetie. We can manage this as long as we keep our heads."

"What a choice of words." Jovianna curled into a tighter ball, wishing she could disappear into the blankets. She held her breath as the latch rattled and the door hinges creaked.

"I shall carry her in and lay her down," Tobias said.

Jovianna found herself scooped up and nestled against his chest before Amaranth could respond. She kept her eyes covered with one hand and held tight to his shirt with the other. Wherever they were, it sounded like a hub of activity. A deep drone of several conversations swirled all around. The racket of carts and animals. Even with her eyes closed, she cringed at the curious gazes she felt drilling into her.

"It will be all right, lass." Tobias carried her up what felt like a short flight of steps, then angled to one side and bumped into something. From the sound of a deep, metallic groan, she envisioned a heavy door with sturdy iron hinges swinging open.

"Saints alive!" A woman's voice, followed by the hurried clicking of heels on hardwood flooring. "How bad is she hurt, and where did ye find her?"

"Devil's Pulpit." Tobias grunted as he pushed through another door. "We thought her drowned but were able to snatch her from death's door. Quite the goose egg on her forehead, and a cut with a redness that worries me. Could be festering."

He lowered Jovianna onto a soft, padded place that felt like a small cot. She curled into a tighter ball.

"Has the same fearsome headaches I have. The pain empties her stomach for her if she uncovers her eyes. The herbs ye sent helped, but she hasna had a brew of them since before dawn."

"Since before dawn?" the woman repeated in a scolding tone. "What did I tell ye about the dosage and their timing, Master Tobias?"

"We needed to get back here before Tellerston's visit. Ye ken that well enough, Mrs. Gibb."

Tobias sounded not only agitated but defensive. Jovianna didn't know who Tellerston was, but that visit was clearly not welcome. She risked easing her hand away from her eyes, squinting to avoid any sudden intrusion of sunlight. Relief filled her as she discovered the room softly lit by a single, small window set up close to the low ceiling of exposed beams covered in hanging bundles of dried herbs. She opened both eyes fully. "It's my fault they were delayed. I don't know what my mother and I would have done without Tobias and his men's kindness."

The middle-aged woman wearing the white kertch turned and stared at her. "An Englishwoman?" She arched both her dark brows and aimed a stern look back at Tobias. "Here?"

"Ye would rather I left her for dead?" He glared at her, almost baring his teeth.

"Of course not." She shot an irritated scowl right back at him while donning a fresh white apron over her simple black garb. She lit a candle and brought it to the bedside. "I am Mrs. Gibb. Housekeeper and healer here at Risk Manor."

Jovianna shied away from the light but tried to smile. "A pleasure to meet you, Mrs. Gibb. I'm Jovianna Jacobs."

"Well, Mistress Jovianna, I can tell the light pains ye. Begging yer pardon for it, but I need to see this cut and bump on yer head that's causing ye the trouble." Mrs. Gibb peered at her, then muttered something under her breath and set the candlestick on the bedside table.

"Is it that bad?" Jovianna couldn't believe Amaranth hadn't warned her.

"No, mistress. 'Tis just I canna see a blessed thing up close anymore without my spectacles." She reached into a small linen bag tied to her belt and pulled out a pair of delicate wire-rimmed glasses with small oval lenses. After rubbing them clean with their bag, she put them on and picked up the candle again. The older woman offered a kindly smile. "Much better. Now let's see what we have to deal with."

"Ye see the redness?" Tobias said from behind her shoulder.

"I do." Mrs. Gibb shooed him away. "'Tis naught but irritation. Ye rinsed it with Cade's whisky, I suppose?"

"Aye."

She shook her head. "'Tis a wonder that man hasna burned a hole clean through his middle. Ye ken that stuff he drinks is about a minute's worth of fermenting into pure poison? Ye burned the poor woman's skin. If her husband doesna shoot ye for scarring her beauty, ye'll be lucky." She gave Jovianna a sad shake of her head. "I am sorry to be the one to tell ye, lass, but ye will carry that scar to the grave."

"At least I'm alive," Jovianna said. "That's all that matters, and I don't have a husband who would care about it, anyway."

"I see." Interest sparked in Mrs. Gibb's lively brown eyes. She turned and peered over the tops of her glasses at Tobias. "No husband?"

"Dinna start, woman." He pulled up a stool beside the cot and sat. With a sorry shake of his head, he cupped Jovianna's chin in his hand and studied her forehead. "I am truly sorry, lass. But I dinna think it will be a bad scar."

"I'm not that vain. Just grateful to be as well off as I am." She swallowed hard against a sudden surge of nausea. "I don't mean to sound ungrateful or be a bother, but might I trouble someone for a cup of those lovely herbs that make me feel so much better? I'm about to start vomiting again."

"I have a better batch that I think will suit ye, mistress." Mrs. Gibb went to a worktable against the far wall and started pulling down crocks and jars. "I keep water on the fire. The brew will be ready in no time."

Jovianna caught hold of Tobias's hand as he took it away from her chin. "Thank you. For everything."

He frowned down at her, but as he held her hand, he gently squeezed it as though trying to reassure her. So many shadows filled his eyes, as though he battled with himself. "Ye are quite welcome, lass. I must leave ye for a bit, aye? There is much to be done, I fear." After a moment's hesitation, he brushed a quick kiss to the back of her hand, touched her cheek one more time, then rose and went to the door. After opening it, he paused. "I shall send yer mother to ye." He cut his eyes in Mrs. Gibb's direction. "I'm quite certain she and Mrs. Gibb will take to one another right off."

Then he was gone before she could respond.

Mrs. Gibb crossed the room to the hearth and ladled steaming-hot water from an iron pot into a stone cup. With the smallest black pestle Jovianna had ever seen, she slowly stirred the contents as she made her way back to the bedside. "Master Tobias seems quite taken with ye." She set the cup on the table, helped Jovianna sit up, and put several pillows behind her.

Not sure just how much she should share, Jovianna adopted a guarded smile. "He is a good man, and very kind. His men are as well. I'm thankful they were the ones to find me and my mother."

"As ye should be, mistress." The matron offered the cup. "Take care. 'Tis verra hot."

Jovianna took a hesitant sip, surprised when her lips numbed even quicker than they had with Tobias's mixture. Had the housekeeper poisoned her? "My lips are already numb."

"'Tis stronger than Master Tobias's mix. I also added comfrey and nettles. This tonic will help with the soreness from bruising as well as ease yer poor aching head." With her hands primly clasped in her lap, the housekeeper wrinkled her nose to adjust her glasses. "How did a pair of Englishwomen come to find themselves at the Devil's Pulpit with none to protect them?" Her head tipped the slightest bit and her thin lips pursed as she leaned forward, perked to listen intently.

"My husband owed a great deal of money to some very bad men," Amaranth announced from the doorway. "And when he died, they came after us, chasing us from London to Glasgow, where the last of our family lived, and then on to the Devil's Pulpit, where they left us for dead and will hopefully continue to believe we are." She stepped forward and took a proud stance at the foot of the cot. "I am Amaranth Jacobs. Jovianna's mother."

Mrs. Gibb offered a hesitant nod. "I am Mrs. Gibb. House-keeper and healer here at the manor."

Amaranth seated herself on the cot beside Jovianna's feet. "Thank you for helping my daughter. She is my only child, and even though she's a woman grown, I cannot imagine losing her."

The taut lines of Mrs. Gibb's stern expression noticeably softened. "I am glad I could help her."

"And we are both indebted to Tobias and his men," Jovianna added. "I know we're English, but we would never do anything to bring harm to him, his men, or his people."

"Good. Because Master Tobias has been harmed enough." The housekeeper's face went stony again, and she rose and returned to the worktable.

"I can tell he's been hurt," Jovianna said without thinking. She stared down at the brew remaining in the cup, wondering if the wily housekeeper had added an herb to make her say whatever came to mind. Not that she needed such a thing, since she already possessed that dangerous habit. "He has been so kind, yet when I thank him and tell him what a good man he is, he refuses to hear it. Even said that the goodness in him died long ago."

"He is a good man," Mrs. Gibb said without turning from her mortar and pestle. "His brother is the wicked bastard determined to end us." She turned and faced them with a sour look. "And I should not speak so freely with those I have just met."

Jovianna couldn't resist. She pointed at her cup and nodded. "It's the herbs. I think they make us say whatever is on our minds. You probably absorbed some when you mixed them."

Mrs. Gibb cracked a wry smile. "Ye dinna act like any English I have ever known."

"Thank you," Amaranth said. "We try to treat people the way we wish to be treated."

"A rare quality in an English." The housekeeper's gaze settled on Jovianna's ankles, then swept up the rest of her body. She frowned and adjusted her glasses. "I daresay that if those are yer clothes, ye either need a lesson in measuring cloth or ye need to take a stick to yer seamstress and beat her for such poor workmanship. That skirt is a hand too short, and the seams of yer jacket are stretched close to popping."

"When we ran from Glasgow, we left with nothing but the clothes on our backs. Breeches and shirts so small and tight they made riding and running easier but were quite inappropriate for meeting good people." Jovianna smoothed out the folds of her skirt. "Tobias let us wear these clothes that were in the trunks of the coach he and his men procured. I'm so tall; these are the only ones that came close to fitting."

"Procured," Mrs. Gibb repeated with a damning roll of her eyes. "I see Master Tobias has already educated ye on the language of the highwaymen."

"The trunks also held several bolts of cloth." Jovianna finished the tea and carefully slid the mug onto the table. "Lace, ribbons, and threads. Tobias said you'd be quite pleased with it all."

The housekeeper nodded. "Many are in need here. Anything is always appreciated." She pointed at the pillows. "Rest whilst yer mother and I visit Telfa, Maudie, and Agnes."

"Who are they?" Jovianna asked before Amaranth could.

"Risk Manor's washerwomen and the keepers of clothing no longer used. With any luck, we'll have ye dressed proper before dinner." Mrs. Gibb pinched out the candle and motioned Amaranth toward the door. "Sleep will do her good. Come. Ye can tell me more about yer trip here."

As the door closed behind the two older women, Jovianna realized the previous owners of the clothing they fetched for her were probably dead. A shudder stole across her as she curled over onto her side and prayed for the wisdom to survive this historically dangerous era.

CHAPTER SEVEN

"Pag wishes to speak with ye," Fitch said from the doorway.

Tobias didn't look up from the ledgers spread across his desk. Entries had to be made to look legitimate before Matthew Tellerston's arrival to collect the rents. Only proper records would keep the lying bastard from trying to steal Risk holdings as he had stolen so many others by pocketing the rents and saying they were never paid. How else could a lowly rent collector own so much acreage covered in the finest sheep?

"Tobias," Fitch said louder.

"What?" Tobias jerked and threw a disgusted wave at his overflowing desk. "Can ye not see I am busy?"

"I can see ye are working yerself into one of yer headaches." Fitch entered and waved for Pag to follow, then pointed the lad at the liquor cabinet on the far wall between the bookcases. "Whisky."

"There is not enough whisky in the world to help this moment." Tobias sagged back into the depths of his worn leather chair and scrubbed a hand across his eyes, racking his mind for a simpler way to keep his land and people safe.

Fitch accepted a glass of the amber liquid from Pag and made a curt tip of his head to hurry the lad over to Tobias. "I thought ye said we had enough to cover the upcoming payment?"

"We do," Tobias said. "But just enough. There'll be none to spare for repairs, more animals, or anything else the estate sorely needs." He downed the whisky and thumped the glass onto the small table beside his cluttered desk. "What do ye want, Pag?"

The lad emptied his glass before stepping forward. His round, fair face went so red from the sudden heat of the strong spirit that his many freckles seemed to melt together.

Tobias fought not to smile when the boy coughed and thumped his chest. Pag Mackinley, seventeen summers of age and the only member of his immediate family still alive, constantly struggled to appear much older. Tobias figured the boy wanted him to speak to the smithy on his behalf in asking for the man's daughter. "What is it, lad? I've much to do and but one lifetime in which to do it."

The young man stood taller and threw out his chest. "'Tis about the Englishwomen. Mistress Jovianna in particular."

Tobias clenched his teeth, determined to maintain control over the most powerful of his demons. Unreasonable jealousy had cost him too much in the past. "Aye?" He didn't trust himself to say anything else.

"Seems to me they've got nowhere else to go." Pag shuffled in place and cleared his throat. "With Mistress Jovianna as my wife and her mother living with us, I could make a go of it on Da's croft he used to let from yer father before ye. That way it would bring the estate some earnings rather than lying fallow, as it has since my parents died."

"Pag, ye should go." Fitch took hold of the lad's arm and turned him toward the door as he shook his head at Tobias. "I had no idea the wee fool had that on his mind."

"I willna go." Pag yanked his arm free. "What I propose makes good sense."

Tobias slowly rose, unable to remain seated while his un-founded yet unrelenting jealousy churned stronger every minute.

"Ye should listen to yer uncle, boy," was all he trusted himself to say.

"Why?" Pag took an ill-advised step toward him. "Because ye kissed the woman? We all know ye did it just to make her be quiet. My da did that to my ma all the time."

Tobias cut his eyes to the door, then looked back at Fitch.

Fitch nodded, dragged the lad out, and slammed the door shut behind him. He turned and leaned against it, then lazily reached down and flicked the lock. "I appreciate ye not killing my sister's only son." He crossed himself. "God rest her soul. I promised her I'd do my best to protect him."

"God rest her soul, indeed." Tobias picked up his glass and headed for more whisky. "And God give me the strength to overcome the curse of this foolish jealousy that has cost my people so much."

"The time of which ye speak was not yer fault." Fitch joined him and filled his glass as well. "Was Mrs. Gibb able to help Mistress Jovianna?"

"I dinna ken." Tobias upended his glass, then filled it again. "I left after she scolded me for using Cade's whisky to clean the lass's wound."

Fitch shrugged. "Aye, well, 'twas all we had." He slid the decanter out of reach as Tobias went for it again. "Talk it out, old friend. By yer own admission, we dinna have time for ye to disappear into the bottom of that bottle for however long it takes ye to climb back out again."

Fitch was right. But then, the man usually was. Tobias turned his empty glass upside down on the tray beside the decanters. He strode to the broken window behind his desk and stared at the courtyard below. Donnor, Silas, and Cade were busy unloading the coach while stable master Josiah Risk checked out the new horses. "Josiah looks pleased with the additions to the stable."

"He should. Even I could tell those bloodlines are good." Fitch stepped up beside him. "Out with it, man. We all saw that kiss, and not a one of us thought the same as Pag." He tipped his head forward, trying to get Tobias to look his way. "Near as I can remember, ye have not kissed a woman that way since Rebecca."

"I'll thank ye not to utter that name in my presence." Tobias turned back to his desk and leaned over the ledgers, slowly turning each of them to the same page. Every fiber of his being tensed as he fought not to bring to mind the face belonging to that name. "Tellerston is due here any day. Have Donnor and Pag watch for him at the ridge. That's far enough out to give us ample warning in case we should need it."

"I will," Fitch said. "Now, what about the Englishwomen? The young one in particular, because I believe Cade has plans for the older one." Fitch cast a glance toward the heavens and shook his head. "God help the man with that one."

Tobias glared at his friend, at the man who was more a real brother than his own brother had ever been. "Why is everyone so interested in the welfare of these Englishwomen? Have ye already found yer Aggie and told her ye are home safe and whole?"

"Dinna be worrying about me and my Aggie." Fitch swelled with pride and winked. "The bairn should come any day now, and she said old Telfa swears it will be a boy."

"Full moon tonight," Tobias said. His friend's excitement filled him with a mixture of joy, wistfulness, and resentment. He had once looked forward to holding his own bairn in his arms. But now he no longer bothered to even hope for such a blessing. "Of course, I will be yer son's favorite uncle."

"That ye will be." Fitch's lightheartedness turned solemn. "Ye know as well as I if the Englishwomen choose to make a home here, there are those besides Pag who might want Mistress Jovianna as their wife. She is a fair lass and seems to possess a pleasant demeanor."

"Tell me who might wish such a thing." Without thinking, Tobias strode forward as though ready to chase them down.

Fitch pinned him with a broad smile. "Yerself."

A snort escaped Tobias as he realized too late he had fallen into Fitch's trap. "Do ye not have anywhere else to be, man?"

"Aye, I do. But I thought to make a suggestion to save a few lives before my fool nephew risked his own." Fitch widened his stance as though readying himself to be tackled. "Shall I spread the word that the wee lass is under yer personal protection to keep others from expressing any interest?" He held up a finger. "Mind ye now that personal protection doesna mean anything other than that, and I will make that point clear to all. What with her being on the run and still recovering from the death of her father and cousin." He added a convincing nod. "That should keep the young stallions from pawing around the fine new mare for a while."

"And ye will educate Pag and remind him of my temper?" Tobias didn't want to hurt the lad but couldn't guarantee he wouldn't.

"I will."

Tobias nodded, thankful that his friend was so wise. "Aye, do as ye said. And there is one thing more ye can do for me, old friend."

"And what might that be?" Fitch asked.

"Check these entries to ensure I updated them all correctly. I tried to make them look original, but with my weariness, I could have easily erred." Tobias headed for the door, unable to ignore an unyielding desire to seek Jovianna's company.

"Ledgers." Fitch eyed the desk as though it were a pile of manure. He waved Tobias on. "Ye owe me."

"Aye. I do." Tobias chuckled to himself as he strode down the hallway leading to Mrs. Gibb's healing room. As he passed what had once been his father's private solar, he noticed several chickens had once again found their way in through the broken windows. He closed the door to keep them from roaming deeper into the manor. Glass windows all the way from Edinburgh were one repair they could ill afford right now. They had boarded up the broken windows to keep out the elements and the animals, but sometimes both still found a way inside. The sight rankled him. Especially when he knew his brother's home in the finest part of Edinburgh remained pristine and fully intact.

A child's high-pitched crying led him down the hallway to the pantry.

"Moggy willna come to me," the wee one sobbed.

"Where is Moggy?" asked a familiar voice that made Tobias's heart beat faster.

He slowed, then eased around the corner and peeped inside the pantry.

Jovianna knelt beside a distraught lassie that he thought was one of Mrs. Albright's grandbabies, although the bairn's name escaped him.

"Under there?" Jovianna pointed underneath a cabinet loaded down with crocks and cloth bags of salt and flour.

The teary-eyed tot nodded and pointed a chubby finger under the furniture that possessed a crawlspace of about six inches or a little more. The perfect refuge for a cat.

"Maybe Moggy is after a mouse?" Jovianna reasoned. She crouched with her back to the door, unaware of Tobias's eavesdropping.

The bairn shook her head hard. "No. Moggy be too fat to catch mousies. Grammam said so. I afeared her stuck under there. We must save her."

Admiration and amusement filled Tobias as Jovianna stretched out on her belly, wormed closer, and peered under the cabinet. "Uhm, Tildy?"

"Aye?" The tiny lass plopped down on her belly next to Jovianna.

"Moggy is not stuck. She is having babies. We need to leave her alone until she's ready to come out." Jovianna pushed up onto her elbows and eyed the little girl. "How about if we find her a nice saucer of milk and leave it here so she knows we love her and want her to be the best mum she can be?"

"Moggy is having wee ones?" the lassie repeated in an awestruck tone.

Jovianna nodded. "And she needs her privacy so she can take

good care of them."

The child hopped up, then reached down and tugged on Jovianna's sleeve. "Come wi' me. Grammam will give us some cream for her."

"I'm coming." Jovianna tried to stand but got tangled in her skirts and fell back on her bum. Her eyes narrowed as she noticed Tobias standing in the doorway. "It is very rude to eavesdrop, sir."

With a smile he couldn't resist, he reached down, lifted her up, and set her on her feet. "Shall we get the cat her promised reward for being a good mother?"

"Pick me up, Masser Tobias!" Tildy gave him an irresistible smile while hopping in front of him.

"And how are ye today, Tildy?" He swept her up and settled her in the crook of his arm.

"Moggy's having babies."

"Aye, that's what I understand." He led the way to the kitchens, pleased to know that Jovianna followed close behind. He pushed through the swinging door and held it for her. "Mrs. Albright. A saucer of cream, if ye please. For Moggy. She is having babies in the pantry."

"Tildy Grace!" Mrs. Albright rushed forward and pulled her granddaughter out of his arms. "What have I told ye about bothering Master Tobias? And him just back from his trip and weary as can be."

"I wasna bovvering him," Tildy said, then pointed at Jovianna. "I was bovvering the English lady in Mrs. Gibb's healing room, and she is nice as can be."

"She wasn't a bother at all," Jovianna hurried to clarify. "But Moggy is having babies in the pantry. I counted two kittens so far and promised a saucer of cream for the mother's efforts."

"God bless ye, ma'am." Mrs. Albright set Tildy's feet to the floor and turned her toward a stool beside the hearth. "Sit ye down until yer ma comes in from the fields. We shall be having a quiet word, we shall."

"What did I do this time?" The child scowled at the stool, then aimed her frown at her grandmother.

"I will explain later," the older woman said.

"But Moggy needs her cream," Tildy argued.

"I did promise," Jovianna said. "Sorry."

Mrs. Albright threw her hands in the air and glanced upward, as though seeking guidance from above. "I shall get the cream, and Tildy and I will put it in the pantry. Thank ye, ma'am, for yer patience with my wee one."

"She's precious, and I look forward to being her friend." Jovianna waved. "We'll talk later, Tildy. All right?"

Tildy nodded, then tipped her head toward her grandmother. "I will try."

Tobias caught hold of Jovianna's arm and led her out of the kitchen. "Come, before we get the wee one into even more trouble than she's already stirred for herself."

Jovianna laughed as they walked along. "I dreamt someone was staring at me, and when I opened my eyes, there she was."

"So, ye are feeling better, then?" Her transformation lifted his heart. No longer was she pale and cowering away from the light. Good health pinked her cheeks, and the brilliant blue of her eyes sparkled with life.

"So much better," she said. "Mrs. Gibb is a miracle worker. She and Amaranth went to see the washer ladies to see if they had any clothes that might fit me better."

"*Washerwomen*, lass." Her ignorance of the terminology surprised him. "Did ye not have at least one washerwoman in Glasgow or London?"

"Amaranth and I have washed our own clothes for a very long time." She seemed uncomfortable with the admission.

He changed the subject for her sake and was also curious to see her reaction to Fitch's plan. "There is something else you should know."

She eyed him with a leeriness he hated. "And what is that?"

"I have advised Fitch to tell everyone ye are under my personal protection."

Her leeriness shifted to almost panic. "Why do I need your protection here?"

"Pag has already asked for permission to take ye as his wife. If yer mother and yerself choose to remain here at Risk Manor, there could be others asking as well." He struggled to keep the jealousy out of his tone.

"Whom did Pag ask?" She frowned up at him as they reached the end of the hallway.

"Me."

"Why? I don't belong to you."

Her statement cut him as surely as a knife. He forced himself to pull in a deep breath and ease it out before answering. "Aye, that is so, but this is my home. My people. They come to me about such matters." Did she not understand how things were done? Frustration and jealousy simmered hotter within him. Inside he roared that she did belong to him. She had responded to his kiss and given back fully in return. Was she now saying she hadn't? "Ye are under my protection, ye ken?"

She stared up at him for a long moment, then slipped her hand in his and squeezed. "Thank you once again for protecting me."

His irritation with her immediately cooled, settling back to the lonely yearning he could control. At least, that was his hope. "Ye should always be protected," he said softly. "Even from me."

She touched his face with a gentleness that frightened him. "I know in my heart I have nothing to fear from you. Not now. Not ever."

"Ye dinna know me, lass."

"I know enough." She shocked him by wrapping her arms around his middle, hugging in close, and resting her head on his chest. "I have never felt as safe and contented as I do when you hold me."

Reluctantly, he gave himself over to the dangerous gift. He closed his eyes, rested his cheek on the silkiness of her hair, and slid his arms around her. "I would always have ye safe and contented," he whispered.

She hugged him tighter, then shifted and smiled up at him. "You are a good man, Tobias Risk," she said so softly he read it on her lips more than heard it. "And whether or not you know it, you deserve to be happy."

"God help ye," he uttered, before taking her mouth with his.

Once again, she opened up to him. Lent wings to his heart and made him want her with an unbearable intensity as she clung to him.

Someone nearby cleared a throat. In fact, two someones cleared their throats several times.

He lifted his head and glared at the fools risking their very lives. "What?"

Amaranth and Mrs. Gibb held up arms loaded down with clothing.

"We have better-fitting clothes for the lass," Mrs. Gibb said. "She'll be more comfortable at dinner, ye ken? But I need to know where ye wish me to put them. What rooms shall they have?"

He stared at the woman, debating whether or not she enjoyed seeing him suffer. After a hard swallow, he stepped back and placed a proper amount of distance between himself and Jovianna. "Verra well, Mrs. Gibb. What rooms do ye suggest? Ye ken the condition of the floors better than I." It shamed him to admit that some levels of Risk Manor had deteriorated to an uninhabitable state. But it couldn't be helped. Lack of coin, raids by the English, and time itself had ruthlessly transformed the once glorious Risk Manor into a crumbling, chicken-infested shambles.

"The only rooms fit for them are either on your floor or mine with Lettie, Jennet, Sarah, and Frances. And they'd have to share a room with either me or one of the maids." Mrs. Gibb leaned toward Amaranth with a knowing dip of her chin. "Ye dinna want to share a room with Frances. The woman never sleeps, always smells of what she's cooked that day, and has a perpetual case of the winds."

For one of the few times in his life, indecision paralyzed him. It wouldn't be proper to have them share rooms with the maids, but if they took up residence on his floor, that would put Jovianna so close, so dangerously accessible. The prospect both tempted and terrified him.

When he failed to respond, the housekeeper strode forward with the determination of a general advancing troops across the battlefield. "There are two perfectly suitable rooms on yer floor. The one adjoining yers and the other across the hall from it. I dinna think ye wish to cast Cade out from his room on the end, aye?"

Tobias wrenched himself free of the daze clipping his tongue. "I willna have Cade displaced. He has no one but his son, and Bennie's apprenticing with Sutter and sleeps in the shop." He stepped aside and waved the women toward the stairwell. "My floor, of course, Mrs. Gibb. As I'm sure ye already knew."

With flagrant smugness and a sly smile, the housekeeper jutted her chin higher and marched past him. "Follow me, Mistress Amaranth. We'll put these things away, then fetch the maids to give the rooms a proper airing so yerself and yer daughter can settle in."

"I can clean," Jovianna said. "There's no need for the maids to have extra duties."

"Oh no, dear," Mrs. Gibb called out without looking back. "I ken ye're feeling better because of the tonic, but it will wear off soon. Ye should rest." As she climbed the stairs, her voice increased in volume. "Ye should rest as well, Master Tobias. I can tell by that crease in yer brow that one of yer headaches is coming on. Hie to my healing room, the both of ye. Fix yerselves another tonic each and sit till I come and fetch ye. Just add the hot water to the bowls I left out. Ye canna miss them there on my worktable."

Jovianna cut a wide-eyed glance at him, looking as though

she was about to burst out laughing.

He offered his arm, slightly perturbed that the housekeeper had read him so easily. A headache *was* coming on, but so far, he'd been able to ignore it. The intriguing lass at his side somehow made the pain easy to forget. "Mrs. Gibb is a verra controlling woman. We must always do as we are told with her. I have learned that the hard way."

"I like her. She's a force to be reckoned with."

"That she is. The woman had five sons and a husband who never crossed her because they both feared and worshipped her." A heaviness settled across him at their memory. It made the pounding in his head increase. "She lost them all at Culloden."

"I am so terribly sorry." Jovianna bowed her head and kept her gaze locked on the floor as they walked.

"Aye, lass. We all are." The excruciating pain he hated, the one that always split his skull like a battle ax, surged stronger and blinded his right eye, making him stumble.

"Tobias?" Jovianna ducked under his arm, supported him with her shoulder, and wrapped her arm around his waist. "Lean on me. I'll steady you the rest of the way."

"The feckin' headaches always blind me on the right." He hoped the soldier who had nearly cleaved his head in two was burning in the hottest part of hell.

"Here's the door." Jovianna bumped it open without letting go of him. "We won't fit through together, but if you want to close your eyes and give me your hands, I'll lead you to the cot."

"It appears I have little choice." Another searing bolt of pain shot through his skull, bending him over and making him clutch his head.

"I have you." With a gentle tug on his elbows, she steered him across the room, turned him, then helped him ease down onto the narrow bed. "Do you want to lie down, or do you feel better sitting up while I mix the tea?"

"This is best," he managed to utter. He leaned forward, propped his elbows on his knees, and pressed against the sides of his skull. "I hate this weakness."

"It is not weakness." Her voice sounded farther away. "It's a problem you have to manage as best you can."

"Where are ye?"

"Over here at the workbench, trying to decide which of these bowls I'm supposed to use. I don't want to poison either of us."

"She always leaves the pestle with the proper herbs beside the bowl. Did she not do that this time?" He struggled to keep his voice level and not lash out like an animal in pain. This feckin' curse wasn't the lass's fault.

"I know you're miserable. I'm so sorry to be so useless."

Even through the pain, he felt her warmth close to his face. He cracked open his left eye and discovered her kneeling in front of him with three bowls. "Ye are not useless, lass. Yer presence alone helps me."

"I'm glad." She held up one of the bowls. "These three bowls were all that she left out. I thought maybe you could sniff them and tell me which is yours. I'm pretty sure I know which is mine."

"'Pretty sure' can be a dangerous thing with Mrs. Gibb's herbs." Another surge of pain made him hiss. At this point, he didn't give a damn which bowl she mixed as long as she gave him something. But he wouldn't tell her that. She did not deserve his wrath. "Bring it closer." She did as he bade, and he smelled the herbs. "No. Try another."

"This is the one I think is mine. If all else fails, we can share it." She lifted it close to his face. "Or you can have all of it. I don't feel bad at all."

"Not that one either. Mix water with the last one, aye?"

"Shouldn't you smell it first to be sure?"

"Just mix it, ye ken!" He closed his eyes tighter and rocked with not only the pain but the shame of losing control and shouting at her. "Forgive me," he rasped. "I beg ye."

When she didn't answer, he knew for certain she had left him there alone, and he deserved it. But when he barely opened his left eye again, his heart hitched with a dangerous thing that resembled hope.

She walked toward him, her eyes glued on the steaming bowl in her hands. When she noticed him watching her, she smiled. "I filled it too much and don't want to spill. Sorry."

"Forgive me for shouting at ye," he said quietly as she carefully knelt in front of him. The caring and concern in her eyes made him wish his head would stop pounding so he could take her into his arms.

"You do not owe me an apology." She lifted the bowl to his mouth. "Careful. It's right off the fire."

He cupped it in his hands and sipped. "Thank ye, lass."

"I hope it's the right one. I don't want to cause you more harm than good."

"The taste is right."

"Thank goodness." She rose to her feet.

Momentary panic seized him. "Where are ye going?"

"I'm going to fix mine, then sit beside you and drink it." She carried the bowl to the pot over the fire and ladled hot water into it. "I wonder why she left three bowls?"

"With Mrs. Gibb, who could know?" But he did have a theory. The meddling housekeeper knew if she left a puzzle that he and Jovianna would have to work together to sort it out.

She returned to his side and eased down onto the cot beside him. "Risk Manor is very nice," she said after a long, awkward pause.

"Ye dinna have to lie to me, lass. I am not on my deathbed, I assure ye." He breathed in the steam from the bowl as he drank. He'd learned long ago that the combination of the steam and liquid brought him relief much quicker.

"It's very rude to accuse a guest of lying when they compliment your home." Her teasing tone almost made him smile.

"Not when I see the state of my home with my own eyes. Chickens have taken roost in the first-floor solar."

"Well…" She paused for a sip of her own tonic, then shrugged as she lowered the bowl from her mouth. "Chickens in the solar will be handier. Closer to the kitchen for eggs." She took another sip, choked on it, and almost spat it back into the bowl. After several minutes of coughing and wheezing, she turned to him with an apologetic look. "I'm so sorry. I know I shook you."

"Ye didna shake me badly, but ye should take care. I'm in no condition at the moment to save ye from drowning again." He risked opening his right eye and was pleased to discover the foggy darkness was gone.

"Can you see?" Jovianna sat with her bowl halfway to her mouth, frozen in the act of taking another sip.

He offered her a smile. "Aye, lass. I can see, and the pain is not as fearsome."

"It's amazing how fast her remedies work." Jovianna frowned down into the bowl as if suspecting it held magic.

"It is at that." He eyed her, yearning to ask about what she had said earlier. Her words nagged at him. Nettled him like vicious, barbed hooks. "Have ye kissed many men the way ye have kissed me?"

She choked again and sprayed a mouthful of tonic every-where. Setting her bowl aside, she pounded on her chest and coughed harder. "What?" she said, wheezing out the word. "Why would you ask such a thing?"

He finished his remedy, set the bowl on the floor, then turned to face her more fully, since the vision in his right eye was still a bit blurry. "When I told ye of Pag's request to marry ye, ye wanted to know why he had asked me. Then ye said he should not have done so because ye dinna belong to me."

Still clearing her throat and occasionally thumping her chest, she fixed him with a bewildered stare.

"Ye kissed me with a passion, woman. As though ye yearned for an end to yer loneliness as badly as I did. Have ye ever kissed another man that way?" He hardened his heart against the hurt in her eyes. Such games had duped him once before, and he had sworn to never lose to them again.

But then she squared her shoulders and sat taller. "Before I answer that, I have a question for you. Why do you care when you can't seem to decide whether you want to pull me closer or shove me farther away?"

"There is much ye dinna ken about me." As much as he hated to admit it, her question was a fair one.

"Well, there is a lot you don't know about me either." She sounded like a bairn trying to out-boast her playmates. "Like—I don't eat meat, and most perfumes make my head all stuffy, so I never wear them." She gave him a curt nod. "Tell me some things about you."

"Ye dinna eat meat?" How did the woman survive?

She shook a finger at him. "No. We do not comment or condemn. We only enlighten, and it's your turn. You started this. Now, two things about you. Go."

"Even though I am the eldest, I am not the laird."

"That doesn't count. You already told me that." Her scolding tone reminded him of Mrs. Gibb.

He rose from the cot, crossed the room, then turned and faced her. This was not a game to him. She needed to understand that. "I lost my birthright because I broke my brother's jaw when I discovered him in the stable bedding my betrothed. At first, she claimed he had forced her. But when she discovered he would be my father's heir, she married him instead of me and died while bringing my son into this world. The babe died soon after. The wants of my cock blinded me to the woman's fickleness. My temper not only cost me my son but also put my clan in their current position of possibly losing their homes and scattering their families to the winds. All because of me. All because I was a weak and trusting fool."

Jovianna sat there staring at him, her lips parted, her hand clutched to the base of her throat. Just as she started to speak, Mrs. Gibb burst into the room.

"Out!" he roared.

CHAPTER EIGHT

Mrs. Gibb scooted back out and slammed the door behind her.

Tobias strode over and locked it. "And I shout at people when I should not, but ye already knew that as well, aye?"

Jovianna slowly stood. "Yes, I had noticed. So, that doesn't count either." With a determined tilt of her head, she walked over to him, took his hand, and tugged him back to the cot. "Forgive me for making light of what's bothering you. Please sit."

He forced himself to sit even though he preferred to stand.

She sat beside him, wrinkled her nose, then emitted a strained hiss like a teakettle with a clogged spout. "We have a misunderstanding, you and me. To answer your question, no, I have never kissed another man the way I kissed you." She offered him a sheepish gaze. "But I am not a virgin. At least, not technically. I don't think the poor fellow knew what he was doing any more than I did, and the entire five minutes of the act was rather a letdown for us both." She shrugged. "To be perfectly honest, the whole thing was more a matter of us getting it over with because we were too old to still be virgins."

"How old is too old to be a virgin?" He never realized such an age limit existed.

"That is not the point." She reached over and rested her hand on his. "I was surprised when you said what you did about Pag, because I always thought any man who wished to marry me would ask *me* first. And, after I agreed, go to my father for permission." A sadness crept over her, making her smile small and faint. "Father is gone now, though, so no one can ask him anything." A sheen of moisture in her eyes made her blink faster. She gave him a sympathetic frown. "I am so sorry that dreadful woman treated you the way she did. And that you lost your son. I'm also sorry about your birthright and your monstrosity of a brother." She chewed on her bottom lip while eyeing him. "But none of that means I would ever treat you as badly as they did."

"Ye said ye didna belong to me," he whispered, unable to get her declaration out of his head.

She reached out and touched his face, then slowly shook her head. "I didn't know I did. Men kiss women all the time and don't mean it. They pretend. They lie to get what they want and then off they go. How was I to know that this grumpy Scottish highwayman—who, against his better judgment, had saved my life—decided he wanted more than a quick tumble? I have met very few honorable men in this world. I thought them a rare and quite possibly mythical beast."

When she explained it like that, he understood.

"And you must admit you didn't exactly make things clear." She squeezed his hand. "You'd be tender and sweet one minute, then the next you'd act as if you were trying to save me from yourself."

"I was." He lifted her hand and kissed it, then rubbed his cheek against its softness. "I have the foulest of tempers, headaches that turn me into a raging beast, and unreasonable jealousy I canna always control."

"Have you ever been cruel to a child, a woman, or an animal? Purposely hurt them or used your authority to mistreat them?"

"Never," he said with a halfhearted shrug. "Well, my brother. But he was a man grown. And I would be lying if I said I didna hate Rebecca for betraying me." He hurried to cross himself even though he had his doubts the woman could ever be prayed into heaven. "God rest her soul," he muttered without meaning it.

"You had every right to hate her, but it doesn't sound as though you retaliated directly against her." Jovianna leaned closer, forcing him to look her in the eyes. "Yes, you broke your brother's jaw, but I would say he reaped what he sowed there. You are not the bad guy here, Tobias."

He slid his hand along her cheek and up into her hair, loosening the tidy weave of her braid. "I willna let ye belong to anyone else," he said softly. "I fear I cannot."

She smiled and covered his hand with hers. "My great, wounded bear. So gruff. So possessive. So in need of understanding."

He brushed the lightest of kisses across her mouth. "I already understand that I need ye to be mine, lass. But I need ye to come to that understanding as well."

Her auburn brows quirked closer together, but she didn't frown as her gaze searched his face. After what seemed like forever, she offered him a hesitant smile. "I understand."

While he ached to do nothing more than lay her back across the cot and show her that loving could last a damn sight longer than five minutes, he held himself back. It wouldn't be right. Not here.

"Mrs. Gibb is probably standing right outside the door," she whispered as if reading his mind.

"Undoubtedly." He consoled himself with another chaste kiss, not trusting his willpower with anything more. He rose and unlocked the door. When nothing happened, he opened it.

The housekeeper stood there with her eyes snapping. She shook a finger at him. "Daren't ye ever roar at me like that again! I dinna care how bad yer head is hurting."

"My apologies."

"Hmmpf." She blew past him, frowned at the bowl of herbs remaining on the counter, then turned to Jovianna. "Which did ye drink?"

Jovianna held up her empty bowl. "The red one."

"Good. That one was yers."

"Why did you leave out three?" Jovianna took her bowl to the worktable and dumped the dredges into the bucket Mrs. Gibb pointed out.

"Master Tobias usually drinks two doses when his headaches first start. Did he not tell ye?" The housekeeper nodded at the unused bowl still on the table and then at the empty bowl on the floor beside the cot. "And I always give him the blue ones."

Jovianna shot a scolding glare his way.

"Dinna give me that look. I was already blind in one eye with the pain and not fit to know my own name. And I never pay attention to what that woman does. 'Tis a wonder she's not used it as an opportunity to poison me." He held out his hand to Jovianna. "I assume all is ready for Mistress Jovianna and her mother to settle into their room, aye?"

"Rooms," Mrs. Gibb said, then turned and smiled like a cat that had just lapped up the last of the cream. "Mistress Amaranth is in the room across the hall from her daughter. Mistress Jovianna is in the room adjoining yers." She turned to Jovianna and attempted an innocent expression that failed. "Of course, the door between the suites locks on yer side, mistress. I left the key on yer bedside table. Dinna fear."

Tobias clenched his teeth to keep from groaning aloud at the possibilities. And all thanks to the insufferable Mrs. Gibb and Jovianna's mother. He turned aside and adjusted his coat, thankful for its length that hid his painfully hard rising.

Color riding high on her cheeks, Jovianna proffered a nod. "Thank you, Mrs. Gibb. And is my mother in her room?"

"She and the maids are drawing ye a bath in yer chambers. We both felt sure ye'd wish to rid yerself of the roadway's grime before ye changed into the clothes we found for ye." The matron turned back to her worktable. "I feel certain Master Tobias wouldna mind showing ye the way."

"I would be happy to escort ye." He offered his arm, feeling certain that Jovianna wished to escape the meddling old woman as badly as he did. As they hurried out of the healing room, he swore he overhead the housekeeper quietly chuckling to herself.

"She's worse than Amaranth." Jovianna lengthened her stride, almost running.

He tugged on her arm to slow her. "Never run from her, lass. It makes her even hungrier for the chase."

"I blame my mother." She pumped her free arm as she walked, clearly fuming. "I'm sure Amaranth told Mrs. Gibb about our kiss and filled her head with ideas. Why else would your housekeeper try to pave the way for you with a stranger she just met? An English stranger at that!"

"I wouldna lay the entire blame upon yer mother. For years now, Mrs. Gibb has not only hated the fact that I've remained alone but also done her damnedest to change it." He couldn't resist a grin as he added, "Even if it meant resorting to an Englishwoman to pry me from my loneliness."

He released her arm, lit a candle from the table just inside the stairwell, and aimed the light up the stairs. "Take this to light our way and mind the seventh step. The board split last time I was here, and I dinna ken if Sutter or Bennie has mended it."

"How long has it been since you've been home?" She paused and tapped her toe on the seventh step. "It seems to be fixed." Then she continued climbing.

"Several weeks." The new board squeaked under his weight as he tested it for himself. "The king's higher taxes mean lighter purses on those traveling the roadways."

She came to a stop at the landing and looked back at him. "Which floor?"

The soft glow of the candlelight lent a golden hue to her beauty and almost made him forget to answer. Heaven help him. He had not been this obsessed with a woman since... He shook his head and refused to finish the thought. Jovianna deserved better than a comparison to a heartless she-devil. "This is the floor."

He stepped up beside her and paused with his hand on the latch. "The rooms are shabby, but they are clean and dry and, in the winter, not too drafty. And hopefully, the chickens havena made it to this level."

"Never apologize for your home. I believe it is proud and strong like the man before me." In the shadows, her sapphire eyes took on the deepest shade of a midnight sky. The candle's flame danced in their depths.

He leaned closer and kissed her, unable to keep from it any longer. His heart fell when she gently pushed him away.

"I'm afraid I'll accidentally set you or the house on fire with this candle," she said.

"Ye've already set me burning, lass."

She caught the corner of her bottom lip between her teeth, then breathed in with a shudder. "Me as well," she whispered.

He drew up every ounce of self-control he possessed to keep from carrying her to his bed. Instead, he shoved open the hallway door and nodded for her to go ahead of him. "This first room on the left is Cade's. The next, according to Mrs. Gibb, is yer mother's. The door on the end is to my suite of rooms, and the only door here on the right is yers."

As they drew even with her door, it swung open and Amaranth stepped out. "I thought I heard voices. Hurry, Jovianna. Letty and Sarah have the hot water ready so you can freshen up before dinner."

Tobias never wanted to bellow so loudly in his life. His fists tightened until his knuckles popped.

"My goodness." Amaranth looked all around. "What on earth was that?"

Jovianna turned to her mother, handed her the candle, and nudged her back into the room, then shut the door behind her. "I'll be along in a moment," she called through the closed door. "Wait for me in there. Understand?"

"Yes, dear," Amaranth said from the other side.

Before Jovianna had time to face him, Tobias spun her around, caught her close, and poured every ounce of his need into a searing kiss. She tangled her fingers in his hair and clung to him, melding the bond between them with her own fire. He walked her back against the wall and pressed into her, grinding his hardness into her soft, inviting curves.

"Saints' bones, I need ye," he rasped against her mouth.

She wrapped a leg around his hip and squeezed him closer. "And I you, but it's your first night back. You shouldn't miss dinner with your people."

He knew she was right, but it sorely pained him to put duty ahead of claiming her with a great deal more than a kiss. With a frustrated growl that came from the very depths of his being, he pushed himself away and retreated to the other side of the hall.

"Go," he begged. "Before I change my mind and tell everyone else they can just be damned."

"Tonight, the door between our rooms will not be locked. I promise." Then she slipped through her door and closed it.

Tobias threw back his head and roared.

JOVIANNA CRINGED AS Tobias's anguished bellow seemed to rattle the door on its hinges. She swallowed hard, imagining the passion he would be capable of. A passion she had only read about or seen in movies.

Amaranth charged in from the adjoining room. "What on earth was that?"

"Uhm…" Jovianna stalled, not quite sure how to put it. "I believe it might have been Tobias."

Her mother arched a sleek brow and gave her the look that always pulled more information from Jovianna, whether or not she wanted to give it.

"He and I would rather not go down to dinner," she said.

"But duty calls, and I believe his frustration got the better of him for a moment."

"I see." Amaranth's expression let on that she understood fully. She waved Jovianna forward. "Come along. Your water's getting cold. I've run off the maids, so we can speak freely."

Jovianna followed her mother into the next room but came up short at the sight of a steaming copper tub lined with a padding of linen. She'd seen no servants toting buckets of water, and indoor plumbing was not yet a possibility. "How on earth did they get hot water up here without using the stairs?"

"An ingenious pulley system." Amaranth opened a tall cupboard and revealed a chain and bucket system. "Of course, it's hand-operated, but still. They said Tobias designed it when his father made renovations to the estate. It comes directly up from a cistern, so if any spills on the way up, none goes to waste. A resourceful drainage system under the bathtub directs the used water out under the floor through a series of mortared sluices and sends it outside. Cade told me all about it. He's quite proud, since he had a part in helping Tobias enhance the design. It's not indoor plumbing as we know it, but they've gotten very close." She pointed at a small hearth beside the tub. "Water is drawn. Those three kettles are filled and set over the fire. It doesn't take as long as you'd think to get a nice bit of hot water. Hurry and get in. I'm sure a bit of a soak will help those bangs and bruises the Devil's Pulpit gave you."

Hot water did sound lovely. And a scrub would be welcome too, because she felt a bit grimy. As she peeled off the clothing that was too small, she took care not to tear it. Someone might be able to use it. "How did you get on with Mrs. Gibb?"

"Quite well once she realized I approved of Tobias's interest in you." Amaranth moved to unlace the stays. "She told me the most horrid story about the poor man. He has not had an easy way of it, Jovianna."

"He told me." Jovianna wouldn't elaborate. She had seen the pain the conversation caused him and refused to dishonor it with gossip.

"It's a wonder he's alive," Amaranth continued. "They smuggled him home from the battlefront in a wagon of straw with his head almost split in two. Several times while he was on the mend, Mrs. Gibb and the maids had to drug him and put him in the crawlspace under her healing room to hide him from the British when they ransacked the house."

Jovianna halted in the middle of pulling off one of her stockings. "Why did they drug him?"

"Do you honestly think that man is capable of being quiet and hiding rather than fighting?"

"Fair point." Jovianna stepped into the hot water. Even though it was less than six inches deep, it felt like heaven. As she piled her hair on top of her head and leaned back against the padded end, a happy sigh escaped her. Then she remembered something she'd been meaning to ask as soon as they were alone. "For the life of me, I can't remember the name Tobias Risk or *Diabhal Dubh-Chridhe* in any of the history annals. Can you?"

"No. And I can't decide if that is a good thing or bad." Amaranth pinned Jovianna's hair to keep it in place, then handed her an opened crock of a creamy substance and a rag. "This soap smells divine. Like freshly bloomed roses."

"Our never reading about him could mean our presence here saved him," Jovianna suggested, hoping with all her might that was true. "After all, if he was arrested for assault and robbery, they would more than likely hang him rather than ship him off to work as an indentured servant somewhere. Don't you think?"

"Considering the man's temper, I feel sure they would have drawn and quartered him." Amaranth tapped her shoulder. "Lean up so I can scrub your back."

Grudgingly, Jovianna sat up from her comfortable reclining position and leaned forward.

Her mother gasped.

"What?"

"Either the hot water or time has caused your bruises to

surface. Your back looks as though someone beat you with a flail. The skin isn't broken, but it looks wicked. Does it not hurt?" Amaranth gently sponged warm water across her shoulders.

"I guess with everything going on and my headaches, I hadn't really noticed." Jovianna rolled her shoulders, discovering an achy soreness that would have been better off left undiscovered. "You should never have told me. Now, I feel it."

"I am certain you would have noticed eventually," Amaranth retorted. "Or Tobias would." Her pleased chuckling made her sound like a happily nesting hen.

"Stop it." Jovianna splashed her. "Hypocrite."

"Hypocrite?" Amaranth rinsed Jovianna's back, then leaned around to fix her with an indignant glare. "How am I a hypocrite?"

"I've seen the way you are with Cade, and your room is conveniently next to his. Are you saying you won't be taking advantage of that situation?"

"I think you need to revisit the meaning of a hypocrite, young lady." Amaranth held up a length of linen and motioned for her to stand. "I would be a hypocrite if I were to tell you to remain chaste and not let Tobias touch you. Actually, I'm more of a partner in crime. I think you and Tobias should take that door between your rooms off the hinges. I fully intend to if there is a door between mine and Cade's."

Knowing her mother was an active sexual being was one thing. Talking about it was just...unpleasant. "I would really rather not have this conversation." Jovianna scrubbed herself dry, flinching as she discovered more sore spots.

"You, my dear, are the hypocrite." Amaranth helped her dry with another bit of linen, then stepped back and frowned.

"What now?" Jovianna touched her unwashed hair. "It's not that bad, is it? I didn't want to stir up another headache by washing it." She bent forward. "Smell it. I don't want Tobias to think I stink."

"This is the eighteenth century, dear. Everyone has an *earthier* aroma." Amaranth flinched as she touched Jovianna's forehead. "The swelling isn't going down as quickly as I'd like. And that cut. I do not want infection setting in."

Jovianna delicately patted her fingers across the wound that had somehow become rather sticky even after washing her face. "I think Mrs. Gibb put a salve of oil or something on it. I know she checked it quite thoroughly. She said Cade's whisky was too strong and burned the skin."

"Well, it bears watching." Amaranth waved her back toward the bedroom. "Come now, we found you the loveliest things that will fit so much better." She spun about and clapped her hands like an excited child. "And I promised Mrs. Gibb that you'd be happy to entertain everyone with a song after the meal."

"*Mother.*"

"I have noticed of late that you say that like a curse word." Amaranth selected a gown of the richest burgundy and held it up. "This one, I think. We'll save the skirts and jackets for every day."

"You know I do not like to sing in front of people." Jovianna cringed at the thought. She hated it, in fact.

"I didn't tell her you were gifted with perfect pitch." Amaranth placed the gown on the back of a chair, then added a shift, stays, petticoat, hose, ribbons, and a pair of slippers too. "I told her you could play the violin. Any song they wish. As long as someone hummed it to you, you could play it as though you wrote it. But I called it the fiddle. I remembered that seemed to be the preferred name for the violin in this era."

"Sometimes, I hate you. You know that, right?"

"I have known that since you were thirteen years of age, my dear." Amaranth went to the door, then turned and pointed at the clothes on the chair. "Hurry and dress. Those stays do up in the front, so you shouldn't need any help with them. Call out when you're ready to fasten your dress. It has the tiniest buttons I've ever seen in the back. A most unusual design for 1760. Apparently, the fashion historians were wrong about that style. Anyway, you'll definitely need help with them. Until then, I'm off to freshen up a bit and see about a few of my own preparations."

Jovianna stared at the door after Amaranth exited and shook her head. Once again, her mother had had the last word. Determined not to be outdone, she dressed as instructed and grudgingly agreed that the fit and color were perfect. She touched her messy hair piled high on her head and panicked until she noticed a brush and a set of tortoiseshell combs on the table beside the bed. Freeing the braid from the pins that had kept it high and dry, she pulled the leather tie off the end and combed her fingers through the plaiting. Then she went still, staring down at the simple tie. It made her smile. It was like Tobias. Tough. Weathered. Broken yet perfect. Perhaps she should thank the Fates for sending her back in time. With a lighter heart, she brushed out her hair and let the wavy tresses fall down her back and shoulders, hoping he would like it that way.

A noise in the hallway caught her attention. Hopefully, it was Amaranth coming back to do up the higher buttons she couldn't reach. A heavy step on the creaking boards of the flooring gave her pause. No. That was not Amaranth. She pulled open the door and caught her breath. Tobias stood there. In all his glory. Black hair shining and secured back in a neat queue. Clothed in a fine embroidered waistcoat, polished black boots, and snug breeks that outlined his muscular legs.

"My heavens, but you are lovely," she said without thinking.

He crooked a half-smile and tipped his head her way. "Lovely?"

She nodded. "Definitely the loveliest man I have ever had the pleasure of knowing."

With a slow, sultry step closer, he offered her a gallant bow. "And you are the most breathtaking vision I have ever seen, m'lady."

She pressed a hand to her pounding heart. "Oh my. No one has ever said that to me before."

"Have ye known only blind men, then?" He gallantly tucked her hand through the crook of his arm.

"Apparently so." She fell in step beside him and shivered. "Is my hair all right? I don't want to seem improper." Remembering her not-quite-done-up dress, she pulled him to a stop and turned while sweeping her hair to one side. "And could you finish the last of my buttons?" Nothing happened for the longest moment, so she cast a glance back at him. "Tobias?"

With a jerk, as though breaking free of a trance, he hurried to fasten the last of the buttons. "I love yer hair loose. To hell with what anyone else thinks." He gently settled it back in place, then stepped up beside her and offered his arm again.

She held tight to him to keep from stumbling. The lace of her petticoat kept catching on her heel, but she ignored it, hoping the silly thing would rip enough to stop getting snagged. "Amaranth promised I would play the fiddle after dinner. That will make our *meeting* even later than we hoped, I'm afraid."

"Meeting?" He huffed a silent laugh, then shook his head. "It willna be a mere meeting, lass." As they approached the stairwell door, he stopped and fixed her with a look that took her breath. His voice fell to a deep, husky whisper. "It will be a claiming, my own. A joining of two lonely souls. I promise ye."

"Oh my." A shuddering breath left her.

He gave her a wicked smile. "And when we are done, there will be no doubt in yer mind that ye've been truly and completely loved for a damn sight longer than five minutes."

She had no proper response to that. So, she settled for shyly ducking her head and concentrating on maneuvering the stairs in the long gown that threatened to trip her.

Tobias stopped her three steps down. "Come here afore ye break yer wee neck." He swept her up into his arms and gave her a quizzical glance while cradling her like a babe. "To watch ye, one would think ye had never walked down steps in a gown before."

What could she say? She hadn't. Mainly because she'd never exactly been the epitome of gracefulness when out in public. Anything that threatened to trip her was to be avoided at all costs.

Whenever she'd attended formal functions, she'd always opted for the much safer yet still stylish slacks or wide-legged pants. Safety and comfort always trumped high fashion, as far as she was concerned.

She patted his chest and decided to play off his remark with a laugh that didn't come out as lighthearted as she intended. "It's my height, you see. I am so tall my skirts and gowns never really reached the floor. Took too much material."

He halted again, staring at her first in disbelief and then with a crestfallen look, as though she'd told him to go straight to the devil. "Forgive me for such a thoughtless remark. It could not have been easy for yerself and yer mother with yer father losing everything to the gambling dens."

A mixture of guilt, shame, and relief filled her. She hated all the lies. Hated portraying her wonderful father as a gambling loser. And hated making Tobias feel bad about something as ridiculous as the length of a skirt. She patted his chest again. "There's no time like the present for me to learn the ways of a proper lady now that my hemline reaches the floor. Set me down and hold tight to my arm in case I stumble. You can be my safety net."

Still seeming a bit angry with himself, he eased her down to her feet, helped her fluff out her skirts, then held tight to her arm. "Take yer time, lass. Slow and steady. They canna start supper without us."

"I can't understand why my mother told Mrs. Gibb that I'd play the fiddle after supper. It's still back—" She cut herself off, locking her jaws against saying something she shouldn't. With a frustrated huff, she kicked at the folds of material bunching up between her right leg and the wall.

"It's all right, lass. I know ye lost everything." The gentle understanding in his tone made her heart hurt about all the deception even more. He wrapped an arm around her waist and held her hand as if she was an invalid. "Mrs. Gibb probably told her I usually play after the meal the first night back. She also knows I keep my grandfather's fiddle primed and ready to play. 'Twould dishonor the old stoat for me to do otherwise." He caught her just as she stumbled, then bent to untangle her hem. With a gentle nudge, he directed her to sit on the step. "What infernal eedjit puts lace in a spot where yer heel catches it when ye walk?"

"Shall I pull off the shoe? Will it be easier?"

His jaw tensing, Tobias hissed a stream of words under his breath as he worked to free the delicate lace of her petticoat from the base of her heel. With a frustrated growl, he looked up and tipped a curt nod. "Forgive me for such language."

Struggling not to laugh, she leaned forward, grabbed hold of the hem, and ripped it free. After a bit of plucking to ensure all the loose threads no longer dangled, she smoothed it out and stood. "No one will ever know. And if they notice, they're looking entirely too close at my petticoat."

"Agreed." He took hold of her arm again and grinned. "Most women wouldha had a fit about tearing their precious lace."

Even though he said it in a lighthearted way, she wondered if she had erred yet again. "It's not that I don't value it," she hurried to explain. "But I'm sure your people are ready for their supper. It would be rude to prioritize the well-being of my lace over their stomachs."

He tugged her to a stop again and pulled her into his arms. With a gentleness that made her catch her breath, he tilted her face up to his and stared into her eyes for the longest time, drawing her deeper into his powerful gaze. "Ye are a rare woman, Jovianna Lillian Jacobs."

A surprised laugh escaped her. "You know my full name. How?"

He gently teased his thumb back and forth across the fullest part of her bottom lip. "When we thought ye drowned, yer mother shouted it when she demanded ye turn back from death's door and rejoin the living." He sealed this confession with a kiss so tender, she felt it to her soul. "I am glad ye heeded her call, lass. This world would be a darker place without ye."

"I'm glad you were there at the gorge to save me." She reached up and pulled him down to her again. "May I have another kiss before we go to supper?"

"Aye, m'lady," he answered in a deep, throaty whisper that sent a shiver up her spine. "I will give ye anything ye wish." He pulled her tighter against him, leaving no doubt as to what he had to offer.

The kiss ignited a heat that made her ready to rip away the layers of clothes between them. She might not be an expert in the art of love, but she knew what she wanted, and contemplated going after it right there on the staircase. As he deepened the connection, she frantically worked out the logistics of such an act. The only unknown she couldn't factor in was the amount of traffic on the staircase and if they would be interrupted.

A loud *ahem* from the steps above them made that unknown a very real known. "If we dinna feed the ladies, they will surely faint dead away," Cade said. Amaranth stood at his side, her arm looped through his.

Tobias didn't loosen his embrace. Instead, he pressed his forehead to hers. "I canna kill him. The old devil comes in handy at times."

Jovianna allowed herself a despondent sigh. "And she *is* my only mother." As she eased out of his arms and started moving, she shot a narrow-eyed glance back up the stairs. "And I would hate for her to starve and waste away to nothing."

Amaranth shooed them onward. "Anticipation is one of the best aphrodisiacs. You'll thank me later."

Heat flushed Jovianna's cheeks, her throat, and her décolletage. Even without a mirror, she felt sure she resembled a boiled lobster. She fanned herself and tugged on Tobias's arm. "Slow down. I don't want to meet everyone looking red as a beetroot."

"Dinna fash yerself, lass. Supper is outside tonight. The gentle kiss of the midsummer eve will cool ye 'neath the torchlight." He leaned so close his lips brushed against her ear. "And then later,

I'll leave the windows open wide so the breeze can cool our bodies once we're sated."

Jovianna found herself breathing in short huffs and fanned herself harder.

CHAPTER NINE

T HE TORCHLIGHT TURNED her hair into shimmering curls of copper and gold. It mesmerized him. Tobias followed Jovianna with his gaze as she moved among the people of his clan, smiling and reaching out to them. He understood her intent. The lass wished to put them at ease that she wasn't like the other English they knew. Some would take longer than others to accept her. Some never would. He hoped she understood that.

She turned and smiled at him, unleashing a flood of emotion and wanting with that simple act. He resettled his footing and took a deep draught of his ale. It would be a while before they could return to their rooms and love away their loneliness. He blew out a heavy sigh. He had never been a patient man.

"Everything is so lovely," she said, hurrying back to him like a wayward duckling realizing it had wandered too far from its mother. "Absolutely beautiful here. So simple. So pure."

He cast a sweeping gaze across the grounds, trying to see it through her eyes. They had set tables and benches from the main hall in a comfortable circle so everyone could enjoy each other's company. The manor house stood tall and proud in the moonlight, like a brave sentry watching over the people. Even with some windows boarded up and a corner of the roof collapsed, the soft evening light somehow healed the old place, helping its strongest features to shine. Children scampered and played among the tables. Their mothers and the servants shooed them away while cleaning up after the meal. Hounds waited for scraps, following the women with expectant yips. All was well and good on this mild Highland night, making it easier to set aside the worries of the day.

Some of the tension eased from his shoulders as he allowed himself to relax and accept the blessing for what it was. "Mrs. Gibb and Mrs. Albright did a braw job with that fine supper on such short notice."

"Indeed, they did." Jovianna kept glancing all around, as though excited to take in everything at once. "Stable. Smithy." She stood on tiptoe and squinted at something past the glow of the torchlight in the courtyard. "What is that place down there by the stream? With the windows lit?"

"Gristmill. Maudie's family has ground the manor's grains for as far back as I can remember. Her daughter runs it now." A heaviness settled over him. One he couldn't shake. "Ye will find we are almost self-contained here in our wee glen."

"Why do you sound so unhappy about that?"

"Because I dinna ken how much longer it will be this way." He sadly shook his head. "My brother is hungry for coin. I fear Risk Manor's days are numbered even if I can cover the rents. Jamison champs at the bit to either cover the place in feckin' sheep or sell it outright to someone else who will."

"I'm so sorry." She rested a hand on his arm and squeezed. "I wish I knew of something that would help."

"No long faces tonight!" Mrs. Gibb marched toward them with a pair of fiddles and their bows held high. "I believe we were promised music." Shouts and clapping accompanied her announcement.

"Aye, Mrs. Gibb. And music there will be." Tobias accepted his fiddle and handed his grandfather's to Jovianna.

"Oh, she's lovely." Jovianna reverently touched the instrument, put it to her shoulder, and tested the strings. She adjusted the pegs the slightest bit, then tried the notes again. "I love her tone. Thank you for letting me play her."

"Shall we play them a reel?" Tobias tuned his as well, finding comfort in once again holding his old friend.

Without meeting his gaze, Jovianna played a short bit of a lighthearted tune. "I don't believe I know any reels, but after you play for a bit, I can join in. As long as I listen long enough to get the gist, I'll be able to accompany you."

Interested to see how she could manage such a feat, he set into a lively song he knew his people loved. Clapping started, and couples soon danced and spun to the toe-tapping reel his grandsire had taught him. Jovianna joined in and almost caused him to lose his place in the tune.

Her fingers flew across the strings while she raced the bow back and forth, making the already lighthearted reel into an even more boisterous melody. Eyes dancing and color high on her cheeks, she whirled in place, playing as though born humming the Scottish song.

Together they played tune after tune, joining one into the next until folks started dropping to the benches and on the ground to catch their breath. Only then did they end the performance and lift their bows from the strings.

"Oh my goodness, it's a wonder we didn't burst into flames." Jovianna laughed as she lowered the fiddle from her shoulder. "That was wonderful."

"Indeed, it was, lass. We make beautiful music together."

She ducked her gaze as though suddenly shy. Good. She understood his unspoken intent.

Amaranth hurried over with two overflowing tankards. "I believe the fiddlers earned a drink," she called out to the crowd.

The crowd shouted in rousing agreement.

As she handed an ale to Tobias, she whispered, "Jovianna sings even better than she plays."

"Is that true, lass?"

Jovianna looked his way after taking a deep drink. Foam coated her upper lip in a tempting mustache he would happily lick away. He almost groaned as she swiped the tip of her tongue across her lip and beat him to it. "Is what true?"

"Do ye sing better than ye play?"

Her eyes narrowed into a spiteful glare aimed at Amaranth's back as the woman scurried back to Cade as though seeking his protection. "I can sing, but I don't enjoy doing it in front of a lot of people." She shot another irritated scowl at her mother. "And she knows that."

Her reaction made him even more determined. Setting their fiddles aside on a table, he held out his hand. "Come. We'll go off to ourselves while everyone is catching their breath. Ye can sing to me alone."

"Please don't make me do this."

"Jovianna. 'Twill lift my heart. One wee song?"

She grudgingly took his hand and let him lead her away from the crowd, down to the low stone fence surrounding the kirkyard of the family's small chapel. She sat on the fence as though dreading her turn in the confessional. "I don't know what to sing."

"Anything ye like." He sat beside her and made a show of staring straight ahead. "And I willna look at ye if that will make it easier."

She snorted, but he took that to be a *yes*. Especially when she started humming a lonely, lilting melody that made his heart rise to his throat. And then she sang,

"Wish I may
Wish I might
Whisper this wish to the moon tonight.
Send a love for me alone.
A love to keep and call my own.
Truer than the stars.
Stronger than the tides.

Loving only me
Till the end of time.
Mighty moon
Hear my plea
Please send a wondrous love for me."

Captivated not only by the words but also her ethereal voice, Tobias slowly dropped to a knee in front of her. He took her hands in his, unable to speak as he stared up at her. The moonlight set her face aglow like the finest porcelain. Her sapphire eyes sparkled like a midnight sky strewn with stars.

"Jovianna," he whispered, then stopped. He had no words.

"Was it all right?" Her shy smile and the way she tucked her head made his heart clench, as though fearing to lose this precious soul that fate had dropped into his midst. "I wrote it a long time ago. You're the first person to hear it."

He pressed tender kisses across both her hands and leaned in close. "I would be that love for ye," he promised softly. "If ye will have me."

She stared down at him in silence for so long that he feared she would refuse, but then she barely squeezed his hands. "Are you sure?"

"More sure than I have been about anything."

Her smile made him want to roar to all of Scotland that this rare woman had not found him wanting. "I will gladly have you as long you will have me," she answered.

He rose, swept her up into his arms, and headed deeper into the darkness.

"Uhm, Tobias?"

"Aye?"

"Where are we going?"

"To be alone. For the night."

"In the woods?"

"No, m'love." Tempting as that was because of its proximity, he chose the more difficult solution that would guarantee them privacy for the entire night. He took the path leading around the unlit side of the stables, the smithy, and the dovecote. Before stepping out from the shadows of that stone tower, he peered around it to ensure no one at the tables had noticed them. As he had hoped, Donnor had taken up his clarsach and launched into a story, augmenting the tale with an occasional plucking of the instrument's strings.

"I can walk," she whispered as he dashed across the only part of the route where he feared they might be discovered.

"Forgive me, my own, but ye have a difficult enough time walking where it's well lit. I dinna have much faith in yer agility in the shadows. But I blame the shoes. Ye've yet to become accustomed to them." He prayed that would lend a kinder tone to his criticism. She'd come close to landing flat of her arse several times since they had come outside for dinner.

"It *is* the bloody shoes," she said. "I almost lost one of them in the soft ground behind our table."

He set her over into the private garden that adjoined the library, then leaped over the fence and joined her. Catching her hand in his, he hurried her across to the double doors, pushed through them, then closed them securely behind them. Before they continued on to the staircase, a delayed sense of gallantry booted his conscience. He didn't want her to think that he was like those men she had described. The ones who said whatever the woman wished to hear just to lure them into their beds. If he said something, he meant it. She needed to know that. "Jovianna?"

"Yes?" She glanced all around as if afraid someone might overhear.

"I dinna wish ye to think I'm just some buck in rut."

The blue-white light of the full moon shining through the doors lit her confused expression. She frowned at him for a long moment, then shook her head. "What?"

Perhaps now was not the time to explain it. Instead, he led her to the hall, cracked open the door, and peered out. "The stairs are close. Can ye run for it, or do ye wish me to carry ye?"

Without answering, she gathered her skirts up out of the way and yanked off her shoes. "I'm ready."

So was he. Especially at the sight of her lovely, long legs from the knee down. "Ye go first, aye?"

She nodded.

He opened the door, and she bolted down the hall and up the staircase. He ran after her, somewhat amused to find himself forced to behave like a lad sneaking up to a maid's room for a quick tumble. It couldn't be helped. If they'd not snuck away, there could have been hours of revelry left to endure.

"Shite! Shite! Shite!" came from up ahead in a hissing whisper.

There on the landing, crouched in a ball, Jovianna rocked back and forth, holding her foot.

"I knew I shouldha carried ye." He picked her up, shouldered open the door, and strode down the hallway to his room. All the while, she held tight to her foot, her face filled with pain.

"What happened?" He angled to the side, trying to open the latch without setting her down.

"I caught my pinky toe on the post. I think I tore it off."

Even in the dim lighting from the single candle sconce beside the door, he could tell there was no blood but didn't want to seem hardhearted. "Open the latch, aye? I'll light more candles, and we'll have a better look at it inside."

She let go of her foot long enough to push the latch and open the door. He carried her to the bed and eased her down, noting somewhat grimly that this was not the arrival to his bedchamber that he had envisioned. In a matter of moments, he had every candle in the room lit from the night candle on the mantel. He brought the one from the bedside table closer and almost groaned as she hiked her skirt up to her thigh.

"Well, there's no blood. So that's good." She untied the ribbon above her knee, rolled down the white stocking, and slipped it off. "Poor pinky toe. It hurt like the dickens." She rubbed the little red appendage, then looked up and gave him a sheepish smile. "Sorry. I didn't mean to be so dramatic. But it did hurt."

"Now that ye're in my bed, lass, I can forgive ye anything."
He shoved the windows open wide, remembering his promise
about letting the nighttime breeze cool their sated flesh.

She hugged her knees and twitched as though nervous. "We
should lock the doors, I suppose. Can you lock the one between
our rooms from this side too?"

He teased her with a wink. "Of course. There are times when
the lord of the manor doesna wish to be bothered."

"Like when he's taking liberties with one of the maids?" she
asked in a tone that revealed she wondered if he ever did so.

"I never take liberties with the maids." He hoped she believed
that. After locking the adjoining door and the one leading out into
the hall, he returned and held out the key. "Now, ye shall have
both keys to the connecting door. I'll have no privacy at all, I
fear."

She looked up from the ribbon on her leg still sheathed in its
stocking. "Just put it on the table, please. This dratted thing is
knotted."

He pulled his dagger from his boot and cut through it. "Yer
freedom, m'lady." Before she could pull off the hosiery, he did it
for her, relishing the satin of her skin sliding against his fingers.

"Oh my." She wet her lips, inflaming him even more.

"Can ye stand, m'love?"

"Stand?" She stared at him as though she didn't understand
the question.

"Aye." He gently took her hand and steadied her as she
scooted to the edge of the bed. "If ye'll stand and turn, I'll undo
yer wee buttons so ye can slip off yer dress. That is, if ye wish."
He understood she might have a change of heart, but for his own
sake, he needed her to halt their evening before it went any
further.

She eyed him as she stood, looking as though he'd scolded
her. "Of course I wish. Do you not want me here after all?"

"Lore a'mighty, lass. I want ye with a fury." He framed her

face with his hands, then buried them deep in her hair. "A fury," he repeated in a rasping whisper as he hungrily closed in for another kiss.

She slid her hands up his chest and stretched tighter against him, molding her softness against his aching hardness. Then she broke the bond and drew back. "You're wearing entirely too many clothes too." She untied his neckcloth, tossed it to the floor, then started unbuttoning his waistcoat.

Unable to resist another quickly stolen kiss, he slid his hands up her arms, then spun her in place and hugged her back against him. "Ye first, m'love. Let's get to those wee buttons, shall we?" Her shudder delighted him, making him seriously consider getting his blade back out and parting the fasteners from the dress in one quick slice. But instead, he settled for undoing them one by one while nibbling across her nape. The gown fell away from her, and she shuddered again as she stepped out of it.

As she grabbed it up off the floor and shook it out, she twitched a nervous glance his way. "I'll soon be down to my shift, and there you stand fully dressed and still in your boots."

"Forgive me, m'lady." He gave a dramatic bow, then sat on the edge of the bed, removed his boots, and stood them beside the bedside table.

"They look like they're standing at attention," she said while fumbling with the laces of her stays. "Bloody hell! Why does everything always end up in knots?"

Even though she had denied it earlier in the day, she behaved very much like a virgin. It fanned his wanting of her even hotter. Made him cherish the gift of her coming to his bedchamber even more. An inexperienced woman who trusted him to show her the way. She would know and remember only him.

After stripping off his waistcoat and tossing it over a chair, he went to her. "Let me try."

"No knife," she said. "We can't be slicing through everything I manage to tangle."

"No knife," he promised. After a few moments of working

with the strings, he shook his head. "'Tis either the blade or ye wear it till it rots off."

"Mrs. Gibb is going to think me an addlepated fool. We've cut the garters and now the stays. I'll look like an ungrateful wretch." She tossed the stays onto her pile of discarded clothes and stared glumly down at her petticoat. "At least this waistband has a button." She looked up at him with a horrified frown. "But the shift ties in the back."

He stopped her fussing with a long, slow kiss. "If anyone thinks ill of ye, they'll have me to answer to. Ye're down to yer shift and I'm down to my léine. What say ye we have a wee drink to calm ye, aye?" He ached to bed her but wanted even more for her to enjoy it as much as he did.

"A bit of wine would be lovely if you have it."

"I have a fine bottle of port procured from a gentleman out of Edinburgh." The strong, sweet wine would be the perfect thing to settle her nervousness. He went to the liquor cabinet beside the hearth and poured them each a drink.

She waited for him on the bench beside the window, her hair caught in the steady breeze, gently floating all around her shoulders.

"Here ye are, m'lady." He handed her the glass with the larger portion.

Swirling the liquid, she eyed it, then shifted her gaze to him. "And why does mine have more?"

"Because I have already enjoyed a great deal of ale and whisky this evening." He touched his glass to hers. "A toast to ye, Jovianna. For bringing light to where only darkness lived."

She hitched in a quick breath, took a sip, then leaned over and slid it onto the bedside table. With a hesitancy that endeared her to him even more, she rose and circled him. As her fingers lightly trailed across his back, he set his glass beside hers, then turned and pulled her into his arms.

"Such a beauty," he whispered while kissing his way from her jawline to her shoulder. He couldn't help but smile as the tie to her shift gave way with a simple tug of the string. "I would see ye, m'love. If ye would allow it."

"I will," she said softly. With a step back, she slid the shift off her shoulders and let it fall to the floor.

A groan left him of its own volition as he took in all her glory. Creamy skin made golden by the candles' glow. He had known she would be breathtaking. Her revealing clothes at the Devil's Pulpit had hinted as much. "Ye are even lovelier than I imagined."

She smiled and ducked her head. "I've always been tall and gangly, like a knobby-kneed colt."

"Nay, m'love." He gently lifted her chin back to a proud slant. "Long and lithe, with the lissome beauty of a goddess. Never doubt that, my own."

She gathered his léine in both hands and slipped it off over his head. Then she slid her hands down his chest to his muscled stomach and smiled. "Climbable."

"Climbable?" The prospect sounded promising.

With a kiss to his collarbone, she outlined the cut of his muscles across his middle. "Amaranth describes muscles like these as climbable."

He picked her up and settled one arm under her lovely arse while pulling her legs around him with the other. "Climbable enough?"

She held on tight, squeezing him with her thighs while hugging her arms around his shoulders. "Very nice, indeed."

"We shall explore that more later," he promised, while walking her over to the bed and laying her across it. He stared down at her for a long moment, then started kissing his way up her legs, starting with the inner part of her ankle. "I think I prefer climbing yerself at the moment, ye ken?"

"Oh my." She wriggled beneath his gaze, clutching at the bedclothes bunched around her.

By the time he nibbled his way up to her inner thighs, he noticed she was holding her breath. He spread himself over her, not touching but bringing his body close enough to feel her heat. The slow, steady loving was agonizing but would be so worth it. He leaned down and brushed the lightest of kisses across her mouth. "Breathe, lass. Ye'll be needing air."

"I was afraid I was about to shout," she confessed with an innocence that made him smile.

"I sincerely hope ye do." He returned to where he'd left off, gently blowing across her dainty curls as he lifted her legs farther apart and draped them over his shoulders.

"Oh my." She bucked as he sampled a wee, teasing nibble, then drove his tongue in deeper. The longer he tasted and teased, the livelier and louder she became, until she screamed, and wave after wave of violent shuddering overtook her.

He climbed up her body and settled down where he belonged but didn't enter yet. Even though the ache had become an agonizing urge, he had more work yet to do to convince his lady love that she had not erred in coming to his bed.

"I am a man of terrible temper," he whispered as he cupped her breast in his hand and tickled the tip of his tongue around her nipple. "But I swear it will never cause ye harm—only the greatest passion."

Her breath coming in panting gasps, she hugged her legs around him and guided his mouth back to hers. She kissed him hard and deep while arching her body to hurry him along with the claiming.

"I need you," she uttered against his mouth. "Now."

He slid in slowly, taking his time even though the method was pure torture. Then settled hard and ground in fully, leaving no part of her wanting. "Ye are mine, Jovianna," he said, straining for control. "Say it."

She dug her fingernails into the cheeks of his arse and squeezed. "Yes!"

Almost shaking with the need to pound, he eased out, then took his time easing in again. Unable to resist, he treated himself to a few more strokes, then settled in and stopped again. "Say ye are mine. Say it."

"I am yours, Tobias. Yours alone." She rocked into him, tangling her fingers in his hair and pulling him in for another kiss. Then she broke the bond and glared at him. "I really need you to move right now. A lot. Hard. And fast. Please?"

"Aye, m'love. Gladly." He pounded long and hard until his need to roar drowned out her ecstatic shrieks. Barely able to think, he had the foresight to lock his forearms in place to keep from crushing her when he collapsed. He buried his face in the curve of her neck, gasping for breath.

"Oh, my heavens." She ran her hands up and down his sides, caressing him as she hugged him. "My, my heavens."

He couldn't resist laughing as he raised his head and looked down at her. "Are ye all right, love?"

"I am indescribably all right." She framed his face with her hands and smiled. "You are…amazing."

He rewarded the compliment with a kiss, then rolled to his side and curled her close against him. With her head nestled in the dip of his shoulder, he brought her hand to his mouth and kissed it. "I am glad ye were not disappointed."

She draped her leg across his middle, then grew still except for the slow, lazy tickling of her fingers through his chest hair. "You weren't disappointed, were you?"

"I was not." Idly stroking her hair, he let the silky strands slip through his hand. "I dinna believe I could ever be disappointed in ye," he added quietly.

"Give it time." She shifted with a heavy sigh. "When I've fumbled your favorite something and shattered it to bits, you might feel differently."

"Ye try too hard, lass. Think too long before taking action. Everything has its own rhythm and canna be forced. Ye must learn to relax, do what ye can, and let everything fall in place."

"That's much easier said than done, I'm afraid." She propped herself up and smiled at the opened window. "The breeze is lovely. Just like you said it would be." Then her eyes rounded wide and she bit her lip.

"What is it?" He turned to see what had caused such a look on her face.

"The window is open," she said louder, as if that explained everything.

"Aye." He scooted higher in the bed and eyed it. "What of it?"

"Everyone is still outside. I can hear them." She glared at him as if he deserved a scolding.

"Aye, most will probably be there for a while yet." He reached for her wineglass, helped himself to a sip, then offered it to her.

"If I can hear them, I would be willing to bet they heard us. You roared like a lion, and I shouted like the room was on fire."

His smile came of its own accord and grew wide and proud. He couldn't help it. "The room *was* on fire, m'love."

She smacked his chest and hopped up onto her knees, making her pert breasts jiggle in an irresistible way. "You are proud they heard us."

"Aye. I am. Every man wants his clan to know he's served his lady well." He pulled her back into his arms and rolled until she lay squirming beneath him. Then he kissed her neck with loud, squeaky kisses until she started giggling. "Louder, m'love. I want to make sure they hear ye again."

"You have to earn my shouts," she challenged.

"Consider it done, m'lady." He settled back in and started rocking his hips with hard, teasing thrusts. "'Tis time again for both of us to roar."

CHAPTER TEN

"I BROUGHT YE some tea," Amaranth said. "To help with that hoarseness plaguing you this morning."

Jovianna pulled her attention from her bowl of parritch and narrowed her eyes at her mother, willing the woman to behave.

Amaranth's smile only grew wider as she returned to her seat.

"Ye feeling poorly this morning, Mistress Jovianna?" young Tildy called out from her place farther down the long table in the main hall.

"Dinna fash yerself, Tildy," Mrs. Gibb said before Jovianna could answer. "Sometimes shouting can leave ye with a bit of hoarseness even though ye're in good health." She placed a platter of fried bread on the table while quietly chuckling to herself.

"Mrs. Gibb." Tobias glared at the housekeeper until the woman bowed her head and meekly returned to her seat.

Jovianna pushed away the bowl of boiled oats and concentrated on sipping her tea, hoping it possessed enough caffeine to keep her awake until she could steal a nap. Last night had resulted in very little sleep but had been thoroughly worth the sacrifice. She flashed hot all over again at the memory of finally stumbling from Tobias's bed in time to wash her face and dress for breakfast. After several fortifying sips of her tea, she offered him an expectant smile. "I thought I could help with some chores. Is there anything, in particular, you'd like me to do for you?"

Across the table, Donnor choked, coughing and wheezing for air while Fitch snorted with mirth and pounded him on the back.

Tobias stood and brought his fist down hard on the table, rattling everything on it. "Never in all my days have I witnessed such crudeness among my own. I am ashamed of the lot of ye. No wonder the English consider Scots to be uncivilized beasts. Ye've proven them right."

Jovianna reached toward him and patted the table. "It's all right—"

"It is not all right." He held out his hand and motioned her forward. "Come. Stand at my side, my own."

Even though she didn't want to, she did as he asked, wishing he would just let it go. They meant no harm. Did he not realize he'd just make them resent her? She took his hand and turned so the others couldn't read her lips. "It's all right," she whispered. "Please don't scold them. They don't mean anything by it."

He turned her to face everyone seated in the hall. "I dinna intend to scold them even though they deserve it." His voice boomed the length of the long formal room that had gone uncomfortably silent. He ripped off his neckcloth, bound her wrist to his, then lifted them for all to see. "This woman is my wife, and ye will treat her with the respect she deserves, ye ken?"

Jovianna bit the inside of her cheek to keep from asking him if he had lost his mind. Such a drastic reaction was completely unnecessary. Because of the irregular marriage laws of Scotland at this particular time in history, if she agreed—well, even if she didn't—she was legally his wife. Did he really want to do that? She locked eyes with her mother.

Amaranth barely shook her head, a warning that helped nothing.

"Will ye serve as witnesses to our union?" Tobias asked those gathered in the hall.

A chorus of *ayes* echoed through the room.

He turned and gave her such a tender smile that her heart melted. "Truer than the stars. Stronger than the tides. Till the end of time." His deep voice rang out like the loud tolling of a great bell, touching her heart and making it pound. It was her song. He had remembered the words. Tears slipped free before she could stop them.

"Dinna weep, my own. I know I didna ask ye and this is not a kirk. But life in the Highlands can slip through yer fingers before ye know it. It can end before it even gets started. I didna wish to waste any moments we could share." He gently wiped her tears away. "Dinna weep," he whispered. "I beg ye."

Overcome with emotion and unable to speak, she pulled him down for a kiss.

Tankards pounded on the tables, and clapping filled the room. Mrs. Gibb rushed over and hugged Amaranth as though the two had planned the breakfast nuptials all along.

Everyone congratulated them as they finished their meal and rose to go about their day. Jovianna smiled until her cheeks ached, hoping she could make this man she barely knew not regret the rash decision he'd just made for both of them. She cared about him. Might even go so far as to say she loved him, and believed that love would deepen. But was it the same for him, and would it be the same as time passed? Especially if he ever found out the truth about her and Amaranth?

As the room emptied to nothing but the maids clearing away, he helped her back to her seat without untying their wrists and sat beside her on the bench. "I surprised ye?"

She eyed him as she unwound the neckcloth from around them. "Yes. You definitely surprised me."

"I thought it the best way to save yer name and ensure ye are treated properly."

That gave her pause and made her heart lurch with a disappointed dip. She handed him the neckcloth while kicking herself for being foolish enough to believe in something as silly as love at first sight. "So, that's the only reason you did it, then? To save my reputation and keep them from calling me your English whore?"

His dark brows slowly drew together over his pale blue eyes, and his lips parted as though he was too confused or shocked to speak.

She stood and picked up her cup. "Excuse me. It's gone cold." She wasn't entirely referring to the tea as she hurried toward the kitchen.

"Jovianna Lillian!" His bellow halted everyone remaining in the hall and made them turn and stare.

After a deep breath to maintain control, she faced him but didn't move to return to him. "Yes?"

He slowly rose and walked toward her as though approaching his prey. "Ye misunderstand."

"You said that claiming me as your wife was the best way to preserve my reputation and ensure everyone treated me with respect—yes?"

"Aye."

"Then how did I misunderstand?" She ignored Amaranth and Mrs. Gibb standing in the archway making frantic hand gestures as though trying to flag her down and help her avoid the train wreck she was about to cause.

His glare still locked with hers, Tobias pointed at the two matrons. "Out. The both of ye. This is between me and my wife."

Jovianna clutched her cup tighter, determined to keep a level head. She was tired. Her head was starting to hurt again. And this marvelous man who had loved her so fantastically the night before had just hurt her feelings and was too big of an ass to realize it. She blinked against the threat of tears. She would not cry.

The muscles in his jaw flexed as he moved closer. Fire flashed in his icy eyes. He glared at her, opening and closing his fists as though pumping up his courage. "Have ye already forgotten the words I used to mark our vow?" he asked quietly.

She twitched a nonchalant shrug. "I figured you said it for

them. So they'd be impressed that you remembered my song."

He slowly jutted his chin higher and folded his arms across his chest with a smugness that tempted her to throw her cold tea in his face. "And how would they know the words of yer song when they had never heard it?"

A disgusted huff deflated her. "Shite," she said through clenched teeth.

"Exactly." He took the cup from her, set it on the floor, then pulled her close and held her. "We are new together, you and me, and have much to learn about one another. Ye will learn I do nothing that I dinna mean to do, nor do I do anything only for appearance's sake." He tipped her face up to his. "I wanted ye as my wife because ye made me realize it might be a verra fine thing to grow old beside ye. Did ye only accept my offer to save yer name?"

"I accepted because I think you're making me love you, damn you, and I'm so bloody tired right now—because of you, I might add—that I can't even think straight." She took another deep breath and continued, "And my head hurts. And my tea is cold." Without meaning to, she sniffed and lost the battle to hold back tears of frustration. "And you hurt my feelings when you said you just did it to save my reputation."

He unleashed a heavy sigh and shook his head. "I apologize for hurting yer feelings. That was not my intent, and I fear there will be a great many more of these misunderstandings in our future as we learn one another's ways. Forgive me, aye?"

She sniffed again, suddenly feeling very foolish. "Well, I am a little oversensitive because I'm tired and my head hurts."

"And yer tea is cold."

"And that is no small thing to an English." She bent to pick up her cup but instead grabbed her head as the aching within it pounded harder. "Bloody hell."

He caught her up in his arms and cradled her like a babe to his chest. "Leave it. The maids can fetch it. It's off to Mrs. Gibb with ye for a bit of tonic, and then ye can have yer tea once ye feel better."

"You carry me like this an awful lot," she complained, but closed her eyes and rested her head on his shoulder.

"I like carrying ye."

"How is it that you're not tired?" A hitching yawn escaped her as she rubbed her pounding temples.

"I am tired. Men handle it better than women."

"Oh, really?" She lifted her head and glared at him.

"Dinna start, woman. We just finished our first wee squabble. Wait till ye are better for the next, aye?" He kicked open the door to the healing room and gently deposited her on the cot. "Close yer eyes and rest while I fetch Mrs. Gibb." He kissed her forehead and was gone before she could argue.

She lay back and draped an arm over her eyes. Maybe all she really needed was a nap.

"I wondered if yer poor head would bother ye further," Mrs. Gibb said. Her heels tapped with efficient authority across the wood floor. "Dinna fash yerself, mistress. I'll have ye better in no time at all."

Jovianna almost dozed, relaxing to the sounds of Mrs. Gibb rustling around the small room preparing the tonic.

"And dinna fret," the housekeeper continued. "This different mix of herbs willna hurt a bairn that may be taking seed."

Wide awake now, Jovianna lowered her arm and stared at the woman. "Surely not after just one night."

Mrs. Gibb chortled out a happy sound as she added hot water to the bowl. "Anything is possible." She gave an excited bob of her head. "That would properly bless the new union, aye?"

Jovianna pushed up to a seated position while damning herself for being so naïve. Of course it could happen after just one night. Thankfully, she'd been on her prescription birth control long enough that even missing a few days shouldn't be too disastrous. At least, she hoped not. Jumping into dubiously wedded bliss was one thing, motherhood quite another. Hopefully, Amaranth had background knowledge about birth control possibilities in the eighteenth century.

"Himself would be overjoyed with a wee bairn of his own." The housekeeper held out the steaming bowl, looking almost teary-eyed with happiness. "He's endured so much sorrow. 'Tis time his life took on a happier course." With a caring, motherly touch, she rested a hand on Jovianna's shoulder. "I dinna ken if ye realize it or not, what with the way he hides his feelings, but ye've brought him great joy. He hasna been this content for a verra long while. My dreams proved right, after all. I never shouldha doubted them."

Jovianna risked a sip of the brew that didn't smell nearly as tolerable as the previous ones. Thankfully, it didn't taste as noxious as it smelled, but it did possess a cloying sweetness that made her rake her tongue across her teeth to get rid of the taste. She couldn't help but shudder. "Dreams?"

"Hmm...appears I added too much honey. I'll use less next time." The animated woman hurried back to her shelves, plucked down a stoppered jar, and added a pinch of its contents to Jovianna's bowl. "That should curb the sweetness a mite. Try it now."

Jovianna did as instructed and nodded. "Much better." It still amazed her that the kind lady who appeared as protective as a grandmother over Tobias had so readily accepted a pair of strange Englishwomen. Perhaps it had something to do with those dreams she mentioned. "You said your dreams were right after all?"

The housekeeper smiled and seated herself next to Jovianna. After a glance at the door, she leaned closer and lowered her voice. "My dreams tell me about things that have yet to happen."

Gooseflesh rippled across Jovianna's arms. After her traveling back through time, her belief in things that couldn't be explained had changed exponentially. "And you dreamed about Amaranth and me?"

Mrs. Gibb chuckled and rocked back and forth as though quite proud of herself. "I did. Course, I didna ken it at the time."

She held up three fingers, and her eyes widened with excitement. "Three nights in a row I saw Cade and Master Tobias striding side by side, wrapped in England's colors, and each of them carrying a single red and white rose. After that first night, I woke up with chills. Quite beside myself just knowing that the English had discovered Master Tobias to be the Devil of the Highlands and Cade and the others his accomplices." Still rocking, she shook her head and rubbed her arms as though reliving the terrible feeling. "Then the second night was exactly the same dream, except they both looked happy as could be. And the third night they were laughing and singing while wrapped in those colors and waving the roses all around." With a decisive nod, she tapped Jovianna's arm. "Next day was when Master Tobias showed up with ye in his arms. Soon as I kent ye to be English and saw how gentle he was with ye, I knew what the dreams meant." She clapped her hands and hopped to her feet. "And when I saw Cade smitten as a young laddie over yer mother, I knew I was right." She clucked like a contented hen as she wiped down her worktable with a damp rag. "My dreams have never led me astray. Never doubt the sight, mistress. 'Tis a gift from above."

Tobias appeared in the open doorway. "What is a gift from above?"

"Bairns," Mrs. Gibb answered without missing a beat. "I told her I changed the herbs in her tonic so as not to harm any bairns that could be taking seed."

Jovianna hid behind her bowl and took another deep sip. She wasn't ready for a conversation about having children any more than the housekeeper appeared to be ready to share her prophetic dreams. She understood why, from how Tobias reacted when she'd told him she and Amaranth had the sight. Unlike most Scots she'd known, he didn't appear to appreciate or believe in such things. Distracted by the observation, she sucked in a glob of honey-matted herbs and choked.

Tobias took away the bowl, lifted her arms, and started thumping her back. "They may not harm a bairn, but they're about to strangle her."

Coughing and wheezing, Jovianna batted him away. "My fault. I tried to drink it too fast." She cleared her throat and gladly accepted a cup of water from Mrs. Gibb. "Thank you. Much better, indeed. And my headache is already easing."

"Perhaps ye should go to yer room and rest, aye?" Tobias kept rubbing her back, as though loath to stop touching her. "Earlier, ye said ye were verra tired."

"I can't lie about while everyone else is busy with chores, and actually, I'm feeling quite refreshed. I must have gotten my second wind." She eased out of his reach and caught his hand to make him stop fussing. "I meant what I asked earlier. Surely there are things I could do to help. Cleaning? Gather eggs? Repairs? I'm quite good with a hammer."

Tobias shot her a dubious look and shuddered.

"What is that supposed to mean?" She sat straighter. "I'll have you know I helped build..." She snapped her mouth shut, knowing he would never understand why anyone would build shelters for a community of feral cats.

He hiked a brow and tipped his head. "Aye? Ye built what, dear wife?"

"Shelters. For animals. With feeder boxes and such." Of course, she'd broken her thumb on the first day of volunteering, but that could happen to anyone. "I know which end of the nail to hit."

Mrs. Gibb cleared her throat and offered an apologetic dip of her chin in Tobias's direction. "After speaking with Mistress Jovianna's mother, Cook feels the kitchen might not be the safest place for extra helpers."

"I'm not clumsy all the time." Jovianna rose and shook out her skirts. She couldn't help her occasional fumbles, and they didn't happen all the time. Now, thanks to Amaranth, everyone feared her. "What about cleaning, then? Or washing clothes? I could help with that."

"Ye can come with me." Tobias tucked her arm through his.

"I need to have a word with Josiah about the new horses."

She tried to find some solace in his offer to let her tag along like a child no one wanted to play with. "Josiah, the stable master?" She thought she'd met the man at dinner the night before but didn't remember for certain.

"Aye. I want the beasts reshod. Just in case."

"They do have distinctive tracks. Looks like there's a letter or something on the left bracket of their shoes." She shielded her eyes as they stepped outside, leery that the sun's glare would resurrect her waning headache.

"Ye noticed that, did ye?"

She preened a bit at his surprised yet impressed tone. "I love animals and often volunteered and helped them during my off-hours."

"Off-hours?" He halted just inside the stable and frowned down at her. "Off-hours from what?"

Heaven help her. What was a task he might find acceptable for a woman to do for money in this day and age? "Basket weaving," she said, borrowing Amaranth's idea. "Every bit of coin earned helped the household."

He visibly relaxed and nodded. "I'm quite familiar with the effort it takes to earn two coins to rub together."

A burly man with hair as black as Tobias's and eyes almost the same shade limped out of the shadows, leaning heavily on the handle of an upright pitchfork as if it were a walking stick. He tipped a curt nod at Jovianna and offered a strained smile. "Well wishes to the union, mistress." But his tone and expression relayed that he didn't mean a word of it. Without giving her time to respond, he turned his attention to Tobias. "Fine horses ye found there, cousin. Good bloodlines, I'd say. Strong. Will help grow the stable."

"Promising news, indeed. Have ye spoken to William yet?" A loud squeal then a hard bang and rattling of boards made Tobias stand taller and scowl across the stalls. "One of the new ones?"

"Aye." Josiah frowned in the same direction. "That one refuses the feed and hates the stall. Trying to kick his way free."

Jovianna headed down the center aisle toward the sound. The poor animal was scared to death. Maybe she could help.

"Jovianna!" Tobias caught up with her. "Ye need to stay back, ye ken? Josiah said it's as though the beast was never properly broken. Such stallions can be dangerous."

"That's the problem. He *is* broken." She pulled free. "I know what I'm doing. You and Josiah stay back. You'll only make it worse."

"Jovianna Lillian!"

She reeled around and pointed at him. "Use my full name like that one more time, and you and I are going to have a quiet word. Understand?" She'd let him slide earlier, but he needed to realize that using her first and middle name in the tone of a parent was not acceptable. With a flip of her hand, she shooed both him and the stable master back. "I've worked with abused animals many times with great success. Leave me with him for a while."

Animals were her second greatest love next to studying history. She smiled to herself. Of course, now she supposed Tobias would be first and history and animals would be second and third. Maybe. It depended on whether Tobias knocked himself farther down the list by being a stubborn ass.

She found the stall holding the magnificent, yet enraged, Clydesdale. Its coat was a deep mahogany brown, and its thick black mane whipped all around as it fretted. Instinctively, she knew its wonderfully feathered hooves would be a lovely white. It tossed its head, bared its teeth, and glared at her. Terror shone in its eyes.

"I know it's frightening to find yourself in a place you've never been before." She didn't move to touch it, just kept her voice low and calm. "Everything smells different. Strange people and other animals. It's hard to know whom to trust, isn't it?"

It squealed again and kicked the back of the stall but didn't seem as frantic as before. Still tossing its head, the beast grumbled and swayed back and forth as if ready to be shed of the place and race across the Highlands.

"I've never been here before either," she continued. "I'm still trying to get to know everyone and trying to make friends." She eased closer and rested her hands on top of the stall door, knowing she risked a vicious bite. "It's scary when you don't know if people are going to like you or if they're going to hurt you."

The beast moved closer and snuffled her hands. She slowly turned them palms up and waited. It was the horse's choice whether or not to be touched. "I'm kind of lonely here too and would love to have you as a friend. I would never be mean or hurt you. No matter what."

The animal nipped her palm, pinching the fleshy part at the base of her thumb.

She wanted to flinch but forced herself not to react. If the horse had wanted to bite her hard, it could have. The stinging pinch was to see if she meant what she said about being kind. "That wasn't very nice, you know, but I understand why you did it. May I rub your nose now, or are we still feeling a bit pouty about our situation here?"

The beast grumbled and stomped, but stepped forward and shoved her with its nose.

She couldn't help but laugh as she scratched the petulant animal behind the ears. "Such a lovely, brave boy. I'm so proud of you for trusting me."

He hooked his head over her shoulder and leaned against her as though wanting a hug. She was happy to comply. "I'm very glad to meet you too. I've needed a friend I can trust."

"She has the gift," Josiah said from farther down the aisle. His tone clearly conveyed that he hated making the admission.

"Indeed. I shouldha known she possessed the ability to tame raging beasts." Tobias eyed her with a faint smile that said he meant himself as well as the horse. "Do ye think ye can convince yer fine new friend to tolerate William shoeing him?"

"I'd like to exercise him first." She could almost feel the animal's need for open spaces. "I don't think he's used to being in a stall and definitely doesn't like it."

"I ken what's best for the horses," Josiah said. "He is safer there."

Jovianna hated that the man took it as an insult. She'd not meant it as one, but had concluded that no matter what she said, the stable master wouldn't approve. She remembered him now from last night. Cold and distant almost to the point of being rude. He didn't like her, and wouldn't no matter what she said or did. She felt it deep in her bones.

Without further attempts at explaining, she took a firm hold on the bridle, opened the gate, and led the animal out into the paddock adjoining the rear of the stable. "Here now. Let's have a nice walk and some fresh air, shall we?"

The stallion lifted its head and flared its nostrils as if pulling in a deep breath, then bounced a nod and fell in step beside her. She kept a light hold on the reins, gently guiding the animal as they ambled around the large pen. As they walked, she talked about the weather, the scenery, and whatever else came to mind, just as if she was visiting with a human. After a while, she noticed the beast was limping and halted. "What's hurting you, sweet boy?"

She eyed the horse's joints but didn't notice any swelling. Then she caught sight of a split in the front left hoof. "No wonder you're in such a state. You've got a sore foot, poor thing."

"What have ye found?" Tobias called out from the fence where he and Josiah watched her.

"He has a cracked hoof. It must be cleaned and sealed before a deadly infection sets in, if it hasn't already. Did you notice his limp?" She had no idea what they used in this century to repair hooves. She'd watched the process while volunteering, but without access to acrylic patches or fiberglass, she didn't know how to help the mighty beast.

Tobias turned to Josiah. "Fetch William and his son. Have them look at the lad out here while Jovianna keeps him calm."

"*Fetch* William?" Josiah glared at him and didn't move.

"Josiah." Tobias squared off and stood his ground, scowling right back at him.

Eyes narrowing to slits, the man swung about and gimped away, stabbing the ground with his pitchfork's handle with every step.

"He doesn't like me," Jovianna said as the man disappeared inside the smithy's lean-to.

"'Tis because ye are English." Tobias stared after the man, then sadly shook his head. "His wife deserted him after he came home from an English prison with naught but one good leg and an inability to father any children. She probably wouldha stayed at his side if he'd not lost his way into a bottle every night and raged at the world about all that was wrong with him. She couldna bear the shame."

"That's terrible." She eyed the smithy's place, dreading when Josiah returned. The poor man had a right to his anger and hatred. "I'll bear that in mind."

Tobias blew out a heavy sigh. "He is only a danger to himself. But that is why ye should never expect him to accept ye."

"I understand."

She barely recognized William Harper and his son, Willy, as they emerged from the dilapidated structure attached to the forge. She had met the smithy and the lad last night as well, and was relieved to remember that they'd been quite cordial. But last night, both had been a great deal cleaner and fully dressed. Today, they were shirtless, grubby, and wearing leather aprons. They both ambled up to Tobias. Josiah passed the men without a word and disappeared inside the stable.

William stared after the man for a brief moment, then shook his head and turned to Tobias. "Josiah said to hie me arse out here and see what ye wanted?"

Tobias pointed at Jovianna. "My wife has discovered our newest lad here has a cracked hoof that's hurting him."

"Yer wife?" William rubbed his shiny, bald head while turning to stare at her, then quickly recovered his manners and politely bowed. "Congratulations to the two of ye. May God bless ye with many years of happiness and twice as many bairns."

His toothy smile and jovial tone made Jovianna smile with the knowledge that he meant every word. "Thank you, Mr. Harper." She tried to ease the horse closer to the men, but the beast locked in place and snorted. Releasing the tension on the reins, she rubbed the horse's nose. "We'll stand here a bit longer, but then Mr. Harper needs to see your foot so it won't hurt you anymore."

"I canna believe they had him as part of a team pulling that carriage," Tobias said.

"Bastards probably beat the devil out of him, and he's determined not to allow it again." The smithy rubbed his smooth head again and turned to his son. "Fetch our things and wait here until the lad is ready to let ye near him. By then, I should have some shoes ready for him." He turned to Tobias. "I assume ye want the entire team reshod?"

"Aye," Tobias said. He propped his arms atop the fence and arched a brow at Jovianna. "Will ye be staying with yer new friend there or coming back inside?"

"I'll stay with him. I want to make sure he eats and drinks a bit too."

"Good enough, then." Tobias fixed her with a pointed look. "Remember what I said about—" He cut himself off and tipped his head toward the stable.

She knew he meant Josiah. "I'll remember and do my best to not vex him anymore."

CHAPTER ELEVEN

EVEN THOUGH THE hours in the paddock had passed quickly, Jovianna ached with satisfied weariness as she led the much more peaceful Clydesdale back inside the stable. But as she made the turn toward his stall, Josiah blocked the aisle. She braced herself, hoping Tobias was right about the man not being dangerous.

Josiah pointed at a large corner stall beside the wide door to the paddock. "Put him in that one. 'Tis larger and where he can see outside." Then he wheeled about and limped away, stabbing his pitchfork into the ground with every step.

Jovianna didn't speak, just accepted the act as kindness to the animal and was grateful. "You see?" she said to the horse as she led it into the nicer stall already fitted with fresh feed and water. "Mr. Josiah is a good man who only wants what's best for you."

The stallion grumbled as if dubious about her assessment, but as soon as she removed its bridle, it dug into the feed. Unsure whether the animal liked being brushed, Jovianna decided rubbing it down with a cloth would be best for the time being. The horse thanked her with a gentle whicker.

"I'm glad you like it," she answered. "Maybe tomorrow we'll try the brush. You've had a big day today, so we don't want to push it." The sweet Clydesdale surely had to be tired and ready for some quiet time.

"Well, what have we here?" asked an unfamiliar voice from deeper in the stable. "Who might ye be, my fine lassie?"

Jovianna exited the stall and secured the gate without turning her back to the strange man. Tall, with a sharp, beaklike nose, and beady eyes that reminded her of a rat, he had a greasiness about him that set her on edge. "I am Mistress Jovianna Risk. And you are?"

He gave her a lewd up-and-down ogle. "Risk, ye say? I know all the Risks, and ye are not one of them. And the only Risk I know who'd bed an English wench is the earl himself." He swaggered a step closer and gave her a smile that made her want to gag. "Course, I dinna have no such prejudices myself. My cock likes a hot, wet scabbard no matter the country."

Jovianna had no doubt that Tobias would kill the loathsome fool. But the current problem was escaping the isolation of the stable or finding a makeshift weapon that would buy her more time. The revolting wretch had already pulled his dagger, since he seemed to realize his pickup line had failed to impress her.

"My husband is Tobias Risk." She backed into a shovel propped against the boards of the stall. As the intruder stepped closer, she closed her hand around the handle. "I advise you to take your leave while you're still able."

The man guffawed. "Tobias Risk done married him an English?" He twirled the dagger higher and nodded. "Poor lovely. He probably got ye for me. Thinking ye'd convince me to look the other way when he couldna pay the rents." He licked his lips and bared his rotting teeth. "Are ye that good, my lovely? Make a man forget his duty?"

"I'll make you forget your duty!" She swung the shovel hard and fast, aiming for his head.

He ducked and lunged, pinning her in the corner between the stall and the doorway to the paddock. With the tip of his dagger jabbed up under her chin and his knee shoved into her middle, he yanked the shovel out of her hand and threw it aside. "Now, is that any way to welcome old Matthew? Ye'll have to serve me even better now for me to forget any coin that's owed."

"Tobias!" Jovianna screamed long and loud, but the bastard cut her off by slamming his filthy hand over her mouth.

He shook his head and raked the tip of his knife down the length of her throat. "I like screamers, but I'd rather ye say my name. It's Matthew, lovie. Matthew Tellerston."

Tellerston. The one whose visit Tobias had dreaded. And Mrs. Gibb had told her why. Jovianna tried to bite his hand, but apparently, he'd done this before and knew how to silence a woman without getting bit. She kicked and fought, screaming even though the sound was trapped and couldn't get past his hand.

"Get away from her!" Josiah shoved the tines of his pitchfork into the side of Tellerston's face and throat, jabbing hard enough to draw blood. "And if ye scratch her with that blade, I'll shove this through ye."

"Get off me, ye damned cripple." Tellerston swept his arm up and knocked the pitchfork away, then kicked Josiah backward.

"Help!" Jovianna screamed again and again as she retrieved the shovel and bashed Tellerston as he went to stab Josiah. As the devil shied away, she kept beating him and screaming. Every animal in the stable lent their voices to the battle, squealing and rattling the stalls.

"I will kill ye, ye bastard!' Tobias roared as he swooped in and took over.

Jovianna fell back against the stall and sank to the ground, her chest heaving to pull in enough air to keep from passing out. She crawled over to Josiah, dragging his pitchfork along with her. Blood covered the man, but she couldn't tell whose. "Are you all right? Did he cut you?"

"No, m'lady. Thanks to yer wee shovel, I am unhurt." Josiah flinched as Tobias slammed Tellerston against the wall and clutched the man's throat between his hands. "He must not kill him. He'll lose the land for sure if he does."

Jovianna forced herself to her feet, ran to Tobias, and tried to pull him away. "You can't kill him. It'll cost you everything."

Teeth bared, his face blood red, and the veins bulging in his forehead, Tobias didn't loosen his grip. "He must die." The words came out in the low, guttural growl of an enraged beast consumed by bloodlust.

"His life is not worth losing your land or your people. Please. You can't kill him." She locked her arms around Tobias's waist and pressed her cheek to his back, willing him to see sense through the red haze of his anger. "Let him go. Pay the rents and let him go." *But get a receipt.* She didn't trust Tellerston and knew deep down that somehow the rat would retaliate. She tried to pull him away again. "Tobias. Please."

Josiah appeared at Tobias's side and clapped a hand on his arm. "Listen to yer wife, man. Ye ken she is right. Listen to her."

Tobias shook with a bloodthirsty roar before wrenching his hands away and letting Tellerston drop. "Get to yer horse. Tender a receipt that says the rents are paid in full. I'll order the bags brought out to ye, and then ye will leave and thank God Almighty for staying my hand."

Curled on the ground, Tellerston coughed and spat while holding his throat but didn't try to rise.

"Move, damn ye!" Tobias bellowed.

Tellerston looked up at him with a scowl of pure hatred, then pushed up from the ground and staggered out of the stable.

"I'll tell Fitch to fetch the bastard his money," Josiah said while hitching away with a gait that appeared even more pained than before. He turned back, looked at Jovianna, and offered a respectful tip of his head. "Thank ye, mistress."

"Thank you, Josiah," she said, "for stopping him when I couldn't."

He accepted her thanks with another nod, then went his way.

Jovianna turned back to Tobias where he stood glaring out the wide doorway to the paddock as if still trapped within his rage. She eased over and barely touched his arm. "Tobias?"

He remained silent, didn't even blink.

She did the only thing she could think of—draped his arm around her shoulders and hugged in close to his side. "You did right," she whispered while holding him tighter. "You did what you had to do."

He came to life, crushed her to his chest, and pressed his face into her hair. "Forgive me," he whispered. "Forgive me, I beg ye."

"For what?" She lifted her head and made him look her in the eyes. "You did nothing wrong."

"I shouldha got here sooner. Never left ye alone to begin with."

The torture in his eyes broke her heart. She held tight to him, framing his face between her hands. "No love on earth can tolerate constant togetherness. Absence makes the heart grow fonder and familiarity breeds contempt. I read that somewhere. Pretty spot-on, if you think about it. We all need to exist as individuals. Even when we're half of a loving pair."

"He couldha—"

She stopped him with a hard shake of her head. "But he didn't, because Josiah attacked him with the pitchfork so I could get the shovel and beat the daylights out of him."

He drew in a ragged breath and pulled her close again. "Thank God," he whispered. "Thank God Almighty ye are unhurt."

"And thank you and Josiah for protecting me." She closed her eyes and tightened her embrace, worried not only about Tobias but also about what Tellerston might do once he left. "Why doesn't he collect the king's taxes from your brother in Edinburgh? Save himself a trip to the Highlands."

"Jamison pays the man for services other than collecting the rents and extra taxes." Tobias spat the words with contempt. "I ken his plan is to be rid of our crofters, cover the lands in sheep, and set Tellerston over it all." A heavy sigh left him. "But I canna prove it. All I can do is cover what's owed and pay off contacts in Edinburgh to legally foil them at every turn. But they're getting cannier. I dinna ken how much longer this game can be played."

Jovianna remembered testing her students about the politics involved in the Highland Clearances, but she had to take care about sharing too much with Tobias. What if she headed off one event and kept it from happening only to trigger a worse result than history had already reported in her time?

"We will play the game as long as we can," she said, hoping with all her heart that she and Amaranth could somehow help prevent the clearing of Risk lands.

"I must see the bastard on his way." He gently squeezed her shoulders, then his eyes narrowed and rage returned to his face. With his teeth bared, he lifted her chin and turned her head to the side. "He marked ye with his blade."

She caught his hand and held it tight. "A mere scratch. Nothing compared to what he might already plot to do because we stopped him. You cannot react. For the sake of your people and your land. Promise me."

Tobias bowed his head, sucked in a deep breath, then blew it out. "Know that your word alone is all that stays my hand."

"I know you'd snap him in two if I asked." She glanced toward the front of the stable, then looped her arm through his. "Come. Let's see him paid and gone."

"And then ye will let Mrs. Gibb have a look at yer throat, aye?"

"I promise."

Her throat was the least of her worries as they exited the stable just as the vile collector accepted a cloth sack from Fitch. Tellerston shoved it into his saddlebag, then tipped his hat at Tobias. As he rode away, the chilling sound of his taunting laughter floated back to them.

"He's going to do something," Jovianna said, hugging herself against the terrible knowing.

"Warn the crofters," Tobias ordered Fitch. "Tell them if they want their women and children to stay here at the manor for a few days, they're welcome."

"I'll see it done." Fitch turned to Donnor. "Take the west. I'll take men to the east."

"I'll take the north," Cade said from the steps of the estate.

Silas and Pag stepped forward. "One of us can cover the crofts to the south whilst the other stays to help here."

"Cade." Tobias motioned the old Highlander closer. "I need yer help here, aye? Silas and Pag can warn the crofts to the north and south."

Cade glared at him, clearly not happy, but accepted the order with a nod.

Relief filled Jovianna. She liked all of Tobias's men, but Cade's knowledge and experience would be helpful. Not only that, but his age concerned her. He'd survived well past the average life expectancy for a man of this era. He didn't need to push it.

As the men prepared to ride and Tobias and Cade discussed all that could happen, Jovianna eased over to the low stone fence in front of the garden and sat. She'd burned through every ounce of adrenaline she'd ever hoped to have. With her weak in the knees and with her head spinning, it wouldn't take much for her to faint.

Amaranth sat and pulled her into a hug. "I didn't want to fuss too much in front of the men. Tobias still has murder in his eyes."

"Thank you." Jovianna leaned against her mother and patted her arm. "Tellerston is going to retaliate. The man reeked of pure evil."

"An agent of the Highland Clearances along the ilk of the infamous Patrick Seller?" her mother asked.

"I have no doubt Tellerston is as capable as Patrick Seller of burning houses, destroying mills, and wrecking crops to terrorize his own people." A violent shudder stole across Jovianna as the men saddled up and rode away to warn the crofters. "And even if the crofters expect him and his men, I wonder if they'll be able to stop them."

"We can only hope and pray," Amaranth said.

"AND THE CROPS?" Tobias snorted against the foul stench of smoke and singed hair filling the hall. It clung to everything.

"Razed as well," Fitch said. "The bastards spared nothing, knowing it too late in the season for the land to be replanted." He swiped a sooty forearm across his forehead. "We saw them riding away but thought it more important to save as much as we could rather than give chase." He sadly shook his head. "We were nay so lucky with the other two. To destroy so much, Tellerston had to have ordered it done before he came here. The whoreson probably had a hand in it on his way."

The three families displaced by Tellerston's burnings huddled around tables in the main dining hall. Jovianna and Amaranth helped the maids serve them food and drink, while Mrs. Gibb tended to those injured during the fight to put out the fires and save what they could from their homes.

Tobias ground his teeth so hard his jaws cramped. "I should-ha killed the devil when I had the chance."

Cade shook his head. "Ye did right by sparing him. Who knows what wouldha been put into play if Tellerston had failed to meet with the rest of the murderers after his visit here? Pag should be back with the priest soon." He crossed himself and bowed his head. "Three graves to pray over so far." He lifted his head and flinched as his gaze swept across those gathered in the hall. "From the look of it, there may be more."

"We must stop Jamison once and for all," Tobias said.

"Ye canna kill yer brother." Fitch accepted a tankard from a passing maid, emptied it in one long gulp, then rumbled with a satisfied belch as he lowered it. "Ye ken he has the ear of the Crown."

It shamed Tobias to admit that his own flesh and blood had groveled his way into the good graces of not only King George but also the king's youngest son, the Duke of Cumberland, more aptly known as the Butcher for his heinous acts during the Jacobite rebellion of 1745.

"I'm going to Edinburgh." Tobias readied himself to speak to the poor tenant farmers who had lost so much because of his carelessness. He was not good at such speeches, but he owed them an apology and a plan to make things better.

"Ye canna kill him," Fitch repeated.

"I didna say I intended to kill him." Tobias set his jaw and forced a smile. "I mean to talk with him."

"God Almighty help us," Cade said, then scrubbed a hand across his mouth. "Forgive me for pointing out that what some folk consider as *talking* is not a talent ye possess."

"That is why ye will accompany me." Tobias nodded at Cade and Fitch. "The both of ye." Neither caring nor willing to consider any response they might have, he turned and strode down the center aisle between the lines of tables of his beleaguered tenants.

Jovianna met him halfway with a tray of empty plates balanced on her hip. "Poor things are starving after walking all the way here. I hope Mrs. Albright has more bread. Would it be all right if I asked her to make them some soup too? Especially for the children." Compassion and sympathy shone from her as she eyed them all. "How could someone do this to them?"

"Tellerston and my brother sold their souls long ago." Tobias pulled his gaze from his suffering people and tried to focus on Jovianna. "Nothing but riches matter to them. That is why Cade, Fitch, and I are going to Edinburgh to convince Jamison to change his ways."

"Convince?" She arched a brow. "You cannot kill your brother. If the king granted him an earldom, it's likely he has the court's ear. You don't exactly handle such matters with delicacy."

"Ye are the second person to point that out to me in less than an hour, my own."

She rested a hand on his arm. "I'm not trying to be critical, but you know your temper." She moved closer and lowered her voice. "You're a very passionate man, and while I love that about you, it also hinders your ability to reason at times."

"And that is why Cade and Fitch are accompanying me." Her words stung Tobias even though they rang true. He could be a reasonable man if he had to—perhaps. "'Tis a three-day trip, and I dinna ken how long it will take once we get there. We could be gone at least a fortnight or more. But there will be men here to ensure all are safe."

She handed off the tray to a passing maid, then pointed at the closest table of tenants. "They need more bread, please, and ask Mrs. Albright about a soup."

"Aye, m'lady." Jennet Albright, the cook's daughter, dipped a quick curtsy and hurried away.

Tobias braced himself. Jovianna's expression shouted that she was about to say something else he wouldn't like. "Jovianna?"

"What?"

"I thought ye were going to be the one to talk to Mrs. Albright."

"I thought it more prudent to talk to you. I'm coming with you to Edinburgh." She folded her arms over her chest and lifted her chin. "As a matter of fact, I am certain Amaranth will wish to come too. So consider both of us a part of the 'save the Earl of Grampian's soul' plan."

Irritation flashed hot and fast through him. "Ye will not," he said. "Ye will stay here where it is safe."

She pointed at him. "You won't be safe if I don't go, and neither will Cade. Amaranth and I are coming with you."

"And how in the devil's name do ye think that yer presence will keep us safe?"

"If the English or the Edinburgh sheriffs come across you and the other men, they'll suspect you to be the Devil of the Highlands band looking for prey. But if you're traveling with two women, they'll see you as a harmless family of Scots headed for Edinburgh and not looking for any trouble." Victory rang in her tone, making her smugness even more irritating.

"Bah!" Tobias waved away her reasoning like swatting at a midge. "Ye stay here, as does yer mother, ye ken?"

"Have you already forgotten how we fooled the sheriffs the last time? What if you run into them again? Amaranth and I need to go. Do you want me to call her over here to reinforce my argument?"

"I am not afraid of yer mother." The woman annoyed the hell out of him, but he did not fear her. Tobias gave Jovianna a curt nod. "As I said, wife, ye stay here, and so does yer mother."

"Amaranth," Jovianna said so loudly that everyone around them went quiet. "We need to pack. We're going to Edinburgh to address this horrible situation with the Earl of Grampian."

Amaranth straightened from helping a trembling young mother feed her wailing toddler. "I can be ready in an hour, as soon as I finish helping Mistress Robertson here."

"There you have it," Jovianna said. "Amaranth and I will finish helping these fine folks and be ready to leave soon after. I assume you plan to leave at dawn?"

Cade and Fitch walked up and joined them. Both looked more than a little confused. "The women are coming?" Cade asked.

Determined not to look the browbeaten fool, Tobias stood taller. "Aye. That way if we come across any English or authorities, they'll think us families traveling to Edinburgh rather than the esteemed men of the Devil of the Highlands."

Fitch looked suitably impressed. "Not a bad idea."

Cade nodded. "Good plan."

"I thought so," Tobias said while pinning Jovianna with a warning glare.

She smiled and started to walk away, but he caught her by the arm and drew her in close for a whisper. "Daren't ye ever do that again, wife. Understand?"

"I promise." She granted him the peace offering of a quick kiss. "Never again."

Somehow, he doubted she'd be able to keep that promise. It wasn't in her nature.

"Master Fitch! Master Fitch!" Tildy Grace careened into the hall shouting at the top of her lungs, her young voice shrill and piercing.

"Over here, young one." Fitch waved her down.

"Yer bairn's almost here," the little girl said. "In the kitchen. Telfa and Maudie is helping Aggie. Gran sent me to fetch ye. Said by the time ye get there the bairn will be here."

Tobias clapped Fitch on the back. "Ye heard the lass. Go!"

With little Tildy scampering ahead, Fitch hurried after her.

"Aggie's been helping cook all day," Jovianna said. "She mentioned her back aching a little but wouldn't let anyone make a fuss."

"Knowing Aggie, as soon as the wee one is born, she'll try to hop up and finish whatever she was doing before the bairn decided to come." Tobias crossed himself and sent up a silent prayer for both mother and child to be safe and well. The dangers of bringing life into the world were not to be taken lightly. After a hard swallow, he added another prayer for the soul of the son he never knew. Then his gaze settled on Jovianna as she looked toward the kitchen, smiling. What if she were to carry his bairn and fight to bring it into the world? Would they be safe? Would they survive?

"Jovianna." He pulled her closer.

She peered up at him, her brow puckering with confusion. "Tobias? What's wrong?"

What could he say to make her understand he feared for her? That he feared what might happen if she tried to bless him with a child? He opened his mouth to speak, but no words came.

She caught hold of him and frowned, staring up at him with concern flashing in her eyes. "What is it? Tell me."

He glanced all around, realizing that those sitting nearby

were staring. "I canna speak of it here." He pecked a quick kiss to her forehead and gave her a smile he didn't feel. "'Tis nothing. Dinna fash yerself, aye?"

He turned to go. He had to get outside, clear his head before he spoke to those made homeless by his brother. And the last thing he needed right now was to confess to Jovianna that he prayed she would never get with child. Without another word, he headed for the door with a long, hurried stride. As he pushed out the doors and charged down the steps, she called after him, "Tobias!"

Damn his foolishness for caving to his fears during a moment of weakness. He halted and stared downward, wishing she would go back inside. "There is much to be done, my own. Best be about it, aye?"

"Not until you tell me what's wrong," she said quietly. "What happened back there?"

"I'm merely concerned for Aggie and the babe. Fitch would be lost without her. They've been inseparable since they were bairns. We all were children together." He prayed he sounded convincing, and she'd leave it at that.

She eyed him as though debating whether or not to call him a liar to his face. "With the baby coming so fast, chances are that Aggie and the child are both doing well. When there are complications, things usually take a lot longer." She moved closer and rested her hand on the center of his chest. "But I don't think that's what's troubling you. Are you still angry with me about the trip to Edinburgh?"

"I was never angry with ye." He shuffled in place, feeling like a lad forced to confess his misdeeds to his father. "Yer safety is always foremost in my mind." There. That was the truth of it, without revealing everything weighing on his heart.

She touched his face with such caring that it inflamed his guilt about not telling her the complete truth. "We'll keep each other safe. Yes?"

"Aye," he whispered. "We will as much as God allows." As

soon as the words left his lips, he knew he shouldn't have said them.

Her eyes narrowed. "We are not moving from this spot until you tell me what is really wrong."

He stared into her eyes for what felt like forever. "I dinna want ye to die trying to have my child."

She slid her arms around him and held him tight. "I'm not ready to die either, but we've got no control over when or how our time comes." She eased back and looked him in the eyes again. "And if we spend what time we have worrying about when it will end—we waste it."

"I know." Her words brought him no comfort, even though he saw the sense they made. "'Twas easier when I cared for no one and my thoughts centered only on protecting my people and my land."

"If you didn't care about your people, you wouldn't worry about protecting them," she said with a smug tip of her head.

He glared at her. "Ye ken what I mean."

She smiled. "I do. And if it's any consolation, I'm not pregnant and I'm trusting Amaranth and Mrs. Gibb's daily herbal tea to keep me that way until you and I know each other well enough to decide if we wish to be parents."

"Ye dinna wish to have my bairn?" He didn't know whether to be thankful, hurt, or insulted.

She rolled her eyes. "There's no pleasing you today, is there?" She poked him in the chest, backing him up a step. "*Someday* when we're both ready, yes. But not right now. We're too— new." She scowled at him and jabbed him again. "And if it's any consolation to you, the last time I saw my physician, he commented that because of the way I'm built, I should have no trouble having babies."

"Ye saw a healer? Why?"

She rubbed the spot on her forehead where the fresh pink scar had formed. "I was unwell at the time." She let her hand drop and glared at him. "You said we had a lot to do in preparation for the trip. Should you not be getting to it?"

"Dinna take a tone with me." He caught her up against his chest to soften the scolding. "'Tis yer fault. All this—uneasiness. I find myself caring more about ye every day." He tucked his mouth against her ear and whispered, "And every night, I canna get enough of ye." He drew back and attempted a stern glare. "Ye should be ashamed for bewitching me so."

"Oh, I am." With a look that rendered him even more powerless, she eased out of his arms and tugged him toward the stables. "Come help me."

"Help ye with what?" he asked, although he had a fair idea, and the thought of testing the softness of the new hay appealed to him immeasurably.

She smiled back at him. "I'm sure you'll figure it out."

CHAPTER TWELVE

JOVIANNA KNEW THE place as Gilmour's Linn or Touch Glen Waterfall and Charlie's Cave. But those names were from her time, so she kept them to herself. Instead, she reveled in the cold waterfall tumbling down over her, washing the dust of traveling away. Tomorrow, they would reach Edinburgh and all the stress that entailed. But today, she and Amaranth, and Cade and Tobias, would enjoy this hidden gem of the Highlands to gather their thoughts and prepare for whatever lay ahead.

Tobias surfaced in the pool and sent a shower of droplets flying as he tossed his glistening black hair back from his face. He stood and walked toward her, moving through the water like a powerful water god ready to claim his prize.

She stepped out of the waterfall and met him halfway, wrapping her legs around him as she held on to his shoulders. "There's something to be said for the buoyancy of water."

"Indeed." He cupped her buttocks and pulled her closer while teasing his fingertips across her opening beneath the surface. As he kissed a trail across one of her breasts, he paused and gave her a meaningful smile. "But a warm patch of grass will bring us more pleasure than this cold water."

Sliding a hand down between them, she wrapped her fingers

around him. "Still very impressive. Even with the cold."

His low chuckle rumbled more like the purring of a great cat as he carried her to a spot on the bank covered in lush, cushiony moss and feathery ferns.

As he lowered her onto the nest of green, he smiled down at her. "Much better, aye? A bit of sunshine makes everything grow, ye ken?"

"Yes. I do agree." She arched against him as he ran the tip of his tongue around her nipple. "And Cade and Amaranth are where?"

"Not here," he said, then sucked her nipple harder as he teased his fully swollen hardness against her opening.

She took that to mean he wasn't in the mood to discuss it, and agreed completely. She ran her hands down the slickness of his wet back and squeezed his buttocks, loving the play of his muscles beneath her touch as he settled inside her. To keep from shouting and alerting the others, she caught her bottom lip between her teeth, meeting him thrust for delicious thrust until he went still and rose to frown down at her.

"Why did you stop?" Breathless and so very close to ecstasy, she needed him to move.

"Why are ye quiet? Am I not pleasing ye?"

"We're outside, and I don't want Amaranth and Cade to hear us." She tried to urge him onward with a hard squeeze of his tensed behind.

A wildly shrieked *yes* split the air somewhere off in the distance, followed by a deep, guttural roar that almost shook the trees.

Tobias arched a brow at her and didn't say a word. Amaranth and Cade were obviously otherwise involved and wouldn't be paying them any mind.

"My apologies, sir." She stroked his sides and ground herself up against him. "Make me scream now. Please?"

"Gladly, m'lady."

He rocked into her with a hard pounding that made her shout

as wave after wave of tingling bliss exploded through her. His rumbling growl echoed into the depths of the cave behind the waterfall and flushed a brace of birds from the bushes. After a moment of trembling and another endearing growl, he dropped across her while taking care not to crush her deeper into the mossy embankment.

"Oh my." She kissed his shoulder while relishing the warm, contented laziness pulsing through her with every beat of her heart.

He lifted his head. "Oh my, what?"

She smiled up at him. "Oh my, that was wonderful."

"Good." He kissed the tip of her nose. "Ye had me concerned there for a bit when ye didna make any of yer wee yips or growls."

"You make me sound like one of your hounds."

He gave her a wicked grin. "I have known ye to howl a time or two."

She gave his arm a playful swat. "You better behave. Aggie promised to tell me all her secrets about making Fitch do as he's told."

"Aye, old Fitch will be useless for a while. The man's completely besotted with his wee daughter." Tobias rolled and gathered her close, tucking her into the curve of his arm. She nestled her head into the dip of his shoulder and hugged her leg across his middle. His quiet laugh rumbled against her cheek. "That poor lassie will never be able to marry. Fitch willna let anyone close to her." He trailed a fingertip up and down Jovianna's back. "It pleases me greatly that Aggie and the babe are healthy and whole."

"I agree completely." Jovianna stared at the fluttering leaves as the limbs swayed with the gentle breeze and decided to take the opportunity to vocalize her fears about the trip. "How eloquent is Cade?"

A heavy sigh escaped Tobias. "I am not a bloodthirsty fool, Jovianna—contrary to what yerself and everyone else seems to think."

She regretted the question immediately. "No one thinks you a fool. Me especially." She combed her fingertips through the tiny black curls dusting his chest. "If you were a fool, you couldn't have made it through all that you've survived, and your people would have already been scattered." She yearned for him to know beyond a shadow of a doubt that she believed in him. "You are the man for this. No one else can resolve this hellishness but you."

He caught her hand in his and kissed it but didn't speak.

They lay there for a long while, the unknown growing between them like an unfettered beast. Then he spoke so quietly, she almost didn't hear him. "Has yer sight told ye anything about this trip?"

What could she tell him that might help and wouldn't be a lie? She propped up on her elbow and looked down at him. "I have seen nothing about you or the Earl of Grampian." And she hadn't. Nowhere in all her studies had Tobias's or his brother's name ever been listed. Hoping she wasn't making a mistake, she continued, "All I have seen is that the Duke of Cumberland will suffer an attack of apoplexy this month." Actually, it would be the first of several strokes for the duke, but she couldn't call them that. "And on October twenty-fifth, King George II dies because of a severe malady of his arteries." She couldn't remember if artery was a word from this time or if Tobias would know what it meant, so she added, "A worse attack of apoplexy than that which strikes his son the duke. His grandson will take the throne. King George III."

He stared at her as if she spoke a language he didn't understand. Finally, he said, "Pray tell me the Butcher dies soon too."

She sadly shook her head. "I'm sorry. Not until 1765. He will be an advisor to his nephew, King George III, up until that time."

"Have ye seen Scotland ever become free?" he asked in a rasping whisper.

"No. I haven't." She sat up and hugged her knees, wishing

she'd not answered so truthfully. But then, wouldn't it have been cruel to give him hope? "The important thing is, I haven't seen anything about you or your brother. That means nothing bad happens."

He rose and sat beside her. "Or nothing good happens." He shook his head. "My gut tells me this visit willna go well, and my gut is rarely ever wrong."

"What are your hopes?"

With a huffing snort, he shifted positions and propped his arms atop his bent knees. "If I had the coin, I'd buy the lands from the wee bastard. But knowing that greedy cur, he'd make the price impossible to come by. He's nearly done so with the rents and our share of the taxes."

If that were the case, she failed to see what good their visit would do at all, but didn't voice it. If Tobias thought it worth the effort to travel all the way to Edinburgh, surely he had some idea of a way to bend Jamison to his will. "I'm going to rinse off and dress so I can see if Amaranth is ready to help me forage for some fresh greens to enjoy with our oatcakes this evening."

"If I relented and built ye a fire, would ye cook?" He stood and joined her in the pool.

"Trust me. You do not want me to cook." She fully submerged, then swam to the other bank where she'd spread her clothes across the bushes for a good airing. As she wiped off as much water as she could with her hands, she wished for her favorite body spray and lotion. Herbal substitutes for deodorant were all well and good, but nothing compared to the items she'd always taken for granted. But then a sideways glance at Tobias's naked glory reminded her that her sacrifice hadn't been in vain. And it wasn't just the physical part. He was stubborn, gruff, and as unrefined as a jagged stone, but gentle and loving, with a ferocity that would move heaven and earth to protect her. She'd never known this level of contentment in her time. As soon as he had his léine pulled down over his head, she threw her arms around him and kissed him hard.

As she finished the kiss and eased away, he framed her face with his hands and held her there, staring into her eyes as if trying to see into her soul.

"What?" she whispered.

He shook his head. "When I look into yer eyes, it eases my heart. Makes me dare to hope that there is some peace and happiness left to be had in this world."

She patted his chest and gave him her bravest smile. "We will make our own peace and happiness. I promise." A tall order, but she would see it done if it was the last thing she did. Tobias deserved it after all he'd been through.

He brushed a gentle kiss across her lips, then turned her in his arms. "Fill yer lungs, my own, so I dinna get yer corset too tight."

Jovianna expanded her ribcage with a deep inhale, smiling to herself as he pulled it to the perfect amount of tightness with a single tug. As she bent to step into her petticoat, he swatted her behind and laughed at her yip of surprise.

"I'm off to check on the horses," he said as he donned the rest of his clothes. "And have a look around to ensure we dinna have any unexpected guests." He nodded toward the east, then winked at her. "I believe the noises came from that direction, if ye care to call out and see if yer mother is available for foraging."

"I'll head that way and make as much noise as possible." She raked her fingers through her wet hair, coiled it to the top of her head, and secured it with pins and combs. It could dry later, after they settled down for the night. As she tromped eastward, she rattled bushes and low-hanging limbs. "Amaranth! Are you decent?"

A lazy giggle came from the other side of a dense thicket of hawthorn. "My decency is entirely dependent upon whom you ask," Amaranth called out. A deep chuckle that in no way belonged to her followed.

Jovianna rolled her eyes and turned her back to the thicket just to be on the safe side. While she'd somewhat come to terms with her mother being a sexually active senior, she did not want to witness it firsthand. "I thought you and I could forage for some greens to go with tonight's oatcakes. Tobias has gone to check the horses and make sure no intruders are near."

"He should not have gone without me." Cade came crashing around the thorny thicket while still yanking his tunic on over his head.

"You are a killjoy," Amaranth said to Jovianna as she emerged soon after, tightening the laces of her jacket across her stomacher while she walked. She looked up from her handiwork with a perturbed scowl. "There are much more enjoyable things to be had this afternoon than fresh greens."

"Cade was right. Tobias shouldn't be walking the perimeter alone." Jovianna waved her mother forward and plucked several leaves out of her hair, feeling slightly jealous that she and Tobias weren't still lazing away the day beside the waterfall. "And I don't think Cade is as worried about this trip as Tobias."

"Ahh," Amaranth said. "The truth comes out." She patted Jovianna's shoulder, then looped her arm through hers. "And Cade is very concerned. He fears Tobias won't be able to reason through his rage."

"I'm hoping I can help him with that as much as possible," Jovianna said. "But I fear it will take all of us."

A man's shout in the distance halted them and made them hurry to crouch behind a small rise covered with thick ferns. They held tight to one another as they cowered.

Jovianna squeezed her mother's hands, then eased up, peered all around, then dropped back into the greenery.

See anything? Amaranth mouthed.

Jovianna shook her head, straining to listen to the woodlands around them, but her pounding heart drowned out all other sounds.

"Jovianna!" Tobias shouted. "Come out. Donnor and Pag have joined us."

"That can't be good," Amaranth said as they both stood.

Jovianna agreed—especially when she spotted Tobias's dark

expression. She hurried toward him, running and hopping around anything blocking her way. "What's happened? What's wrong?"

"More fires," he said, catching hold of her when she stumbled. "Two more crofts destroyed. 'Twill be a lean winter indeed at Risk Manor."

Donnor and Pag stood rubbing down their horses after stripping them of their gear. "If they take down any more," Donnor said, "I dinna ken how we'll all survive."

"When did you plant the potatoes?" Jovianna asked. "With this being late August, you should still be able to salvage some of them."

Pag huffed a humorless laugh. "They couldna get the potato fields to burn. Still too green. They took out the ripe oats and barley instead."

"At least no one was hurt this time," Tobias said. He turned to Jovianna and Amaranth. "As soon as the horses are rested, we leave for Edinburgh. I dinna wish to delay until morning."

As the men turned away, Amaranth pulled Jovianna aside. "What does he mean to do once we get there?"

"I have no idea," Jovianna said. "I just pray it works."

JOVIANNA'S FIRST IMPRESSION of the Earl of Grampian's sumptuous estate in the best part of Edinburgh was not a good one. The pristine home, with its impeccably lavish style, made her realize even more the sad state of Risk Manor back in the Highlands. Every elegance, from the sparkling crystal chandeliers to the polished brass stair rods, reminded her of the burned-out ruins of the crofters' cottages. The only redeeming point she'd found in the place was that every servant, be they male, female, young, or old, seemed genuinely overjoyed to see Tobias and Cade, and settled them comfortably into the nicest rooms even though they had arrived at well past midnight. Pag and Donnor had opted to bed down in the stables with the horses, saying they'd rather house with animals than with Tobias's brother.

As she poured water into a basin for a morning refresh, she cast a worried glance at Tobias. He stood with an untouched glass of whisky in his hand, his shoulders squared and his stance wide, as though ready to vault off the balcony and battle the rising sun. He hadn't slept. Not even lain in the bed and rested. He'd thrown open the double doors of the balcony, and there he'd stayed for what was left of the extremely short night.

She went to him, gently twisted the drink out of his hand, and set it on a nearby table. "Is that the one you poured when we first got here?"

He blinked, then looked at her as if suddenly realizing he wasn't alone. His gaze slid to the glass, and he snorted. "Aye. I reckon so."

"What is our plan?" She wrapped her arms around his waist and rested her cheek on his chest. His heart thumped strong and steady, making her wish she knew of a way to make all that threatened him go away.

His arms tightened around her, and a heavy sigh left him. "I will try reasoning with him first. If that fails, he and I shall go for a ride."

She pulled back and stared up at him. "You can't kill him. He's too well connected, even though he's despised."

"Many a rider has broken their neck when their horse fails to make a jump."

"It's too risky. You might still be blamed." The set of his jaw told her that nothing she said was getting through. "You cannot be the only person who wants him dead. Is there not someone else who would kill him for us?"

"And blackmail me for hiring them?" Weariness and worry etched deep lines in his face, chiseling his expression with frustration and pain. "I must do this myself."

"But if you do and are implicated in his death, the Crown will seize everything." She tried to shake him, willing him to listen.

"Then what will happen to everyone you're trying to protect?"

He gave her a sad smile, then pressed such a tender kiss to her forehead that she wanted to weep. "There is no other way," he said in a resigned tone. Stepping back from her, he picked up the whisky, downed it in one gulp, then thumped the glass back onto the table. "I'm going to the stables for a wee look around. If ye decide to leave the room, mind yerself. I dinna ken when the lazy bastard rises, or if he's even here. The servants were expecting him, but that doesna mean he came home last night."

"Tobias." Jovianna started toward him, but he stopped her with a curt shake of his head.

"I must do this, my own."

Then he was out the door before she could argue him back to her side.

She hurried to dress. Well, as much as one could hurry when having to fiddle with so many layers—shift, stays, petticoat, tie-on pockets, bum roll, skirt, jacket, stomacher, stockings, and shoes. And then there was her hair. For heaven's sake, it would be well past noon at this rate. As put together as possible, she hurried out of the room and down the winding staircase. She came up short upon reaching a wide hallway and a closed set of mahogany double doors directly in front of her. She tried to remember which room the weary maid had said that was—a library, dining room, drawing room, or some other name that escaped her at the moment.

As she eased over to the doors, she glanced up and down the hallway lined with portraits and pedestals holding dust collectors that she really needed to be careful and not bump. She felt sure the earl would increase Tobias's rents or taxes if she broke anything. She held her breath and listened at the doors. Nothing but silence rewarded her efforts, and that told her nothing about the room's contents or how it might help her in the plan she had yet to sort out. All she knew for certain was that she had to discover a way to help Tobias and the people counting on the Risk lands to survive.

"In for a penny, in for a pound," she muttered as she slid one of the doors open wide enough to slip inside. Upon turning to discover what the room held, she didn't know whether to be disappointed or glad that she'd found quite the large library, which contained a massive desk and leather chair on one end and an elaborate seating arrangement in front of an ornate hearth on the other. The high-backed chairs and sofa appeared to be empty. It was hard to tell, since they faced the hearth. She eyed the desk. If the earl kept business or personal papers there, maybe she could find something useful.

She tiptoed across the thick Turkish rug, around the desk, then deflated with a disappointed huff. Every drawer sported quite an elaborate brass keyhole, and she'd bet money they were all locked. After trying the center drawer and one on each side, she sadly conceded that she'd been correct and would've won a lot of money on that bet.

A groan came from the couch as the back of a man's dark head slowly rose into view. "Sons-a-bitches," he said, rocking forward to propel himself to his feet.

Jovianna held her breath and debated whether diving under the desk before he turned around would be a good choice or not. Deciding *not*, she sprang around it, rushed to the doors, and tried to exit.

"Hold a minute there!"

If not for the door hanging in the track, she would have made a clean escape. But just as she managed to wrench it open, the man caught hold of her shoulder and spun her around to face him. Even without an introduction, she knew who the foul-smelling bloke was. The family DNA ran strong and true when it came to the Risk black hair and icy-blue eyes that looked even worse when bloodshot. But that was where the likeness stopped. Jamison Risk, the first Earl of Grampian, was a short, chinless, pudgy sort that appeared to be the runt of the litter.

"Forgive me for disturbing you," Jovianna said, refusing to cower. "My husband and I arrived so late last night that I failed to remember the way to the dining room, and I'm absolutely famished. Would you be so kind as to direct me?"

"Yer husband?" The earl gave her a rude, bleary-eyed scowl. "Dressed like that, I'd say ye belong in the kitchens with the rest of the sculleries, not the dining room. Who is yer husband?"

"Tobias Risk." She set her chin to a regal angle, noting she could look down on the sniveling fool—literally. "I am Mistress Jovianna Risk. And you are?"

The man staggered back a step, squinted at her, then rubbed his eyes. "I am yer husband's wealthy and, might I add, *titled* brother. It appears ye married the wrong Risk, dear sister." He hiccupped as though about to vomit and clutched his middle. "What proof have ye that ye married Tobias? My brother would never marry an English." He hissed out a wheezing chuckle. "He hates them as much or more than he hates me, and that's plenty. I'll grant ye that."

"Be that as it may. He is my husband, I assure you." Deciding to take the battle in hand, she squared off, determined to intimidate him. "Are you aware that your man Tellerston ordered the razing of five crofts on Risk land that resulted in three deaths, five homeless families, and lost crops that could very well lead to starvation this winter?"

The earl twitched a shrug, then belched. "What of it?"

"What of it?" Jovianna stared at him. How was this selfish brute Tobias's brother? "That makes him and his men murderers." She jabbed the air, pointing at him. "And you as well, if you ordered it done."

Grampian gave her a chilling smile and stood his ground. "I merely ordered the rents collected, dear lady. If the coin fell short, those responsible were to be evicted, and the lands prepared for sheep." He sauntered toward her, drawing close enough to nauseate her with his stench of greasy, unwashed body, stale piss, and alcohol. "The tenants were warned. Tellerston is merely following my commands."

"We gave the money to Tellerston. Everything owed was

paid in full. Three of the burnings happened before he even arrived to collect the sum. How do you explain that?"

"Fiery wee thing for an English. I'll give ye that." The earl eyed her with an evil smirk that made her want to punch him in the face. He strolled over to a cart filled with fancy decanters and fine glassware. While resting a finger on a bottle filled with a dark ruby liquid, he asked, "Port?" Before she declined, he lifted his hand and shook his head. "No. Not port. A fine lady such as yerself would prefer sherry this early in the day, yes?"

"I would prefer explanations from you, sir. Not alcohol, thank you very much."

His smug, self-satisfied expression became even more pronounced as he poured himself a drink. "What about a proposition in lieu of either?"

Nothing the man could have to say would be good. Jovianna already knew that. She could see it in his eyes. Rather than answer, she glared at him, bracing herself for the worst.

He wheezed out his same annoying chuckle of earlier. "What an intelligent lady ye are. Much too good for the Devil of the Highlands."

She managed not to react. Or at least she hoped she didn't. Instead, she pulled in a deep breath and huffed it out as though insulted and tired of his games. "Apparently, your late night and excess of alcohol have confused you, sir. My concern is for my husband and the Risk clan occupying the lands north of Loch Lomond. That is the topic of our conversation. Not some Highland myth. Perhaps we should speak later, when you are more in possession of your faculties."

Eyes glittering like a predator about to go in for the kill, Grampian took a long, slow sip of his drink, then cradled it between his hands. "Oh, we speak of the same thing, dear lady. Ye ken that as well as I. The only way yer husband gets enough coin to cover the clan's costs is by relieving unwary travelers of their purses." He moved closer, leaned in, and lowered his voice. "What would ye be willing to do to not only save him from the noose but save those weary crofters from eviction as well?"

"I would not be willing to trust you to keep your word," she said without hesitation.

He laughed in her face, then leaned in closer still and sniffed. "I do love yer fire," he said softly, "and ye smell sweet and succulent as a ripe plum waiting to be bitten."

"I bite back," she said, jerking away to put more space between them.

"I would hope so." He lifted his glass as though toasting the offer. "Now, back to my proposition." He traipsed over to his desk, pulled a key from his waistcoat pocket, and opened the center drawer. With his gaze still locked with hers, he took out a piece of parchment and a partially melted stick of red wax. "I shall speak frankly, since that appears to be yer enchanting preference." After another sip of his drink, he smiled. "And I must say, I rather enjoy such brutal honesty myself." He set down his glass, selected a quill, and inked it, then scribbled across the bottom of the paper with a flourish. With an unsteady hand, he melted the sealing wax, dripped it on the page, then pressed the ornate ring on his pinky finger into it.

He waved her forward. "Come, my dear. See what I offer to assure ye my word is worthy of yer trust."

Jovianna moved to the front of the desk, keeping the massive bit of furniture between them. Dread, disgust, and the wish that she'd stayed up in the room churned so hard within her that bile burned in the back of her throat.

"Well?" She had to win this game. Somehow. Some way.

"Oh no, my dear." He crooked a finger and motioned for her to come closer. "Stand at my side to appreciate this rare gift I am prepared to bestow upon ye."

After a deep breath, she eased around to his side of the desk and looked down at the parchment. The page was empty except for what appeared to be his signature at the bottom and the wax imprint of his ring.

"And what is that scrawl?" she asked in a tone she hoped

sounded unimpressed.

"Jamison Risk, first Earl of Grampian. My legal signature, dear lady."

"On a blank page?"

"Aye, my sweet." He picked up the parchment and wafted it back and forth to dry the ink. "And it shall be filled in to say that my brother could not possibly be the Devil of the Highlands and is hereby named as the sole proprietor operating in my best interest over the Risk lands. His word will be law and there will be no more visits from Tellerston as long as Tobias forwards me the rents and taxes. The Risk crofters will be safe as long as my brother sees fit to let them stay."

He reached out to touch her cheek, and she dodged him.

"Now, now, my lovely." He playfully shook his finger. "This page will only hold those words if ye agree to become my mistress. A verra well-kept one, I might add. Ye willna regret it."

"All I see is a blank page. How do I know those words will ever grace it?" She needed time to figure out a way to work this to her advantage without allowing this disgusting fool to touch her.

A light tap on the door interrupted them.

"What is it?" Grampian barked like an irritated dog.

"My lord," a man said. "His Grace, the Duke of Cumberland, has confirmed he will honor ye with his presence this evening for supper. As per yer instructions, we held the guest list and preparations until His Grace's response was received. Shall we proceed posthaste?"

"Of course, fool. See it done." The earl glared at the door as though wishing the man on the other side of it was dead.

"As you wish, my lord." The echo of footsteps on the polished floors faded off into the distance.

Grampian turned back to her. "Now, where were we?"

"A blank page with nothing but your signature means nothing." She tapped on the paper.

He rolled it up and held it out to her. "Take it with ye, my lovely. Write the words. I assume ye can write. If not, I can send someone to yer rooms to help ye. Then present the paper and yerself to my bedchamber this evening after our elegant supper with a few influential guests and we will consummate our agreement, ye ken?" He caught hold of her hand before she could jerk it away and licked the back of it. "Tobias will be safe. His people will be safe. And once again, I will have his woman in my bed."

CHAPTER THIRTEEN

"Jovianna. You can't be serious." Amaranth stared at her with a combination of disbelief, worry, and utter dismay. "If Tobias gets wind of this—"

"I know. That's why I don't intend to tell him until it's all over. By then, if everything falls into place, Jamison will be in jail and, with any luck, scheduled for a short drop and a sudden stop." Jovianna gently blew on the ink, then held up the parchment. "What do you think? Does the wording sound period correct and match his signature enough to pass scrutiny?"

"I still think this is one of your more rash decisions." Amaranth plucked a pair of wire-rimmed spectacles out from behind her stomacher and donned them.

"When did you get those?" Jovianna asked. "They're like Mrs. Gibb's."

Her mother gave her a disgruntled look as she held the parchment first at arm's length, then adjusted the glasses on her nose and brought the paper closer. "She sent off for them for me. Some place here in Edinburgh. I can't read a bloody thing up close anymore, and my arms aren't long enough to read anything without them." Drawing closer to the light of the candlestick, she frowned down at the sheet, her eyes racing back and forth across the page. "I will say you missed your calling. You should have been a forger. The letter matches his hand perfectly."

"Thank you." Jovianna pointed at a particular paragraph in the center of the document. "I know it's flowery, but he talks that way." She almost gagged at the memory. "The man is a self-centered, insufferable bastard."

Amaranth placed the paper on the table, then turned her concerned scowl back on Jovianna. "And you truly think you can pull this off? Cade and I won't be there. Neither will Pag, nor Donnor. Not with Cumberland there. You understand?"

"I understand. And yes. I can pull this off because I have no choice." Jovianna stared down at the letter a moment longer, then carefully folded it and tucked it behind her stomacher.

"And how are you going to get the bitter cascara into the duke's food or drink without getting caught?" Before Jovianna could answer, Amaranth held up a hand. "And how is it you came to have such a dangerous laxative?"

"I went to Mrs. Gibb because my stomach hasn't been right of late. She recommended using it as a digestive tonic." Jovianna pulled the small brown vial from her pocket and held it up to the candlelight, eying the potent liquid. "I remembered reading about it once in a seventeenth-century manuscript and decided not to risk it. Mrs. Gibb was quite adamant that I needed only one or, at the very most, two drops in my tea each morning. The entire bottle should guarantee whoever ingests it an experience they'll not soon forget. That will convince the duke to believe the letter."

"And how are you going to get it into the man's food or drink without getting caught?" Amaranth asked again.

Jovianna frowned. She'd rather not admit she hadn't figured that part out. "When the opportunity presents itself, I'll spring into action."

Her mother gave her another dubious arch of a brow. "That is what worries me." She moved to the window, parted the lacy curtains, and peered outside. "You realize this is going to make you appear to be a British sympathizer?"

"I know." Still sick about that particular sticking point, Jovianna went to the washbasin and started scrubbing at the ink stains on her fingers. "But I can't think of any other way to save Tobias and his people permanently."

"Cade joined him in the stables," Amaranth said. She turned from the window and paced back and forth across the sitting room that connected their opulent bedchambers. "Will Tobias attend supper? He was involved in the '45 rebellion too."

"I don't know." Jovianna scrubbed harder on the last stubborn splotch of ink. "If he does, I fear he'll become unhinged when I get close enough to poison the duke, and rage even worse when I show the man the incriminating letter. But if he doesn't attend, how can I?" She fixed a panicked look on her mother. "I'm damned if I do and damned if I don't."

"I can have a quiet word with Cade. Perhaps he can keep Tobias occupied, and you can offer your husband's regrets. Say he had a previous engagement or was called away to see a dying friend here in Edinburgh."

"Do you think Cade will tell Tobias or attempt to intervene?" The old Highlander and Amaranth had become inseparable, but how strong was their bond? Jovianna dried her hands on a delicately embroidered bit of linen that looked entirely too nice to use. A faint stain remained on the writing callus of her middle finger, but it wasn't as noticeable as before.

"I don't know, sweetie. All I can do is talk to him and hope for the best." Amaranth gave her a reassuring hug, then jerked and glared at the mantel clock as it loudly chimed the hour. "But if I'm going to speak with him, I need to do it quickly. We're nearly out of time."

"But if he and Tobias are together?" Jovianna pressed a hand to her chest. Her racing heart was about to pound itself out of her body.

Amaranth shook her head and threw up her hands. "I don't know, Jovianna. I'm sorry. I just don't know. I'll do what I can."

Before Jovianna could say another word, her mother dashed out and closed the door behind her. After another peek down her front to ensure the note hadn't slipped, Jovianna returned to her and Tobias's bedchamber and did what she could to spruce up her appearance.

Her best everyday skirt and jacket were a far cry from the fanciness such important supper guests demanded but would have to do. The trip to Edinburgh had been one of hurried necessity, not a visit requiring a gown for parties and impressing the right people. She swallowed hard at the realization that she was about to meet Prince William, the Duke of Cumberland. A man she had never liked just from what she'd read about him in the history books.

As she paced around the room, she took the small vial back out of her pocket, unstoppered it, and sniffed the contents. It had a bitter, herbaceous odor, but it was not so strong as to announce itself as soon as she opened it at supper. For the life of her, she couldn't remember what the menu would be for an elegant meal of this era. A soup course would be phenomenally helpful, but if that didn't work, she'd have to go for the duke's wine. Hopefully, the man liked port or something dark enough to hide the drug.

She stepped out on the balcony and pulled in deep breaths of fresh air, praying it would calm her nerves. This plan would work. Tobias would eventually understand when it all worked out. At least, she hoped he would. Even though they had been together a little over two months now, there were still times when she wondered if he had married her out of some misplaced sense of duty to protect her or because he really loved her. Or maybe he'd even married her because of some overzealous attack of chivalry or guilt because he'd taken her to his bed. Or all of the above. All she knew for certain was that she loved him so much she didn't know what she'd do without him—and not just because she was stranded in the eighteenth century.

"Jovianna?"

His entrance startled her so badly that she sucked in a deep gasp and choked on the air, exploding into a coughing fit. He hurried to her and pounded on her back. "Saints' bones, woman. Has the ague taken hold of ye?"

"I sucked in a bug," she said, rasping and wheezing to breathe. "When I inhaled fresh air." She fanned herself and coughed some more. "Dratted thing tried to strangle me."

"Dinna die on me, aye? I've got enough on my mind at present." He softened the scolding with a tender touch of her cheek and a faint smile. "I canna do this without ye."

"I'll do my very best not to die on you," she promised. Poor Tobias. He had no idea how much she meant those words. "I assume you've heard about your brother's affair this evening?"

He bared his teeth and looked ready to growl. "Aye. Cade and the others refuse to attend, but I wouldna miss it. With any luck, I can say something that will cause Jamison and the Butcher both to choke to death."

"That would be fortuitous," she said. It would also deliver her from her now even more difficult ordeal ahead. Not only did she have to slip away from Tobias, she also had to figure out how to poison the duke's drink. Or, at least, make him think he was about to be poisoned and give him the letter, making herself appear to be a loyal admirer. Then it would be up to Cumberland to decide whether to believe her and test his food and drink or have someone else test it. "When are we supposed to go down?"

"Now. 'Tis why I came to fetch ye." He gave a disgusted huff and offered his arm. "Jamison conveniently stayed in his chambers all day. Feckin' coward."

Jovianna didn't respond, just held tightly to Tobias's arm. It occurred to her that this must be what it felt like to walk to the gallows. As they reached the bottom of the staircase, the low hum of conversation, like the droning of a beehive, made her clear her throat and cough again.

"Still choking on that midge?" Tobias waved down a servant carrying a tray of goblets filled with wine the color of pale honey. "Might we have some water for the lady, please?"

The young man smiled. "Absolutely, Master Tobias. Right away." He set the tray of drinks on a cabinet and hurried away.

"What a nice fellow," Jovianna said while eying the beverages. Which of the glasses would end up with the duke? But the light coloring of the wine concerned her. It wouldn't hide the tincture of bitter cascara. Something else would have to serve as the vehicle for her plan.

Tobias rolled his shoulders as he looked around, eyeing the place as if expecting an ambush. He suddenly stiffened, and his eyes slowly narrowed. "And there be the Butcher himself."

Jovianna turned and tried to study the man without openly staring. The portraits in the history books had been kind. He was the picture of gluttony, with a double chin and a swollen portliness that the finest clothing in all of England could never flatter. He moved with a slight limp from the musket ball he'd taken in the right leg during the Battle of Dettingen about seventeen years ago. She'd read it had bothered him the rest of his life. Apparently, the historians had gotten that one right. His powdered wig was a darker gray than most and made his longish face and fleshy jowls appear even fuller. She swallowed hard. That man was the means to her happy ending.

"Mistress?" The kind young man had returned bearing a small tray with water in a long-stemmed goblet.

"Thank you so much." Jovianna appreciated he'd given her a glass that matched the others, so she could keep it with her and not look out of place.

The lad tipped a polite nod, gathered up the large platter of drinks, and went on his way.

"Come." Tobias took her hand and placed it on his arm. "Stay close to me, aye?"

She squeezed his arm, not wishing to lie to him and say she couldn't. This evening, she had a part to play. His life depended on it.

"Tobias!"

She almost choked again at the sound of Grampian's voice.

Tobias's arm tensed beneath her fingers, the muscles flexing rock hard as though champing at the bit to be unleashed.

"Forgive me for being indisposed up until now," the earl said with an arrogance that made him even more repulsive. "Nights in Edinburgh are fraught with pleasures to be enjoyed but can be quite exhausting." He shifted his disgusting smugness to Jovianna. "And who is this delectable creature?"

"*My wife*," Tobias stressed as though issuing a warning. "Mistress Jovianna."

Before Grampian continued his subterfuge, Jovianna took control of the dangerous game. "We met this morning, remember? When I entered your library while searching for the dining room?"

The earl didn't falter. Instead, he touched his forehead and laughed. "Ah, yes. I remember now. Forgive me, dear lady. I was not at my best this morning."

"No. You were not." Jovianna turned her attention back to Tobias and gave him a gentle tug. "Everyone seems to be moving into the dining room. I must have missed the announcement that we should be seated."

"Yes, yes." Grampian cut in front of them, occasionally glancing back with a gloating sneer. He nodded at Jovianna. "Ye will be most pleased to know ye're seated next to the guest of honor, my dear." With a cruel cut of his eyes over at Tobias, he added, "I'm sure the Duke of Cumberland will be delighted to meet ye."

When another guest pulled Grampian away, Jovianna squeezed Tobias's arm and whispered, "Above all else, for the sake of your life and the lives back at the manor, please hang on and control your temper." When he continued staring straight ahead as though she'd not said a word, she jerked on his arm. "Please, Tobias. Please do this for me."

Jaw flexing as though he gritted his teeth, he spared her an accusatory glance. "Ye failed to tell me ye had met Jamison."

"I felt it not worth mentioning a drunken fool who stank as though he'd spent the night in a puddle of piss." She kept her gaze locked with his, willing him to believe her. "I find him disgusting and can't believe the two of you share the same parents."

Tobias snorted. "We dinna. His mother was my father's mistress."

Yet another reason for Tobias to hate the earl. Jovianna hugged closer as they tarried at the dining room doorway while the other guests settled into their seats. "This will all be over soon," she whispered, aching to give him some shred of hope. "I promise."

He frowned down at her as she released his arm and hurried to her side of the long formal dining table filled with guests dressed with a great deal more elegance than herself. To the devil with them all. Whether they realized it or not, they sat there gorging themselves at the expense of the good people of Risk Manor. These people laughed and chatted like Nero playing his fiddle while Rome burned or, more aptly, while the Earl of Grampian ordered the crofters' cottages set ablaze.

Jovianna seated herself to the left of the Duke of Cumberland, who paid her no notice as he spoke with Grampian at the head of the table. The gentleman to her left appeared to be absorbed in admiring the lady to his left, who kept leaning forward to provide him a better view down the front of her low-cut gown. Tobias sat directly across from her, and she overheard the man between him and the earl introduce himself as the governor of Edinburgh Castle.

With the vial of poison clutched in her lap, she gave the duke's place setting a passing glance for an opportunity to share it. Unfortunately, the man's wineglass sat to the right of his plate. That dashed that option. Her heart lifted a bit as footmen placed delicate bowls of a pale, creamy soup in front of them. But that hope fell as the duke frowned down at his and pushed it away.

He leaned her way and chortled. "Soup? Bah! I prefer to save my appetite for the fine meats I was promised."

She forced a wan smile, thankful that he seemed so unimpressed with her.

One of the servants hurried back into the room and passed out small silver cruets, placing them beside the soups. Jovianna noticed that the cruet placed to the left of the duke's bowl was gold rather than silver, making it stand apart from everyone else's. Here was her chance.

"Ye were supposed to hand them out at the same time as the soup, fool." Grampian fixed a murderous scowl on the poor young man. "Folk already started eating it without the imported oil I had brought in especially for this occasion."

"My apologies, m'lord." The servant bowed and tried to back away, but Grampian wasn't finished. It appeared the earl enjoyed belittling his people when he had an audience.

Jovianna took the opportunity to pour the contents of the vial into the duke's cruet and prayed Grampian would make a fuss about the duke at least tasting the delicacy he had provided.

"Take yer leave and get out," the earl said to the poor, red-faced servant. "And dinna come looking for any wages or references. Yer laxness makes them forfeit."

The man rushed from the room. Jovianna tensed, waiting for the chance to convince the duke she was trying to save his life. Timing meant everything in this delicate trap.

Grampian stood and held up his own cruet. "Forgive me, my honored guests, for such an embarrassing oversight. Please, I beg ye. For yer enjoyment this evening, I took the liberty of procuring the finest of walnut oils from France that, my cook assures me, will bring great delight to yer pallet when drizzled atop this creamy vegetable soup." He made a slight bow to the duke and smiled. "Yer Grace, yer oil came from the oldest bottle. It cures like a fine wine and never goes rancid. I do hope ye enjoy it."

"I see," said the duke. He cast an indulgent smile Jovianna's way. "How can I refuse such a gesture?"

"You must refuse, Your Grace. I beg you." Jovianna leaned closer and pressed the folded letter into his pudgy hand as he reached for his cruet. "I cannot sit idly by while this man tries to kill you."

"What say you, my dear?" For the first time, the duke seemed to actually see her. He looked down at the letter and wet his lips as though about to eat it. "What is this?"

"It is nothing," Grampian said, his voice filled with mounting panic.

"Proof, Your Grace." Jovianna spoke louder as she tapped on the note, then glared at the earl with every ounce of hatred she felt for him. "Read it. He meant to blackmail me into his bed. Threatened my husband, who, even though he is a Scot, is a loyal subject to your father, His Highness." Not risking a glance at Tobias, she continued. "And then, bragging about his courage and virility, that man swore to poison the infamous Butcher. Read it. It is all there, Your Grace." She knew the duke hated that name and hoped it would trigger even more anger toward the earl. "That cruet is different from all the rest. I believe it holds poison."

"She is a lying whore!" the earl shouted.

"Ye dare insult my wife in such a way?" Tobias jumped to his feet and started toward Grampian.

"Halt, I say!" The duke held up a hand, then fixed Jovianna with a stern look. "I will examine your evidence. For your sake, dear woman, it best be real."

"It is real, Your Grace," Jovianna said. "Not only does it bear his signature but also the seal of the ring he wears at this very moment."

"I have never seen him without that ring," the governor of Edinburgh Castle commented. "Perhaps we should bring in yer guards just in case, Yer Grace." He turned to the footman standing at the edge of the room. "Fetch them at once." The man hurried to comply.

"This is all a lie," Grampian said, showering spittle with every word. He grabbed his wine and slung the contents at the letter.

Hands fisted and teeth bared, Tobias looked ready to lunge into battle.

The duke yanked the parchment out of harm's way, then

hefted himself to his feet and pointed at the earl. "Restrain that man!"

His guards poured into the dining room and did so.

After a narrow-eyed scowl directed at Grampian, the duke unfolded the letter and slightly moved his head back and forth while reading it. He pointed at the earl's hand. "His ring. I would have it."

One guard tried to twist it off while Grampian flailed and fought him. "Forgive me, Your Grace. It appears to be stuck."

"Then cut it off! I would have it." The duke glared at the guard as if daring him to disobey.

"Hold him," the guard said to the other two as he took a knife from the table and started sawing at the earl's little finger.

Those still seated at the table covered their mouths and turned away. The lady with the low-cut gown fainted.

Grampian howled and screamed as the soldier leaned into it and finally broke through the bone with a sickening crunch. The earl sagged over the arm of his chair and vomited.

After recovering the ring and wiping it clean, the guard gave an obedient bow and handed it to the duke.

Cumberland compared it to the parchment. "This evidence bears his seal and signature. I recognize the hand from the invitation to this fateful event." He picked up the cruet, wafted it under his nose, and sniffed.

"There is no poison, Yer Grace," Grampian said, sobbing out the words. "The whore hates me because of her husband's lies."

The duke held out the cruet. "Then drink it."

With his bloody hand clutched to his chest, the earl faltered. He stared at the tiny vessel as though suddenly unsure of his defense.

Jovianna held her breath and prayed there was enough of the herb in there for an immediate reaction. The man's stomach was empty. The noxious laxative should hit quickly. She didn't dare look at Tobias. Not yet.

The guard accepted the cruet from the duke and handed it to

Grampian.

"I command you to drink it, Grampian. If what you say is true, then what have you to fear?" Cumberland resettled his footing and hefted his thick chin to a haughtier angle.

The earl downed the oil in one gulp, then threw the cruet at Jovianna. "See? I told you she lied. The bitch crept into my library and stole that signed paper. It was blank except for my signature. I intended to write a letter later."

"Then how do you explain the fact that the writing and the ink are all the same?" the duke asked.

Grampian winced and clutched his stomach. He fell forward, bounced off the table, and tumbled to the floor. As he thrashed from side to side, he unleashed a long, hard, groaning retch.

"Take him away," the duke said to his guards, then turned to the governor. "See that the lord justice general sentences the man to hang or be gutted. Or both. I care not."

"After his trial, aye?" the governor asked.

"Of course," Cumberland said as he lowered himself back into his seat. "Edinburgh's populace must not be robbed of their entertainment." He gave a jovial nod. "I am not a man without generosity." He turned to Jovianna, took her hand, and pressed a cloying kiss to the back of it. "And thank you, dear lady. You have my undying gratitude." He snorted a belly-shaking chuckle. "My undying gratitude for preventing me from dying."

She bowed her head. "It was my duty, Your Grace."

Cumberland clapped his hands at one of the footmen. "Clear away the mess and bring on the meal. We have much to celebrate, since the Earl of Grampian has so generously gifted me all of his lands and holdings by this act of treason."

"What?" Jovianna said, clutching tight to the table to steady herself.

"What say ye?" Tobias repeated from his seat.

"Why yes," the duke said, then paused for a deep draw from his wine. Smacking his lips, he continued, "On behalf of my father, I hereby seize all accounts and properties currently in the

Earl of Grampian's name."

"But everything should go to Tobias," Jovianna said. "My husband is a loyal servant to the Crown, and I am the one who warned you of Grampian's treachery. The land belongs to my and Tobias's children. It is their birthright."

Cumberland laughed and shook his head, more intent on the platter of meat set before him than anything else. "My dear lady, I am a generous man, but not that generous. The Crown seizes all, as is right and proper." He looked up from cutting his meat and smiled. "But since you did, in fact, save my life, I shall see that you are allowed ninety days to vacate all properties rather than having to leave immediately." While chewing an overly large bite of meat, he nodded again. "And, of course, I shall see you rewarded with"—he squinted and stared upward—"five gold sovereigns. Yes. I believe that would be appropriate, all things considered."

"But all the people, the crofters, the Risk clan. My Tobias." Without thinking, Jovianna caught hold of Cumberland's forearm and shook it. "You cannot mean to displace them. You can't rip their homeland away."

The duke stilled and stared down at her hand on his arm. "Madam, you forget yourself. Kindly remove your hand from my person."

"Forgive me." Jovianna tucked it back into her lap. She had to fix this. "Please. At least let Tobias have the land in the Highlands. You can keep everything else. The accounts. This place. Everything except the land north of Loch Lomond. Please."

Cumberland fisted his hands on either side of his plate and glared at her as if losing patience. "Again, madam, you forget your station. I understand this evening has been quite eventful, so I am willing to overlook your behavior. But understand this—I did not bring the Scots to heel merely to let them forget who I am or what I represent." The hint of a greedy smile puckered his plump lips. "I feel certain my father will grant me rights to all that I seized today due to the terribly personal nature of the incident."

He sucked the meat juice off his fingers and chuckled. "Butcher Cumberland, a Highland landowner. I rather like the sound of that. I shall stock the place with the finest pedigree of sheep and visit them in the milder months. Quite a lovely way to retire, I think. An enjoyable hobby to add interest to my later years."

Jovianna slumped back in her chair and braved Tobias's glare. There it was. In his eyes. Clear as day. He hated her with a vengeance she had never seen in him before. She shoved away from the table and ran from the room, tears burning trails of shame down her face. In a matter of minutes and faulty planning, she had thrown away everything Tobias had fought to protect for the last ten years.

CHAPTER FOURTEEN

"TOBIAS, PLEASE." JOVIANNA chased after him, trying to stop him with heartbreaking relentlessness. "You've got to realize I had no idea he would take everything. You have to believe I never meant for this to happen."

"And yet it did!" he growled, shaking free of her for the thousandth time as he headed to the stables. She needed to leave him in peace. No. Not peace. He would never be at peace ever again. Not after he'd given her his heart, and she'd served it back to him broken and well seasoned with betrayal. He bared his teeth and shoved his face into hers, backing her up a step. "Get away from me, woman. I release ye from our bond." He continued on to the stables, lengthening his stride to be rid of her.

"Our bond will never be broken," she shouted after him. "Never! You promised. Remember?"

He halted and jabbed a finger back at her, hating her for the pain twisting the life from his soul. "Plague someone else with yer lies! Ye and yer mother are free of the Risks forever. Go back to England where ye belong." He stabbed the air again, his hand trembling. "Ye made me care for ye, damn ye." His voice broke, but he forced himself to continue. "Never again. Dinna come near me or my own, for I never wish to set eyes on ye again as long as I live."

She dropped to her knees in the middle of the courtyard, covered her face, and sobbed.

Walling up his aching heart, Tobias turned away and charged into the stable. "Cade! Pag! Donnor! We leave. Now!"

Amaranth stepped into the aisle and blocked his way. "I don't know what happened in there, but you know Jovianna would never do anything to hurt you."

"Go to yer daughter, woman. I dinna wish to set eyes on ye any more than I do her." Tobias shoved past her, then halted as Cade moved into his path. "Choose yer next words with care, old man," he warned.

"I dinna ken what happened, but—"

Tobias cut him off. "I will tell ye what happened. The daughter of yer lover, my feckin' *English* wife, just handed the Butcher everything we've risked our lives to protect all these years. Oh, the sly minx finished Jamison for us. She did manage that." He raked a hand back through his hair, reliving the moment when his world had crumbled. "Somehow she made it appear as though he intended to poison Cumberland. Now, while Jamison heads to trial and then the gallows, we have ninety days to clear the lands and the manor house of all who live there so the Butcher can take up a new hobby and stock the place with sheep, since the Crown has seized all Risk holdings."

"I dinna believe it," Cade said. He sagged back a step and steadied himself against a post.

"There has to be some misunderstanding," Amaranth said a little too calmly for Tobias's liking. "Jovianna would never hurt you or anyone at the manor."

"Well, she did it, woman. Right in front of me. I witnessed every cruel moment of her betrayal." Tobias shoved past them, needing to be shed of the place as badly as needing air to breathe. "Where the devil are Donnor and Pag?"

"Gone to the pub." Cade groaned and scrubbed his face with his hands. He let them drop and turned to Amaranth. "Did ye know of this?"

Tobias rounded to hear what she would say. A bitter laugh escaped him. "Aye, she knew of it. Look at her. And she didna warn ye. They betrayed us both."

"That is not true!" Amaranth fisted her hands and charged forward as if ready to fight. "She did it to save you, you thick-headed son of a bitch. Your brother told her that if she didn't become his mistress, he'd have you arrested for being the Devil of the Highlands and burn every cottage that remained on Risk land. She told him she'd never trust him to keep his word, so he gave her a blank page signed and sealed to fill in as she pleased so you and your people would be safe." Amaranth swaggered forward and poked him in the chest. "But she would never go to that disgusting little man's bed. Never. So she came up with a plan to frame him and have him sent to the noose—thinking that if that happened, everything would go to you. She failed to take into account Cumberland's black-hearted greediness." She jabbed him again. "That's why she did what she did. Risked her own life, I might add, while trying to save yours and your people."

"And yet she condemned us all because she refused to believe in me. Refused to trust me to take care of the matter as I saw fit." Tobias bullied his way forward, backing Amaranth up the aisle. "All she had to do was trust me."

"She knew you'd lose your temper and end up doing some-thing stupid. You can't help yourself. Testosterone and pride take over, and you're like a stallion blinded by rage."

Tobias had no idea what the long word meant, but he caught the gist of it and didn't like it one bit. "Get out of my sight, woman. As I said before, I never want to lay eyes on either yerself or yer daughter ever again."

Cade pushed away from the post. "They have nowhere to go, Tobias."

"Neither do we!" Tobias spat on the ground. "We've naught but ninety days to find a place for more souls than I can pray over at the moment. I dinna need the likes of two more. Especially not two betrayers."

"She is yer wife," Cade said.

"Not anymore." Tobias slashed the air with his hand. "I severed that bond. Jovianna Lillian Jacobs no longer bears the name of Risk."

"You can't mean that," Amaranth said. "Jovianna loves you."

"She shouldn't have betrayed me!" Tobias threw back his head and roared out his pain, only to discover that it made his heart ache even more. "I'll waste no more time discussing this." He turned his attention to Cade. "Either come with me or stay with them. The choice is yers. But I bid ye tell Pag and Donnor to hie their arses back home. I need their help with this terrible task."

He went to his horse, launched himself into the saddle, then rode out at a hard gallop. Jovianna reached for him as he passed, screaming his name, but he didn't slow, just clenched his teeth harder and urged his mount to race faster. He doubted Cade would follow. Amaranth had bewitched that old fool even worse than Jovianna had bespelled him.

Tobias cursed the day he'd found them at the Devil's Pulpit. As he cleared the outskirts of Edinburgh, he slowed. He couldn't allow his temper to kill the only thing he had left in this world: his horse. Out of pity for the beast, he halted, dismounted, and walked it to a burn glistening in the moonlight. With a weary rub of its neck, he spoke quietly, as if uttering a prayer. "Drink, old friend. I am thankful to have ye with me."

About to choke on his breaking heart, Tobias went down on one knee and splashed water on his face and the back of his neck. He dreaded the journey ahead. Dreaded the arrival even more. The looks on their faces when he told them they had to leave even though they had nowhere to go. And they would all rightly blame him, because he'd been the one to bring the pair of Englishwomen into their midst. He bowed his head, closed his eyes, and pinched the bridge of his nose, hating himself for being a fool. But, damn his soul straight to hell, he had loved her.

Almost from the moment that he'd spotted her tumbling through that water at the Devil's Pulpit. For some reason, he had loved her. And—may heaven deliver him from this accursed fate—he loved her still.

The sound of riders approaching pushed him to his feet. Pag and Donnor. No sign of Cade. Tobias wasn't surprised. Both men dismounted as soon as they reached him, circling him with leeriness, as though fearing he'd gone mad.

"Cade told us," Pag said, easing closer. After nervously kicking the toe of his boot into the dirt, he yanked off his hat and worried with it. "Ye canna mean to abandon yer wife and her mother. Not to the likes of the Butcher."

"My *former* wife gets along quite well with the Butcher. In fact, he owes her five gold sovereigns." Tobias squared off in front of the men. "We have nothing. Do the two of ye ken that? Not a feckin' thing other than our mounts and the clothes on our backs. And neither will the rest of those we've fought so long to protect—thanks to the woman I made the mistake of trusting."

"From what Mistress Amaranth said, the lass had a good plan," Donnor said. "Outsmarted yer brother and got rid of him without a drop of blood on any of our hands." He jutted his chin at Tobias. "Ye know she did it thinking everything would come to ye, as it shouldha when yer father died."

"The only thing I know," Tobias said, "is that we now have nothing. No land. No manor house. Nothing."

"She did it 'cause o' yer temper," Pag said in a tone that threatened to get his arse thrashed.

Tobias lunged for the lad, then caught himself and stopped. "A wife is supposed to trust her husband to take care of her," he said through clenched teeth. "Not go behind her man's back and try to handle things herself."

"Women have done that since time began," Donnor said, looking at him as if he were a damned fool. "That's how they think they're taking care of us." He snorted. "And most times they're right. Look at ye. If ye'd broken Jamison's neck, ye'd be in the tolbooth waiting to get yer own stretched. Ye've never been one for subtlety, ye ken? Then where would Mistress Jovianna be?"

"Enough!" Tobias glared at the two. They had no idea of what they spoke. "I need yer help to move our people—not nettle me about things ye canna possibly understand."

"So ye still mean to leave here without Cade and the women?" Pag cast a hard look down the hillside at the city. "I willna lie. I dinna feel right about deserting them."

"Neither do I," said Donnor. "Dinna feel right about it at all. One of the servants said the Butcher means to stay in the house till after the hanging. That could be a fortnight. Ye ken as well as I that he'll likely boot Cade and the women out afore then."

"And what if he finds out Cade survived Culloden? What then?" Pag asked. "That be a death sentence for that old Highlander for certain." He scowled at Tobias and shook his head. "How can ye be so hardhearted? The woman made a mistake whilst trying to do good. Ain't ye ever had a plan go sideways on ye 'cause of something ye didna ken till it was too late?"

"If the two of you want to stay, then stay." Tobias mounted up and scowled down at them, unable to believe they held no ill will toward Jovianna. Course, she hadn't betrayed them the way she had him. Lied to her own husband. Well, maybe not outright lied, but held back her plan—a lie just the same. "Ninety days may seem like forever, but all it does is take us to winter's edge. There's much to be done to move so many and see them safe."

"Ye are a damned fool, Tobias," Donnor said. "And I'll have no part of it."

"Aye, me neither," Pag said. "We should all be working together to make things right instead of dividing and running from the Butcher like whipped dogs."

"Ask Cade about the Butcher and what the man is capable of." Tobias shook his head. "There is no reasoning with such a heartless devil."

"Ye got the right of it there." Donnor snorted as he got back on his horse and turned back toward Edinburgh. "There's damn sure no reasoning with a heartless devil. Mayhap Mistress Jovianna is better off without ye."

"Aye," Pag said as he returned to the saddle. "I'll take care of her and keep her safe."

Both men turned their mounts back toward the city and spurred them onward.

Tobias stared at their backs, cursing them under his breath while aching to charge after them. Especially Pag. How dare that wee pup insinuate he would take up with Jovianna? Jealous rage burned hot and dangerous, goading him to do something about it. He'd had his fill of everyone stealing away what was rightly his.

Aye, but ye cast her aside, his conscience whispered in an accusing tone. *Said ye never wanted to set eyes on her again as long as ye lived.*

The memory of his treatment of her made him bow his head in shame. The way she'd looked at him. The hurt and suffering he had put in her eyes. How she had dropped to her knees and wept in the middle of the courtyard, caring not if anyone saw her pain.

"I am a heartless bastard indeed." He lifted his head and stared down at the city. It lay there beneath the stars, shining like a tempting jewel. Not because of the candles flickering in the windows, nor the riches it held. But because a rare woman who had made the mistake of loving him was somewhere within its boundaries, cast out into the streets because of him.

A QUIET TAP on the bedchamber door startled Jovianna and Amaranth where they sat on the small settee holding tightly to each other's hands.

"Is he so heartless as to have the servants toss us out in the middle of the night?" Amaranth asked. She pointed at the door. "Stall them. I'll slip out to the stables and fetch Cade."

"Sit tight until we know for certain," Jovianna said. Emotionally and physically drained from the disastrous day, she plodded to the door and cracked it open wide enough to peer into the next room.

The kind young man who had fetched her the glass of water before supper stood there with a small silver tray bearing a dark blue velvet sack cinched with gold cording.

"His Grace bade me deliver this to ye, mistress." The footman offered a sympathetic smile and lifted the tray higher. "Yer reward," he added.

Jovianna opened the door wider and leaned against it, steadying herself against dropping where she stood. "I see." She waved him into the room. "Please. Come in."

The young gentleman hesitated and glanced inside without stepping across the threshold. "It wouldna be proper, mistress. Not with yer husband away."

"According to my husband, I don't have a husband anymore," she said. "Not since I so artlessly handed his birthright to the Duke of Cumberland." She huffed a bitter laugh at the lad. "Take this advice to heart. If you ever set a trap—check for all the loopholes before you put it in motion."

The servant eyed her with what she perceived as pity, then shook his head. "I thought ye laid out the trap quite well, mistress. Many have tried to dupe the earl and failed." He smiled. "Ye sent him to the gallows, and many toasts have been made in yer honor in the servants' kitchen this night. I grant ye that." He held out the salver again and offered her another sad smile. "At least ye got a bit of gold for yer efforts."

Jovianna opened the bag and dumped the sovereigns on the tray. "Yes. Five pieces of gold. For my life. My marriage. And all the happiness I once knew." She stared down at the coins but couldn't cry. Perhaps all the tears she would ever possess had been shed out in the courtyard, because now she just felt empty.

"His Grace is in the library having a bit of brandy. A great deal of brandy, actually." The gent shrugged and cocked a brow as if that should mean something to her. "When the lads and I took food to his guards, we overheard them talking about how one of his hobbies is the occult. Loves to dabble in all sorts of mysticism and darkness. Has some kind of cards a fortune teller in France gave him, they said." He winked. "After the day he's had, perhaps the spirits will tell him to give yer husband's things back to ye." He gave her a pointed nod. "With some help from the wise lady who trapped the wickedest man I was ever cursed to serve."

Jovianna's mother joined them. "I like the way you think, Mister…"

"Wills." The young man bowed. "I'm simply happy to help the lady who freed me from a despicable tyrant."

"I don't know about that freedom," Jovianna said. "You may have gone from the frying pan into the fire with the Butcher as the new master of the house."

Wills grinned and shook his head. "Everyone knows His Grace loves London best. He'll not be here often enough to be a bother. Not like the earl, who lived here year 'round." He tucked the silver salver under his arm and gave Jovianna a pointed bob of his head. "I meant what I said about trying yer hand at fooling the duke. He's in the library with those cards and well into his second bottle."

"You could foretell his future, Jovianna," Amaranth said with a sly grin. "After all, you do have the sight. And if he's alone and well lubricated with the brandy, he'll be much more pliable to giving you what you want."

"I'd have to have it in writing, or he'll deny it once he sobered," Jovianna said.

Wills held out a small brass key. "To the desk in the library, mistress."

The sight of it sprouted the smallest tendril of hope within her. "Wills, you are an angel."

The lad shook his head. "No, mistress. I am a grateful servant who saw ye weeping in the courtyard. Everyone who works in this household wants to help ye any way we can, and this is all we know to do." With a tip of his head, he backed out of the room, gave her an encouraging wink, and quietly closed the door.

Jovianna stared down at the key in her hand. "You really think I can convince him I'm a white lady with the sight?"

"You can tell him about the stroke he's due to have this month. About his father's death in October and even about his own death in 1765." Amaranth eyed the key with a thoughtful frown. "You could even foretell George IV's birth in August 1762. Maybe somehow link everything with those cards of his. Sounds like a tarot deck to me."

"But will he believe me? And if he does, how will I convince him to revert everything to Tobias?" Jovianna tapped the key in her palm as she paced back and forth across the room. "He could blow off everything I tell him as my trying to manipulate him in favor of my husband."

Amaranth curled her lip as if she tasted something very bad. "Your only other option is to seduce him. He was said to keep mistresses but never married."

Jovianna shuddered. "I can't possibly see that working either. At dinner, he was less than impressed with me, and I am definitely not a seductress."

"Then what?" Amaranth gave her that look Jovianna always hated. The one that said she needed to do something, even if it turned out to be wrong.

"Both, I guess." Jovianna unpinned her hair and fluffed it out. She removed her fichu and tugged her neckline even lower until her nipples risked popping out. "Neither of the two ladies at dinner wore modesty scarves to cover their décolletage. Maybe that's some sort of signal to the men of this era and I came across as a prude." She struck an awkward pose and batted her eyelashes. "What do you think?"

"Wills did say the man was on his second bottle of brandy, so it could work."

Jovianna glared at her. "I've had about all the unkindness I can bear today, *Mother.*"

Amaranth rushed to her and squeezed her shoulders. "I meant it as a compliment. You're not one to go whoring around."

After tucking the desk key into her pocket, Jovianna pulled open the door, then stopped and cast a worried glance back at her mother. "Pray this works. If I'm not able to save the crofts and Risk Manor, I don't know how I'm going to live with myself."

"And Tobias?"

Jovianna blinked against renewed tears stinging her eyes, and the numbness of earlier left her, replaced with an unrelenting ache in her chest. Apparently, heartache had its own reservoir of tears. "All I have to do with Tobias is make sure I never let him set eyes on me ever again. Remember?"

"You can do this, sweetie. Mindset is half the battle." Amaranth kissed her cheek and gave her a gentle nudge. "Hurry on now, before he drinks himself into a stupor."

With a quick nod, Jovianna hurried out, almost running in her haste to get to the library and put yet another possibly faulty plan into action. Wills stood just outside the huge mahogany double doors, holding an unopened bottle of brandy. He handed it to her with a smile, then strode down the hallway and disappeared around the turn.

Jovianna stared at the bottle, then dipped a curt nod. Onward to the battle. She took a deep breath, slid the door open, and slipped inside. Her sight took a moment to adjust to the dimness of the room, which was lit by a lone candle on the desk where the Duke of Cumberland sat. Her heart fell at the sight of him there. She'd not be getting to the drawers with that mass blocking them.

Without lifting his gaze from the tarot card spread, he fluttered his fingers as if shooing a fly. "Must I remind you that if I should need anything, I will summon you?"

"Forgive me for disturbing you, Your Grace," Jovianna said, trying to sound seductive. She sounded pathetic even to herself, so she abandoned that ploy. "I had a vision that my conscience would not allow me to keep to myself."

He looked up from the cards and squinted at her. "And you are?"

"Again, forgive me, Your Grace." She attempted a curtsy and barely pulled it off without losing her balance. "Mistress Jovianna from supper. The one who saved you from the earl's evil ploy."

He frowned and summoned her closer with a wave of his pudgy hand. "I must say, you look a great deal different than you did at supper."

She twirled a tress around her finger as she eased up to the desk. "I was about to retire when I received the vision. I had to come and find you immediately. Please forgive my state of undress." She let her gaze fall to the tarot cards and smiled. "Your cards are trying to warn you as well."

His expression shifted from mild irritation to rapt attention. "You read the cards?" he whispered.

"Oh yes," she lied. "They help me understand my visions." She pointed to the three of wands in the spread. "My vision told me that this month, you will suffer an attack of apoplexy." She tapped on the card next to it. "But it will not be fatal. This time."

"This time," he repeated, but was barely audible. He pointed a shaking finger at another card lying face-up. "But the death card…"

"Your father," she answered. "On October twenty-fifth, 1760. Two months from now."

"And this?" He pointed to the six of pentacles.

"If you wish to be prosperous, you must show the spirits you are capable of being generous." She tried to remember everything her quirky friend from university had ever told her about tarot. "If you do not, the dark side of the card warns of desperation and dependence until you die on October thirty-first, 1765." She prayed he knew even less than she did in case she got it horribly wrong.

"I die on October thirty-first, 1765?"

She nodded.

"I gave you gold." He sounded like a naughty child trying to remind a parent of his good deeds.

"Yes, you did." She reached for the next card to turn over and prayed it would be a good one. "The justice card." She placed it in line with the others. "It reminds you that all you have done will come back upon you times three." She did her best to sound ominous. "You gave me five gold pieces, and yet the plans you have for the estate you seized will cause hundreds to starve to death and lose their homes." She leaned closer and lowered her voice. "Are you familiar with karma?"

"No," he mouthed more than said. Eyes wide, he leaned back in the chair as though fearing an attack.

"Everything is connected," she said softly, then turned over the next card. "Five of cups. Grieving. Sorrow. What you give to others will be given to you."

"Have you no good things to foretell?" He gathered up the cards, shuffled them, and revealed the five of cups again.

Jovianna could almost taste victory. "Your young nephew, the soon-to-be King George III, will look to you for advice. His son, George IV, will be born on August twelfth, 1762."

Apparently, those good tidings weren't personal enough to suit the duke. He scowled and waved her words away. "No. Something fortuitous about me." He thumped his chest. "Personally."

"I have told you everything the visions and the cards have told me." She folded her hands in front of her and waited, knowing if she pushed too hard to revert the estate to Tobias, Cumberland would get suspicious.

"The apoplexy you saw—when? Will it be painful?" He fisted his hands on the desk and started sweating profusely.

"Soon. Before this month is out." She noticed he was struggling to close his hand around his glass and ended up knocking it over. "It will be more frustrating than painful because of the weakness and paralysis." She righted his glass and refilled it, wondering if it was the effects of the brandy or if the stroke was happening now. "There you are, Your Grace. A fresh drink."

His head trembling just enough to be noticed, he threw himself back into the chair and stared at her in horror. "Happen...happen...now."

"I shall have the surgeon fetched." Jovianna started for the door, only to halt when Cumberland repeatedly kicked the desk.

"No," he said, terror in his eyes. "Stay. P-please." His left arm remained limp beside him, but he reached for her with his right. "P-please."

Her conscience forbade her to desert him, no matter the atrocities he had committed. She went to his right side, took his hand, and held it. "I am right here, and here I shall stay. I can shout for help. I'm sure one of the servants will hear. Hold tight while I do that, yes?"

He seemed to nod, although she wasn't sure. Turning toward the doors, she shouted, "Help us! Help! His Grace is gravely ill!"

Wills and another footman came running. As they drew near, their eyes went wide.

"Fetch the surgeon," Jovianna said. At least, that was the one she thought might handle this sort of thing. But with this being Edinburgh, a trained physician might be available. "Or a physician. Whoever is the closest."

Cumberland released her hand long enough to pound on his chest. "My...mine... Tell guards."

"Call for your guards?" She held up a hand and stopped the lads.

He pointed at her as if rewarding her for getting it right.

She nodded at Wills and the other young man, then started to step away.

The duke awkwardly grabbed for her hand but missed and batted at her skirt. "S-stay." Then he hit the desk with his hand and glared at it. "Hide."

"I am not about to hide under the desk," she said. "Wills and the other footmen already know I'm here."

He rolled his head back and forth, spittle slinging down his chin. "Cards."

"Oh. Right." She gathered them up and pointed at the nearest bookcase. "I'll hide them behind the books, yes?"

Sagging back in the chair, he lifted a finger again, which seemed to mean he agreed.

Just as she tucked them out of sight behind one of the thickest volumes, his guards poured into the room.

"S-Stone," the duke groaned, as though saying the word pained him. He squinted his eyes shut, worked his mouth, then said, "Merk."

"Stone and Merk," Jovianna repeated to the nearest guard. "What does that mean? He wanted the lot of you fetched rather than a surgeon or apothecary."

"Stone is his personal physician, mistress," the guard said after pointing at the door and sending the others running. "And I believe he might be trying to say, *Merrick*. That's one of his advisors. A solicitor, in fact. Both men always travel with His Grace. His Highness ordered it so."

"I see." Jovianna glanced at the duke, at a loss for what else to do for the man. "It appears you have it well in hand. I'll leave you to it."

The duke kicked the desk with a loud bang.

"Or not." Jovianna returned to the man's side.

The guard gave her a sympathetic nod. "Thank you, mistress."

"Think nothing of it." She eased back a few steps as two older men rushed into the room. One toted a leather satchel, and the other fumbled with his spectacles that had snagged on the neckline of his nightshirt.

"Apoplexy," she said to the one with the satchel.

The man spared her a glare that said he doubted she knew which way was up.

"No!" Cumberland pointed at the physician. "W-wait."

"Your Grace," the man said, "it is imperative I examine you now."

The duke pointed past him at the other man. "Merk!"

"Looks to be apoplexy to me," Merrick told the physician as he shoved around him. He drew in close and gripped the duke's hand. "What is it, old friend?"

"This house," Cumberland said slowly, fighting to say the words. "Risk...things."

"This house and the Risk holdings?" Merrick repeated. "Yes, Your Grace. I've penned the letter to His Majesty. Just as you requested. And under the circumstances, I will be happy to place your seal on it in front of witnesses."

"No." The duke erratically flung his right hand in Jovianna's direction. "Her. Husband. To him. As is just."

Merrick looked at Jovianna, arched a brow, then returned his attention to the duke. "You wish for everything to go to this woman's husband?"

"Tobias is the Earl of Grampian's closest living relative," Jovianna explained. "If His Grace is making such a generous offer...allowing Tobias to reclaim all Risk properties and accounts..." She knelt at the duke's side and smiled up at him. "We most gratefully accept. And I'm sure all the spirits will surely notice and bless this man sevenfold for such benevolence."

The duke sagged deeper into the chair, as though finally relaxing. One side of his mouth trembled and twitched upward as though he were trying to smile.

"His Highness will have to grant that Master Tobias will also assume the Grampian earldom," Merrick said. "Shall I add that to the letter as well?"

The duke lifted a finger and bobbed it up and down.

"I shall take that as a *yes?*" Merrick gently rested the duke's hand on the arm of his chair and waved the physician forward. "I will see it done and sealed this very night, Your Grace. Rest easy with the knowledge that your wish will be done."

Jovianna's heart soared as she squeezed the duke's arm. "You're going to be all right, Your Grace. I promise."

"P-promise," he repeated softly.

"I swear," she said with a hard look into his eyes. "I have seen it. Remember?"

The corner of his mouth twitched upward again, and he released a heavy sigh.

"I really must insist that you leave now," the physician said.

"Goodnight, Your Grace." Jovianna hurried from the room before he could kick the desk again.

CHAPTER FIFTEEN

"F ROM WHAT I gathered," Mr. Merrick said, "His Grace wishes you to have a copy as proof until the solicitor updates all deeds and accounts to your husband's name. The earldom will be forthcoming, making your husband the second Earl of Grampian and you the Countess of Grampian, m'lady."

Jovianna's hands shook as she looked over the document and all the official seals. Everyone at Risk Manor was safe. All the crofters could stay, and those burned out could rebuild and start again. A happy sob escaped her, and tears streamed down her face.

"Good heavens." Mr. Merrick looked all around as though wishing to escape. "Good heavens, m'lady," he said again while offering his handkerchief. "Do you need to sit? Are you quite all right? Shall I send for your mother?"

Jovianna accepted the square of linen and dried her eyes. "I am more than all right, Mr. Merrick." She tried to compose herself as she carefully slid the parchment back inside its protective sleeve and hugged it to her chest. "Thank you so much for everything. The people of Risk Manor will be elated."

Mr. Merrick bobbed his head. "Of course, His Grace shall stay here until well enough to travel. But I must inform you he insists that you and your husband are to stay here as well to witness the trial and hanging. Although for the life of me, I cannot imagine why. However, it is His Grace's wish, or at least, what I surmise to be his wish." The man's face puckered with a perplexed frown. "And he kept trying to say something that sounded like *cards* and would only calm himself when I pointed to your name on the document. Have you any idea what he might have wanted? Communicating with His Grace can be quite exhausting."

"It's my understanding that victims of his malady are often quite confused for a while." Jovianna offered the man a sympathetic smile. "If you feel His Grace would wish it, send for me after he's rested some, and I'll sit with him and see if I can bring him any ease."

The man seemed to deflate with relief. "That would be most helpful, m'lady, and also most appreciated. I shall see to it immediately and inform you of the best time." He gave her a grateful nod and hurried back up the stairs.

Jovianna watched him until he disappeared around the curve of the stair, her heart both singing and breaking at the same time. Butcher Cumberland had given her everything she wanted—well, almost everything—and it hadn't cost her anything more than making up the meaning of his tarot card spread. Fate had been exceedingly generous with her, allowing all the pieces to fall in place so perfectly. Or perhaps it was Divine Providence protecting Tobias and his people. At least they would have their happily ever after, even though hers was gone.

Amaranth, Cade, Pag, and Donnor emerged from the library, beaming with joyful smiles. Amaranth caught Jovianna up in an excited hug. "You did it, sweetie. You did it."

Jovianna managed a sad smile. "Now, the only one homeless is me."

"Nay, m'lady," Cade said. "Tobias will come around once he learns of all this."

"I'm not so sure I want him to come around." Jovianna dried her eyes again and wiped her nose. Poor Mr. Merrick. She'd have to have his handkerchief laundered before she returned it. After clearing her throat, she lifted her chin. "If he had really loved me to begin with, he would have given me a chance to make things right before *severing our bond*, as he so coldly put it. Tobias made it more than obvious that he had never loved me as much as I loved him."

"Nay, m'lady," Donnor argued, but she held up a hand and stopped him.

"If he *comes around* after learning his birthright has been restored to him," she said, "how do I know he won't boot me out again the next time I displease him?" A bitter laugh escaped her. "Because I guarantee there would be a next time. There always is."

"Jovianna," her mother gently chided. "You're not even going to give him a second chance?"

"Like he gave me?"

All of them looked askance, unable to meet her gaze.

"My point exactly." She held out the precious document to Cade, Pag, and Donnor. "Will one of you see if you can catch up with him before he upsets everyone at Risk Manor? And please make sure he understands I must stay here until the duke leaves, but after that, I will vacate the premises. I should be able to make those gold sovereigns last quite a while if I'm careful."

The three men looked at each other as if none of them wanted the task. Cade rumbled with an irritated growl and took the envelope from her. "I'll take it to the thickheaded bastard and make sure he understands all that he's gained and lost."

"Thank you, Cade." Jovianna tried to roll the tense weariness from her shoulders. "I believe I'll have a cup of tea and a lie-down before I sit with the duke." A sudden wooziness struck, making her stumble to the side.

"Jovianna!" Amaranth caught her and helped her to a nearby bench.

"I'm fine," Jovianna said. "Simply exhausted." Her voice broke and tears overflowed again. She waved the men away, and they ran over each other in their hurry to escape out the front door. "And I'm so very sad," she added to her mother, then forced a smile. "But I'm glad you have Cade."

"Tobias said he never wanted to lay eyes on me again, either." Amaranth hugged her close and gently rocked her as she'd done when Jovianna was a little girl. "You and I will find a nice little place here in Edinburgh. Cade can visit whenever he likes."

"He'll want you to return to the manor with him." Jovianna sniffed and dried her eyes again with the soggy handkerchief. "You know how he hates cities."

Amaranth lifted Jovianna's chin and pinned her with a stern glare. "I won't desert my daughter. Not for anything." She rose and pulled Jovianna up with her. "Come. Let's get you up to bed, and after that, I'll see to your tea. And perhaps a biscuit or two. I noticed you didn't eat a thing at breakfast."

"Too much going on to worry with food." Jovianna held tight to the banister as she slowly climbed the stairs. As they reached their floor, a loud bang came from below, followed by a familiar roar.

"Jovianna!"

"Stall him." Jovianna ran to their suite, dashed into the bedchamber, slammed the door shut, and locked it. After a quick glance around, she angled a chair up under the latch to brace it for good measure. Amaranth wouldn't be able to stall Tobias long. Jovianna's heart leaped into her throat as she spied the open door connecting her suite with Amaranth and Cade's. She closed and locked that door as well but didn't have a chair to block it. She eyed the wardrobe next to it, debating whether to use it as a more substantial barrier.

Heavy footsteps drew closer. Jovianna braced herself, expecting him to pound on the door, bellow, or try to break it down. Or all of the above.

But Tobias surprised her. Nothing but silence followed for so long that she wondered if he had given up and gone away and she hadn't heard his retreating footsteps.

She eased toward the door, wishing she could see through it but wasn't brave enough to open it.

"Jovianna?" The voice was quiet, calm, and controlled. But it was Tobias. His deep baritone rolled across her like a longed-for caress. She didn't answer. Just clutched her fists to her chest in a vain attempt at calming her pounding heart.

Something slid against the door and made a soft rasping noise, as though Tobias rubbed his hand across the wood. "Jovianna, I ken ye are in there. And I also ken why ye willna let me in."

She swallowed hard and clenched her teeth to keep from sobbing aloud. Too distraught to stand, she lowered herself to the floor and hugged herself as she rocked.

"I dinna expect ye to forgive me for being a heartless bastard," he said quietly. "And I agree. I dinna deserve it." Something rubbed against the door again, making her visualize Tobias leaning back against it and lowering himself to the floor. A soft thump and what sounded like a heavy sigh followed. "But ye should know I was returning to beg yer forgiveness even before Cade gave me the news of how ye saved our people. He caught me on the front steps and showed me the papers."

Jovianna clamped her hands over her mouth and squinted her eyes shut. It didn't matter that he was coming back even without knowing. He should never have treated her so horribly in the first place.

"I love ye, Jovianna, and I am so verra sorry."

A sob escaped her as she crawled away, putting as much distance as she could between herself and the door. It was the first time he had ever said the words, ever told her he loved her. But it meant nothing. It was nothing more than guilt and gratitude making him say it. She had granted him all the grace she was going to for his temper. Patience and understanding were one thing, but allowing him another opportunity to treat her badly would not happen. Still sitting on the floor, she huddled beneath the window seat and wept even harder.

The lock clicked on the connecting door to Amaranth and Cade's suite, and it eased open. Amaranth entered with a tray bearing a teapot, a cup, and a small covered plate. Without a word, she placed it on a table, hurried to Jovianna, and helped her climb into the bed.

Jovianna curled around her pillow, hugging it as she cried.

Amaranth sat beside her, gently combing her fingers through Jovianna's hair. "Cry it out, my precious girl. You've earned the right to do so." After a sharp glance at the door keeping Tobias out, she blew out a heavy sigh. "If it's any consolation, he looks like pure shite and just stood and took it when Cade punched him. Twice."

"He hurt me, Mama," Jovianna said, hating that she sounded like a sniveling child.

"I know he did, sweetie. And I'd love nothing better than to give him a swift kick in the bollocks for it. Or watch you do it. Or both of us kick him." She opened the nightstand drawer, drew out a fresh handkerchief, and handed it to Jovianna. "But you do realize that at some point, you will have to come out and face him. Something tells me he won't be going away anytime soon." She huffed a sad laugh. "After all, this is one of his homes now."

"I understand I have to face him, eventually." Jovianna blew her nose. "But I don't want to do it today."

Amaranth shrugged. "Then don't. Stay in here. I'll send word to Mr. Merrick that you're feeling unwell and will sit with the duke tomorrow. Cade is guarding the connecting door and won't let Tobias pass. I'll bring you whatever you need the rest of the day and tonight."

"You don't think I should forgive him, do you?" Jovianna blew her nose again, then curled into a tighter ball. Her heart ached so very badly, and life seemed so bleak.

Amaranth rose to her feet and gave her a grim look. "There is only one person who knows the answer to that, and it is not me." She bent and kissed Jovianna on the cheek, then went to the connecting door and paused. "I love you, sweetie, and you have my support with whatever you decide, understand?"

Jovianna nodded and hugged her pillow even tighter.

Amaranth tipped her head toward the tray. "Drink your tea and force down a bite or two. You're much too pale for my liking. I'll be back later to check on you." Then she left, closed the door behind her, and locked it.

Maybe tea would help settle her nerves enough so she could at least try to think through the situation rationally. After all, Amaranth was right. At some point, she would have to face Tobias. Jovianna pushed herself upright and stared at the tea across the room. That table was entirely too close to the door. But what did that matter? If he'd stayed there during Amaranth's visit and eavesdropped, as she felt sure he had, then at least he had some idea of where he stood and had probably left the sitting room.

Jovianna poured her tea and set the small pot back onto the metal tray, flinching when it rattled the spoon and made it clatter.

"I'm glad ye can drink yer tea," Tobias said through the closed door. "It worries me that ye've gone pale."

"Eavesdropping is rude, and my pallor is no longer your concern. Our bond is severed. Remember?" She added honey to her cup and took a sip, proud of herself for speaking in a level tone and with strength. "Go away."

"Cade told me what ye said about *vacating the premises* after the hanging." He fell quiet for so long that she contemplated kicking the door to make him finish the thought. "It broke my heart," he added barely loud enough for her to hear.

Good. But she didn't say it aloud. Instead, she carried her tea and biscuit to the window seat and stared down into the street below. The first nibble she swallowed did not sit well even after another sip or two of her tea. Her stomach churned the same way it had back at the Devil's Pulpit. Immediate panic filled her. No! She didn't want to go back. She couldn't bear the thought of never seeing Tobias again.

A hard surge of nausea doubled her over, making her clutch

her middle as another bout of dizziness hit and sent her spinning. "No! Don't take me!" she shouted as she hit the floor. Her saucer and teacup flew out of her hands and shattered.

"Jovianna!" The chair wedged under the latch broke into pieces as the doorframe splintered and gave way. Tobias bounded to her side and crouched beside her. "Who was in here? Who was trying to take ye?" He touched her cheek, terror in his eyes. "God help ye, my love. Ye are as pale as death."

He bent closer to pick her up, and she shoved him away. "Get out and leave me alone!"

"Not until I see ye properly cared for." Ignoring her flailing blows against his chest, he scooped her up and carried her to the bed, then rushed to the door and bellowed for help. "Amaranth! Yer daughter! Come quick!"

Jovianna curled onto her side, taking deep breaths and trying not to vomit. If he would just go away for a little while so her nerves would settle... The past two days had her insides determined to turn themselves wrong side out. But thank goodness she was still here. The strange time slip hadn't snatched her away. The stark realization of how badly she'd feared never seeing Tobias again lingered. Damn him, she still loved him even though he'd hurt her.

He returned to her and knelt like a child troubled by a nightmare and seeking the safety of its parents' bed. Amaranth had been right—Tobias looked like pure shite. Blood encrusted his nostrils, and his reddened nose had a crooked bump on it that it never had before. His left eye had almost swelled shut, and his bottom lip was split and puffy. The man looked like he'd just brawled in a pub.

"I thought Cade only hit you twice?" She scooted away from the edge of the bed, keeping an arm's length of space between them.

"Donnor and Pag each got in a fair lick as well." He stared at her as if unable to get his fill.

"Stop staring at me."

"I feared I would never see ye again." Heartbreak filled his eyes.

"Yesterday, that is exactly what you ordered." She couldn't help lashing out. His behavior still stung like an open wound.

"Aye, I remember." He let go of a heavy sigh and bowed his head. "I ken I am a damned fool. Ye'll get no argument there."

Amaranth, Cade, and the duke's physician hurried into the room. Tobias pushed himself to his feet and backed out of the way.

Cade grabbed him by the front of his shirt and started toward the door. "Ye are not wanted in here. Get out and stay out."

Tobias retreated with the meekness of a lamb. "Might I please stand here at the door? Until ye ken what is ailing her? Please?"

Jovianna sank deeper into the pillows as everyone's focus shifted to her. "Fine. Let him stay at the door."

"Another fainting spell, m'lady?" Dr. Stone peered at her as if she were a lab rat.

"I have had a difficult few days, sir." Jovianna covered her nose and swallowed hard. The man smelled strongly of anise oil and an unidentifiable cloying sweetness. "I'm certain after a bit of rest and a fresh cup of tea, I'll be fine."

The scowling physician removed his spectacles and cleaned them with his handkerchief. "Might you be with child, madam?"

Jovianna ducked farther beneath the bedclothes. "I take precautions to prevent that."

"The only precaution that works one hundred percent of the time is complete and total abstinence, m'lady." He perched his glasses back onto his nose and bent closer. "Kindly open your mouth."

With a cut of her eyes over at her mother, Jovianna complied for a moment, then added. "I have no fever or chills. I am telling you it's just a reaction to stress."

"I shall be the judge of that," Dr. Stone said. "After all, I am the licensed physician here."

"And it's my body and I know why it does what it does."

Jovianna pushed up higher among the pillows until she sat leaning back against the headboard. "Thank you for your time, Dr. Stone, but I feel your services are better put to use with His Grace."

The doctor offered her a dismissive nod and turned to Amaranth. "She is with child. I recommend rest, quiet, weak tea, and burnt toast if she will tolerate it."

"You, sir, are a quack! You didn't even examine me." Jovianna glared at the man, wishing she had something other than a pillow to throw at him.

For the first time since their meeting, Dr. Stone smiled. "Your breath, madam, smells exactly like every other expectant mother's breath I have ever treated. I recommend either you or your lady's maid review the last time your courses flowed, and you will discover I am rarely wrong—and this time is not one of them. Congratulations."

As he reached Tobias, standing mute and dumbfounded at the door, Dr. Stone gave him an inquisitive scowl. "You, sir, would benefit from cool cloths to reduce the swelling." He tipped his head to one side and looked closer. "And that nose appears to be broken. Can you breathe through it?"

Tobias didn't spare the man a glance. Instead, he kept his gaze locked on Jovianna. "I canna breathe at all at the moment."

"Ah." The man nodded and pushed on by. "The father. Congratulations, sir."

Her churning emotions about to make her scream, Jovianna pointed at Amaranth. "Get Cade and Tobias out of here. You stay."

"You heard her, gentlemen." Amaranth sprang into action, arms outspread as she swept across the room to herd them away. Cade obliged with haste, but Tobias remained rooted to the spot just past the threshold. "But I want to—"

"No." Amaranth closed the door in his face.

"Why on earth would you bring that quack in here?" Jovianna asked before Amaranth turned to face her. "And now Tobias thinks I'm pregnant. We've got enough relationship issues without adding that to the mix."

"I was worried about you. You have never been a fainter." Appearing entirely too pleased about the whole situation, Amaranth perched on the edge of the bed. "And why do you think the man is a quack? He trained at Edinburgh and serves the duke."

"And probably still practices cupping, bleeding, and leeches." Jovianna covered her face with her hands, then let them drop. "You heard him. He diagnosed me by smelling my breath. I mean, really?"

Amaranth's eyes narrowed. "Methinks thou protests too much. Could it be you already suspected you were pregnant?"

Denial raged loud and strong, but logic shouted even louder. "I'm only a few days late," Jovianna admitted quietly, then closed her eyes. "This cannot be happening. I didn't miss a day of Mrs. Gibb's noxious birth control tea."

"Your father and I never went a time without condoms before you came along and yet, here you are." Amaranth scooted up beside her and leaned back against the headboard as she rested an arm around Jovianna's shoulders. "Some things are just meant to be." She gently shook her. "But now that raises the question about what you intend to do about either forgiving or not forgiving Tobias. This is not the twenty-first century, where being a single mother was difficult enough but manageable. Here and now…"

"I may not even have to worry about it. Did you see the terror in his eyes? He'll probably run again." Jovianna glared at the door leading to the sitting room, once again wishing she could see through it. "Just keep him out of here for now." She scooted down into the bed and turned her back to her mother. "My head's pounding. I may vomit yet, and I didn't get to finish my tea." She sniffed and fumbled with the covers in search of her handkerchief. "And my nose is running and, for the life of me, I can't stop all this bloody crying. I am a proper mess."

"You are indeed." Amaranth retrieved yet another fresh square of linen from the nightstand drawer and dangled it over Jovianna's shoulder. "I shall fetch more tea and coerce the cook into toasting some bread to go along with it. Are you certain you don't want to have a word with the man? Clear the air so you can rest and not lie here dreading it?"

Jovianna wiped her nose again, then waved the handkerchief like a white flag. "I give up. Send him in here and let's get this over with."

Amaranth slid off the bed, went to the door, and pulled it the rest of the way open, since it wouldn't latch because of the splintered doorframe. "She will see you now," she said. "But only until I get back with her tea. You heard the doctor. She needs to rest."

Even with her back to the door, Jovianna knew as soon as Tobias entered the room. His hesitant footsteps. The creak of the floorboards beneath his weight. But more than that, his presence reached out to her, tapping on her heart and soul, begging for permission to exist in the same space with her. She refused to turn and look at him. Shame filled her for behaving like a petulant child, but she had the right to do so. It had been such a bloody awful two days.

"So a bairn is coming," he said quietly, revealing he stood beside the bed.

"Yes." She sniffed and pressed the handkerchief to the corners of her eyes. "Sorry to create a bond you can't sever with just a word."

"Jovianna." His tone dripped with pain and remorse. "I spoke rashly. In the heat of anger. I dinna ask that ye excuse it. All I can do is beg ye to understand it comes from the darkness of my past. A curse I shall fight against all the rest of my days."

"You hurt me."

"I know. And I am more sorry than ye can imagine."

"How could you think I would give away your birthright on purpose?" She rolled over and faced him. "How could you think so little of me?"

He shook his head. "I canna explain my actions, for they can never be justified. Why I reacted the way I did is all a feckin' mess. All I ken is that I regret that day. Regretted everything as soon as it came to pass." He snorted. "I stopped at the outskirts of the city and wrestled with my demons until this morning. It was then I knew I had to come back and beg yer forgiveness. Beg ye to remain the wife of a poor man who owned nothing more than the clothes on his back and his horse."

"How do I know you won't hurt me like this all over again the next time I make you angry?" That was the crux of it. The point she couldn't get past. She knew she loved him, but never would she tolerate a repeat of yesterday. Arguments were a natural part of any relationship, but not the sort they'd had yesterday. She deserved better, and if it turned out that she really was pregnant, their child deserved better too. "How can I trust you to change?"

"All I can do is prove it to ye each and every day." He sucked in a deep breath and slowly released it. "If ye'll but give me the chance."

"I'll think about it," she said softly, then forced herself to speak louder. "But if I agree, that doesn't mean we pick back up as though nothing ever happened." She fixed him with a hard glare. "We're different now. Wounded. And it'll take time for both of us to heal. I will not go through what happened yesterday ever again."

He bowed his head while nodding. "I understand." Then he lifted it and looked back at her with a fierceness that stole her breath. "I will make things right between us, my beloved. Ye will see."

CHAPTER SIXTEEN

TOBIAS COULDN'T TAKE his gaze off Jovianna as they sat together in the garden. It had been a week since he'd been such a damned fool and nearly lost her. And while they still didn't share a bed, the chasm between them narrowed more each day. His heart swelled with gladness. More gladness than he had ever known. He thanked the Almighty that the foul temper he'd possessed since the war hadn't cost him everything.

She cut her eyes his way as she lowered her teacup to the saucer. "You are staring again." Her gently scolding tone made him smile.

He caught her hand in his and pressed a kiss to it. "Not staring, my own. Merely committing to memory the beauty of this afternoon."

She shyly dropped her gaze but glowed with a pleased smile. "Are you having any luck remembering to answer to 'm'lord'?"

"Not as much as I should, I fear." He noticed the nearby rosebushes, heavily laden with blooms, gently swaying even though there was no wind. He rose and moved toward them, his hand on the haft of his dirk. "Who is there?"

"Forgive me, m'lord." A young maid stepped into view with a basket overflowing with cuttings of the pale pink flowers. "Mr.

Ferguson said the vases needed freshening before dinner." She politely tipped her head in Jovianna's direction. "Said ye would wish it done for the Lady Jovianna."

"Aye." Tobias resettled his footing, wishing he had thought of the flowers rather than the butler. "I do indeed." With a wave of his hand, he shooed the lass back to her duties and returned to Jovianna. "Ye do like the roses, aye?"

The amused quirk of her brow revealed she saw his frustration about not noticing the flowers. "Yes. I think they're exquisite." A heavy sigh left her right as she lifted her cup for another sip.

"Tell me what troubles ye, my own." He gently tickled a fingertip across the back of her hand. "Is the weariness still plaguing ye?" Amaranth had assured him that Jovianna being tired was normal, but he wasn't so sure. He'd feel much better once he spoke with Mrs. Gibb about women with bairns on the way.

"I'm a little tired, but it's not that." She frowned down at her tea. "I'm ready for all the *wrinkles* to shake out. The duke to leave, the trial to be done—and forgive me for sounding cold, but I'm ready for your brother's hanging to be behind us." She barely shook her head. "There are still so many things that could go wrong until the trial not only starts but finishes." She gave him a troubled gaze. "Pag said he heard that Matthew Tellerston is in Edinburgh. You know that man will show up in the courtroom and try to cause trouble."

"What I know is that Pag should not have worried ye with such news." Tobias would speak to the lad about that later.

"He was telling Cade and Donnor, and I overheard them. He had no idea I was in the stables." She slid her half-finished tea away and rose from the bench, fidgeting with the odd restlessness she'd exhibited the past few days.

"Why were ye in the stables?"

After pacing a few steps away, she turned and faced him, then flipped her hands with a frustrated jerk. "I am bored out of my mind, so I thought I'd visit the horses."

"Bored?"

"Yes. Bored." She made a harried gesture toward the door, then another at the garden, and then yet another toward the stables. "The servants won't let me help with anything. Whenever I try, they back away from me as if I have the plague." She frowned and rubbed her forehead as if her head was aching again. "At least back at Risk Manor, I could help with the horses to keep from breaking anything in the house."

"Ye helped with the horses because ye are good with horses," Tobias reminded her, a tad uncomfortable that she'd seen through his efforts to keep her from destroying the manor house with her unintentional fumbles. "Do ye not enjoy living here in Edinburgh?" He had half feared she would wish to stay here with all the fineries rather than return to the broken-down manor.

She eyed him as though perplexed. Or perturbed. Or as if she couldn't decide which. Then she shrugged. "It's hard to explain, but Edinburgh doesn't seem as safe as the Highlands. Not unsafe for me, but for you and Cade." She moved closer, cast a glance over at the rosebushes, then lowered her voice. "What if someone recognizes you?"

"Recognizes me?"

She pinned him with a hard glare. Her brows ratcheted up to her hairline, and she flared her eyes wider. "What if you're recognized by a traveler you might have met while they were on the road between here and the manor?"

He leaned in close and whispered, "We covered our faces, ye ken? Tied rags across our noses." This conversation about his highwayman days needed to continue so he could keep pulling her close and pressing his mouth next to her ear. To his delight, she shivered. Perhaps soon, they would once again share the passion they'd known before.

She cleared her throat and glared at him. The rosy flush across her cheekbones thrilled him even more. "You have very distinctive eyes, dear husband."

"I am safe, Jovianna," he reassured her. "But it warms my heart that ye worry for me."

"Of course I worry for you," she said, "I—" She stopped and clamped her mouth shut.

"Ye what, lass?" He ached to hear the words he prayed she had almost said.

She fiddled with the folds of his neckcloth, avoiding his gaze. "You know I have never stopped loving you. The problem is feeling at ease enough to become vulnerable to you again."

He caught hold of her hand and held it between them. After brushing a kiss across her knuckles, he gently tipped up her face and forced her to look at him. "I love ye, Jovianna. So much so that I am willing to do whatever it takes to make you feel safe enough to become vulnerable again. No matter how long it takes." And he meant it, even though living with this wall between them was killing him.

The soft tinkling of a bell interrupted them, pulling their attention to the door leading back inside. Ferguson, the butler, stood waiting for permission to speak.

"I am not a hound to be distracted by a bell. If ye have news for me, just draw my attention and say so." Tobias found his brother's rules for the servants ridiculous and demeaning to them. They were people, not animals to be treated as lesser. Even though most of them were indentured servants trying to avoid deportment or a workhouse, they still deserved civility and whatever compassion he could offer.

But habits ingrained by cruelty died hard. The stoic, white-haired Ferguson, who took great pride in his position, remained silent and waited for the signal to speak.

A huff of frustration left Tobias. "What is it, Ferguson?"

The butler came to life, puckering an angry scowl and waggling both his bushy white brows. "Master Tellerston awaits ye in the library, m'lord." Voice trembling, he dropped his gaze. "Forgive me, m'lord. I recommended he wait on the doorstep or come at another time at yer convenience, but he refused and pushed past me. I fear I am not the man I once was for repelling such unpleasant visitors."

"Ye are a better man than most, Ferguson. Dinna fash yerself about that vermin," Tobias said. "Besides—I prefer to oust the bastard myself." He turned to Jovianna, concerned about leaving her unprotected in the garden. Tellerston's men might be near. "Retire to yer rooms, aye? By the back stair. I dinna wish ye troubled by the sight of that bastard, and I also want ye safe."

She caught hold of his arm and hooked hers through it. "No. I'm coming with you. The duke gave us permission to use his guard if need be. They know to answer to you."

Tobias pulled in a deep breath to avoid a frustrated response. He needed her to do as he asked in situations such as these, but he also needed to word it properly. He would not fail this test. "I beg ye to let me deal with this man, my own. His unpleasantness is too great for ye to bear. Especially..." He lowered his gaze to her middle and allowed it to linger. "Ye've been frail of late because of the bairn taking seed. Think of yerself, love. And the babe. Please."

He feared her stubbornness wouldn't sway. The crease in her brow and the fire flashing in her eyes warned she was not happy. But then she took her arm out of his and squeezed both his hands. "You are right. He is an unpleasant, vulgar man. I shall retire upstairs to our sitting room." She turned and smiled at Ferguson. "Perhaps Ferguson would be so kind as to send up more tea and some of those delicious ginger biscuits?"

The butler responded with a proper bow. "Right away, m'lady. Wills will meet ye there with them."

Tobias pulled her close and pressed a tender kiss to her fore-head. He didn't dare kiss her mouth. Not yet. But he held his lips to the soft sweetness of her skin as long as he dared, then hugged her tighter and nestled his cheek against her silky hair. "Thank ye, Jovianna."

As she eased out of his embrace, she patted his chest and straightened his neckcloth again. "I can't expect you to be the only one who changes. My behavior needs to improve too, so that you know I not only love you but respect and trust you."

"Thank ye, m'love." Her words touched his heart and filled him with a rare calmness. "I shall join ye once I've ousted the man. I'll tell ye everything he says."

"Be sure you do," she said with mock sternness, then hurried inside.

Rolling his shoulders and readying himself for a fight, Tobias strode down the hall and entered the library to find Tellerston helping himself to the port. "This is my home now, and ye are not welcome here."

"Oh, I think I will be." The ruthless evictor lifted his glass in a silent toast, took a delicate sip, then offered a chilling smile. "Found an acquaintance of yers that I'll be bringing to speak at the trial, unless…"

Tobias widened his stance in, the doorway, blocking any means of escape for the devil. "Finish yer threat, man. I've no time for foolish games."

Tellerston chuckled as he pulled an object from inside his waistcoat and held it out. "Recognize this?"

Tobias did, but he wasn't about to react. "Have ye changed yer line of business? Shoeing horses now, are ye?" He shook his head. "There are no openings in my staff. Leave and ply yer trade elsewhere."

"Ye ken where this came from as well as I do." Tellerston turned the bit of iron over in his palm, displaying the unique symbol worked into its left branch by an extremely talented smithy or farrier. "One of my men found this in yer smithy's scrap pile. Ye remember that day, aye? The last time I visited Risk Manor? By the way, how is that lovely English wife of yers? Had yer fill of her yet?"

Tobias clenched his teeth to keep from lunging at the man and snapping his neck, as he should have on that day. He remained silent and glared at the bastard, imagining all the ways he could kill him.

Tellerston's sneer became bolder. "Aye, ye remember that day as well as I. I see it in yer eyes." He tossed the horseshoe into the air and caught it. "Turns out only one man's horses have shoes with that fancy *w* in their left bracket. I believe ye met him and his son on their way back from Glasgow back in June. Lord Wattston?"

"Canna place the name." Tobias contemplated what to do about the blackmailing bastard with a calmness that surprised even him. He almost smiled. His precious Jovianna had tamed his inner beast. "As I said before—get to the point, man. I've business to tend to."

Tellerston's wicked delight shifted to malicious determination. "Lord Wattston will accompany me to the trial. Testify about ye being the Devil of the Highlands. And I'll testify how ye and yer wife sought to send the former earl to the gallows because he threatened to expose ye as the dangerous thief that ye are."

Tobias casually resettled his stance again and folded his arms over his chest. "And yer only proof is that wee horseshoe?"

"It proves ye stole his carriage and team of horses and left his arse on the side of the road with his son."

"And how does it prove that I did such a heinous thing?" Tobias rather enjoyed remaining calm and toying with his prey. He should have adopted this behavior years ago. "'Tis only yer word that yer man found that on my property." He offered a bored shrug. "Or yer man's word. Either is a lie." He couldn't resist a smile. "Are ye such a great friend of the lord justice general that he'll accept yer word without witnesses?"

"Wattston is my witness." Tellerston smashed his glass of port to the floor, sending the ruby liquid everywhere. He pointed at Tobias. "He claims the lead robber had icy-blue eyes just like yers."

"I verra much doubt I am the only man in Scotland with blue eyes." Tobias stepped aside and pointed down the hallway. "Out with ye before I throw ye out. I dinna take kindly to guests who treat my home with such disrespect."

"If ye dinna give me what I want," Tellerston sputtered, "I'll be in that courtroom and tell everything I know. I swear I will."

Tobias grabbed him by the front of the shirt and yanked him forward until they stood nose to nose. "If ye come near me or mine again, the next speech ye'll be making will be to yer Maker, ye ken?" With a hard shove, he sent the man stumbling toward the front door. "See this wretch out," he told Wills as the footman hurried down the stairs.

"Gladly, m'lord." Wills grabbed Tellerston by the back of his waistcoat and the seat of his trews as Ferguson opened the front door. After Wills sent the man tumbling down the steps, he flagged down the duke's guard to escort Tellerston the rest of the way off the property.

"Ye will rue this day, Tobias Risk!" Tellerston shouted as they dragged him away.

Tobias stood in the doorway, clenching and unclenching his fists, aching to finish the task himself. But no, if he ever got Tellerston's neck between his hands again, there would be no stopping until it snapped. And busy Edinburgh was not the place to silence the man permanently. A frustrated huff escaped him. The threat Tellerston had laid at his feet could not be ignored.

"Well done," he told the guards, then nodded at Wills and Ferguson. "And well done to the two of ye as well. If the bastard returns, have the guards oust him, ye ken?"

"Aye, m'lord," Wills and Ferguson said in unison.

Tobias came to a halt at the base of the stairs and stared up them, dreading what he had promised to do.

"Her ladyship said she was expecting ye, m'lord," Wills said. "She had me fetch another teacup so ye could join her."

Tobias curled his lip at the thought of drinking Jovianna's favorite beverage. "I dinna ken why she loves that swill so."

Wills grinned, then offered a kindly wink. "She had me fetch a fresh bottle of whisky for ye too, since she'd gotten rid of all the decanters and glasses after—" He cut himself off and looked as though he wished he hadn't gone down that path. "Uhm…her ladyship's waiting for ye, m'lord."

"Thank ye, Wills." Tobias climbed the steps with the rueful realization that Jovianna had replaced him as the favorite of the servants. While they all still treated him with the utmost respect, some showed a chillier disposition that hadn't existed before the day that would forever be known as one of the worst of his life.

Before entering the sitting room, he pulled in a deep breath and blew it out. He did not want to worry her with Tellerston's threat but had promised to tell her about the man's visit. In the future, he'd make no such foolish oaths. She'd caught him in a weak moment after confessing to him she was willing to change her behavior too.

"I can hear you out there snorting like a bull," she called to him through the closed door.

After rolling his eyes, he entered. "I dinna snort. I was merely breathing."

"You huff and snort like a great beastie from a children's story." Jovianna filled her cup with tea, then smiled and tipped a nod at the bottle of whisky on the tray. "I know how much you *love* tea, but I thought that after a meeting with Tellerston, whisky might be more suitable."

"Ye are as wise as ye are beautiful, m'love." He seated himself beside her on the delicate French sofa that had probably cost his brother an obscene sum. "I must say, I've never had whisky from a teacup before."

"Sorry." She pulled the cork from the bottle and filled his cup. "I pushed the beverage cart into Amaranth and Cade's room after you left that night, and Cade disposed of it." She shrugged as she handed him the drink. "Childish and silly, I suppose, but somehow it made me feel better to have anything you had ever enjoyed shoved out of my sight."

The fine teacup seemed like a wee thimble in his large hands. But the whisky it held hit the spot. He picked up the bottle and tipped it toward her cup. "Would ye like to sweeten yer tea?"

"No, thank you. No more alcohol for me until after the baby

is weaned."

He stared at her with his drink partway to his mouth. "No whisky or wine?"

She shook her head. "Not even ale."

"Why ever not?"

She bit her lip, then fidgeted with the half-eaten biscuit on her plate. "A midwife told my mother about spirits being bad for the baby." While placing the plate back on the tray, she bumped her cup and sloshed out some of her tea. "Oh dear. I've made a mess. I wonder if Wills brought any extra towels."

He stilled her hands before she made things worse. "It doesna matter, love. If ye dinna wish to drink anything other than tea or water out of fear for the bairn, 'tis yer choice. Whatever puts yer mind at rest."

Jovianna sat straighter and placed her hands in her lap. "Tell me about Tellerston. That will put my mind at rest."

"No. It will not." He emptied his cup in a single swallow and refilled it to the brim. "He's threatened to bring Lord Wattston to the trial and have the man testify that I am the Devil of the Highlands who stole his carriage and horses back in June. The ones we had just procured when we found ye and yer mother at the Devil's Pulpit."

All the color drained from Jovianna's face, and she pressed a hand to her mouth. She glanced all around, her eyes rapidly flitting as though she were searching the room for enemies.

Tobias set his whisky back on the tray and pulled her close, steadying her against him. "Saints alive, I knew I should not have told ye." He held her, noting she trembled ever so slightly. Without hesitation, he scooped her up into his arms and carried her into the bedchamber. She clung to him, so silent it terrified him.

When he reached the bed, he ripped back the bedclothes and gently lowered her into the pillows, then pulled the covers back over her. "Shall I fetch Dr. Stone or yer mother?"

She caught hold of his arm and pulled. "No. Just hold me."

He slid into the bed and pulled her into his arms as he leaned back against the headboard. "I will make everything all right, m'love. Dinna fash yerself, ye ken?"

She clung to him, her head pressed to his chest. "I knew that man would try something. I knew it. How on earth did he find out about the horses and the carriage?"

"He has one of the horseshoes. Remember the symbol on them?"

"Of all the things for him to discover. I thought you told Mr. Harper to destroy them."

"He'd not had the time, lass. Tellerston showed up right after the horse had been reshod."

"That's right. He did." She sounded bemused. "Whatever are we going to do?"

"I dinna ken." He kissed the top of her head and closed his eyes, wishing their troubles would leave them alone for just a little while. "I canna have him hunted down and silenced. With Wattston in the mix now, it would look too suspicious."

"Bloody hell." She thumped her fist against his middle. "Are we certain he's contacted that man? Is that really the name of the person who owned the carriage?" She pushed up and met his gaze, hope flashing in her eyes. "Maybe he's just bluffing."

Tobias hated to dash her hopes. He cradled her cheek in his palm and slowly shook his head. "That is the owner of the carriage. We found letters bearing his name among the goods."

"Well, bollocks!" Her eyes filled with tears. "There has to be something we can do other than attend the trial and outbluff them both."

"I would rather ye didna come to the trial." He worried how it might affect her or the bairn. "I will attend and handle whatever happens."

"I have to come." She scooted higher and rested her head on his shoulder. "Not only because the duke has ordered it but for my own sanity's sake." She shifted and kissed his throat. "Please try to understand. I don't want to upset you, but I must attend the trial."

"I dinna ken why the Butcher insists ye go." And if she kept pressing against him and gifting his flesh with sweet kisses, all he would know was that he had to have her. He curled his arm tighter around her. "I dinna like ye sitting with the man each day, either."

She methodically tugged at his neckcloth until she had it untied. With it out of the way, she opened the front of his shirt and slid her hand inside, making him suck in a quick intake of air. "Don't worry about my daily visits with the man," she said as she deliciously tortured him even more by teasing her fingertips through his chest hair and then tickling them lower. "He's still somewhat paralyzed and struggling to regain his speech. I entertain him by giving him hope with his cards."

"His cards?" Tobias struggled to pay attention to the conversation as she unbuttoned his breeks.

"Tarot cards," she said as she curled her leg across him and nudged closer. "Divination is his guilty pleasure that he dabbles in when no one else is around."

"Guilty pleasure," he repeated in a husky whisper as he slid down deeper into the bed and pulled her into his arms. "I have missed ye, m'love."

"I've missed you too." She kissed him with a passion that threatened to undo him. When she drew back, she smiled. "You taste like whisky and an afternoon I've been needing."

"Then allow me to satisfy that need, m'lady." He trailed his lips across her silken flesh to the twin mounds of her breasts swelling above the neckline of her light wool jacket. "Pure delight," he whispered as he nuzzled his way to her nipples, releasing them from their bonds.

"We have come to bed in entirely too many clothes." Her complaint came in breathy gasps as she clutched his head to her bosoms.

"Let us remedy that." He rose long enough to shed his waist-coat and shirt, but then she pulled him back down for another kiss before he could remove anything else. Her impatience stirred him, lending an urgency to the task. He slid his hand up under her skirts. The hot wetness awaiting his touch made him groan.

"I told you I'd missed you," she said while arching into him.

"That ye did, m'love." He ached to take her, ached to return to where he belonged.

She shuddered, bucked against his hand, and dug her fingernails into his shoulders. "I need you. Now. It's been too long."

"That it has." He reared up, shoved his breeks down to his knees, and buried himself inside her with a deep groan that rumbled from his core. "This...this..." No other words made it to him through the ecstasy of her heat.

"Yes," she agreed, meeting him thrust for thrust. "This...oh my heavens...this!" She dug her fingernails into his arse and urged him to pump faster. "More!"

"Aye, m'love, aye." He rocked into her, unleashing all his pent-up yearning with every thrust. A thunderous roar escaped him, and she joined him with a joyous scream. Together, they spasmed and clutched. Together, they spent themselves one into the other, and together, they rode the crest of utter delight.

He rolled to the side with her in his arms, pulling her over with him. "M'love," he groaned. "Lore a'mighty, m'love."

"I agree," she said, breathless enough to make him proud. She draped herself across him, her head on his chest. "I have missed you so much," she whispered.

A warm wetness hit his chest right where her cheek rested. He lifted his head to check on her. His heart lurched with fear. "Tears, m'love? Do ye regret allowing me back into our bed?"

She offered him a tremulous smile. "Happy tears. I have found I cry easily of late, and no, I do not regret this." More tears overflowed, and her smile turned to a worried frown. "But I am afraid of what lies ahead. I can't bear it if something happens to you because of those selfish fools."

He gathered her close once again and stroked her hair while quietly shushing her. "I ken that it's difficult, m'love, but ye must try not to fret overly much. 'Tis bad for ye in yer condition. Bad for our wee one growing inside ye." He kissed her forehead, wishing he knew of a way to soothe her even more. "We will battle the bastards and beat them at their own game. I swear it."

CHAPTER SEVENTEEN

"Y ou must try to eat at least one piece of the toast," Amaranth said.

Jovianna paced back and forth in front of the window in the drawing room, preferring its quiet over the dining room where the duke's traveling companions and their assistants currently breakfasted.

"Is Cade with Tobias?" she asked, ignoring her mother's persistent nudging.

"Yes. They've gone to the stables to bid Donnor and Pag farewell." Amaranth poured the tea, then thumped the table in front of Jovianna's empty chair. "Sit now and eat."

Jovianna continued to ignore her, staring out the window overlooking the street. "I hope they reach Risk Manor quickly. Tobias feels sure Tellerston's men will head straight there to torch everything if the trial goes in the earl's favor."

"And Tobias asked you to eat while he was gone, and you promised you would. There is no way of knowing how long today could last. Do you want to faint in the courtroom?"

"If it helps Tobias, I do." Jovianna relented and grudgingly went to her seat. Maybe if she sipped some tea, Amaranth would grant her a moment's peace. "I have a bad feeling about today."

"I know, sweetie." Amaranth frowned down at her own untouched breakfast. "And this time, our combined knowledge about the past can't help. For the life of me, I can't recall anything about the Risk Clan or the Earls of Grampian."

"And I don't know if that's good or bad." Jovianna swirled a dollop of cream into her tea, mesmerized by the tiny whirlpool changing the dark amber beverage to a gentle shade of caramel.

"At least your storytelling has improved dramatically," Amaranth said with forced brightness.

"I'm not so sure I should be proud of becoming a better liar." Jovianna nibbled a corner off the toast, so when Tobias asked, she could somewhat honestly say she had eaten. "I truly hope since the duke ordered that the lord justice general sentence the earl to hang that the trial will be a mere formality and they won't allow any testimonies on the man's behalf."

Amaranth frowned. "I'm sure that depends on how many palms Tellerston has greased. If the earl hangs, Tellerston knows he's out of a lucrative job."

"Are you certain it's safe for you and Cade to be there?" Jovianna picked at her toast, wishing they had a dog so she could slip her breakfast to it under the table. A puppy would be so much easier than trying to hide uneaten food in plain sight.

"Ye promised to eat," Tobias quietly scolded as he entered the room. "Crumbling yer bread as if ye're about to toss it to the hens is not eating."

Cade rounded the table, bent, and kissed Amaranth's cheek. "Walk with me, aye? There has been a change of plans."

Amaranth shot Jovianna an alarmed glance, then caught hold of Cade's hand. "What do you mean?"

He tipped his head toward the door and helped her rise from her chair. "Come."

"What's going on?" Jovianna asked Tobias as he seated himself beside her.

"Wills got word from his brother. The one who works at the tolbooth, seeing to repairs and such." Tobias slipped his hand under hers and worried his thumb across her fingers. "He overhead that testimonies on behalf of the victim will be allowed today."

"But the duke ordered…" She couldn't finish. Tobias's dark expression cut her off and made her swallow hard. "Either Tellerston paid someone off or your brother has blackmail material on the lord justice general."

"Or since this crime went straight to the High Court of Justiciary, they wish the trial to at least *appear* just. But either or both of yer suggestions is the more likely." His jaw flexed as his mouth hardened to a flat line. With a heavy sigh, he lifted her hand and pressed a lingering kiss to it. "Ye should remain here, m'love. I dinna ken what might happen today. Cade and yer mother willna be attending either. They will stay here, ready to leave immediately and take ye with them if need be. To safety."

"You cannot ask me to do that." She eased her hand out of his and fisted it in her lap.

"It is what I wish, Jovianna."

"I understand it is what you wish, and I also understand you're trying to protect me." She stood and shook a finger down at him. He could not ask this of her. "I am your wife, and I have a right to be there. You cannot deny me the right to stay at your side as you would stay at mine were the situation reversed."

A heavier sigh, more like a frustrated blowing, came from him. "I am not carrying our bairn and havena been as wobbly as a newborn lamb these past few days." He glared up at her, love, caring, and irritation flashing in his eyes. "Think of the bairn."

"I am thinking of the bairn," she said. "I'm protecting his or her father."

"Heaven help me, woman, dinna risk yer life and the life of our child out of pure stubbornness." He scrubbed a hand across his mouth as if blocking off words he might later regret.

She knew this was hard for him, knew he only wanted to keep her and the baby from harm. But on this, she would not yield, even if she had to follow his carriage on foot. She knelt in front of him and took hold of both his hands. "I am going. Not because I don't think you can handle the situation, but because I can't bear waiting here wondering if I will ever see you again. I love you, Tobias. So much so that it frightens me. I never believed I could feel such a love, such a belonging with another soul. I have to go today. To be at your side for good or for ill. At least I'll be with you."

He stared into her eyes with such sadness that her tears welled and overflowed. He framed her face in his hands and tenderly kissed them away. "Ye're going to be the death of me, woman. Ye ken that, aye?"

"I hope not," she whispered. "At least not until we're very old and surrounded by all our great-great-grandchildren. Then we'll take our last breath together."

He huffed out a soft, sad laugh. "One of yer visions, my own?"

"Yes. My favorite vision of them all."

With another heavy sigh and a shake of his head, he helped her to her feet. "Let us hie to the carriage, then."

She rewarded him with a soft kiss. "Thank you."

He made a noise akin to a low-throated growl as he looped her arm through his and tugged her to his side. Poor Tobias was not pleased with her, but he was doing his best to control his medieval urge to lock her in a tower to keep her safe, and she loved him all the more for it. Change could sometimes be the hardest thing in the world to endure.

"Would it help ye if yer mother came? Just in case?" he asked.

"No." Jovianna hugged his arm tighter. "I worry about Cade's safety there. You know Tellerston's men will be there too. They could very well shout something about Cade being a wanted man, even though it was years ago. If anything were to happen to him, Amaranth couldn't bear it."

"Ye take care of everyone but yerself," Tobias said, his tone a shade snappish.

"I'm practicing for motherhood." Jovianna halted and took a

deep breath as they arrived at the carriage, its windows covered. "Can we tie up the shades? Hopefully, the rain will hold off."

"Aye, we can." He helped her up the steps, then gave her a sullen glare. "Although I should leave them down to make ye change yer mind and stay here."

"That would be very childish, and you know it." She rolled up the coverings on her side and fastened them with the strap.

"I dinna care. At least ye would be safe." He opened the windows on his side, then leaned back in the seat beside her and thumped the roof.

She slid closer and rested her head on his shoulder as the carriage took off with a lurch. She needed to touch him. He grounded her, helped her rein in her emotions, and draw on every strength she'd ever possessed for whatever lay ahead.

"I love ye, Jovianna." The somber quietness of his voice made her heart ache for him to be safe. "I love ye more than ye will ever know," he repeated as softly as a whispered prayer.

"I love you more and always will." She hugged tighter against him as the carriage rumbled down the street. It wouldn't take long to get to the tolbooth. She couldn't decide if that was good or bad. Too much time would give her the opportunity to imagine even more worst-case scenarios. "I should've brought my dagger. Slipped it down inside the front of my corset."

"I have daggers enough for the both of us, my own." He tapped his knees, then patted his side. "Both boots and my belt. Just in case."

The carriage rolled to a stop, making Jovianna clench her teeth. She peered out at the tall, fearsome building, remembering everything she'd ever read about the place. How they had tortured prisoners with the boot or pilliwinks. Kept some offenders chained with iron collars and put on public display. Descriptions of the destitution and nastiness of the cells caused her to shudder. She sent up a quick prayer to shield Tobias from it all.

He exited the vehicle first, helped her step down, then tucked her arm in his and kept her close. She noticed onlookers milling around outside carried baskets of rotting vegetables. To throw at the condemned, perhaps? Those allowed into the courtroom were forced to leave their slimy ammunition at the doorstep before entering. The place was packed. The populace of Edinburgh wouldn't miss the trial of a member of the peerage.

Jovianna spotted Tellerston. Beside him stood a portly man dressed in an elaborately embroidered waistcoat and jacket. The garments shimmered when he moved because of the gold and silver threads and embellishments of sequins and beading on his wide cuffs and lapels. That had to be the infamous Lord Wattston. She glanced up at Tobias, but his expression neither confirmed nor denied anything. Somehow, his unreadable mask helped her breathe easier, and she did her best to mimic it.

As they took their seats that were entirely too close to the front for her liking, activity to the right of the tall, forbidding justice's bench drew her focus. Not wearing shackles or chains, but still pathetic with his shorn head and grubby clothing, Jamison, Tobias's brother, shuffled to his seat. A pair of brawny sheriffs guarded him, making him appear even more diminished.

The loud crack of a staff against the floor made her jump as the wielder announced, "All rise."

The lord justice general, with his judge's wig, scarlet robe, black scarf, and scarlet stole, strutted in as if he was the king himself. He wore wire-rimmed spectacles perched high on his bulbous nose but constantly fidgeted with them as if their fit didn't suit him.

Jovianna forced herself to stare straight ahead with a calm demeanor, even though Jamison's murderous glare remained locked on her and Tobias. Tellerston's smug scowl also took some ignoring. The only individual in the enemy camp that appeared oblivious to her and Tobias was the glamorous Lord Wattston.

The lord justice general nodded as a deep-voiced man on the floor read the charges. Once that formality ended, the justice peered over at Jamison and asked, "And how do ye plead?"

"Not guilty, m'lord," Jamison said without shifting his sneer from Tobias.

"But of course ye do." The lord justice's tone held a hint of sarcasm. "Just as ye denied cheating at whist at the club."

That offhanded comment lifted Jovianna's heart. She studied the justice as he scowled down at the sheaf of papers in front of him. His irritated demeanor made her think he would just as soon send Jamison to the gallows and move on to the next case.

The justice cleared his throat, then leaned back in his tall-backed chair as though bracing himself for a long day. "It has come to my attention that there are those who wish to present testimony on behalf of the accused." He stretched his neck forward and scowled down at the papers again. "A Lord Wattston? Is the man present?"

Lord Wattston lifted his hand as though afraid to reveal himself. "I am here, m'lord."

"Move to the box, so all can better hear ye." The justice nodded at the small, raised platform in the center of the room.

After a nervous, yet obviously confused, glance at Tellerston, Lord Wattston took his place in the witness box.

Jovianna found it strange that the man fidgeted as though he were the one on trial.

"Lord Wattston," the justice droned. "Do ye solemnly, sincerely, and truly declare and affirm that the evidence ye give shall be the truth, the whole truth, and nothing but the truth?"

Lord Wattston stared up at him with his mouth slightly ajar, as though struck dumb.

The justice leaned forward and peered down at the man. "Is there a problem, m'lord?"

"I was under the impression I was here to identify and testify against the Devil of the Highlands, m'lord. The highwayman who robbed me in June of this year." Lord Wattston cast a repugnant glance Jamison's way. "That man is not he. As a matter of note, I have never set eyes on that person before this day."

The justice's jowly face wrinkled with even more irritation. He scooped up the papers and shook them at the official to his left. "Who wasted this court's time with this?"

Out of everyone else's view, Jovianna squeezed Tobias's hand.

"There sits the Devil of the Highlands!" Tellerston jumped up and pointed at Tobias. "Him and his scheming wife there beside him! They plotted to end the earl because he was about to turn them over to the authorities."

The courtroom erupted as everyone shifted to better see. Their mutterings and gasps created a loud hum that increased by the second.

The justice rose from his seat and thundered, "I will have order or this room shall be cleared!" He pointed at Tellerston. "Remove that man immediately. I will not tolerate such outbursts. This is not some back alley gaming den but a court of law."

"But it's true!" Jamison shouted. "Tobias Risk is the Devil of the Highlands! Ask Lord Wattston!"

"Ye will silence yerself or be gagged!" the justice bellowed at Jamison. He shot a curt nod at the sheriffs remaining in the room. "Restore order to this proceeding immediately."

Once the place quieted, the justice reseated himself and took great pains to straighten his robes and wide sleeves before leaning forward and calmly clasping his hands together atop his podium. "Lord Wattston, as I see it, yer presence and testimony at this trial was possibly in error." He paused and shot a dark look Jamison's way. "Unless ye see the wanted criminal known as the Devil of the Highlands within this courtroom, ye may take yer leave and go."

Jovianna held her breath and squeezed Tobias's hand even harder, as Lord Wattston turned in a slow circle and swept his nervous gaze around the room. Tobias held his head high, his expression a strong, unreadable mask.

When Wattston once again faced the justice, he shook his

head. "I do not see the criminals who robbed myself and my son earlier this summer, m'lord."

"Ye are a damned fool!" Jamison howled. "There the bastard sits! Right there!" He pointed at Tobias with both hands.

"Silence him," the justice said.

The pair of sheriffs hurried to comply. Jamison fought them as they shackled his hands behind his back and gagged him. As soon as they finished, the sheriff to Jamison's left spoke up. "Yer lordship, if it pleases the court, I can vouch for the gentleman and his wife that the prisoner and the man from the gallery insulted."

"It does please the court," the justice said, adjusting his glasses yet again. "Please do continue."

"Me and the lads came upon Lord Wattston after him and his son had been robbed and left on the side of the road. While Bean and them helped his lordship, m'self and two others rode on in search of the highwaymen who done the crime." He gave a nod that left no doubt he was about to say something about Tobias. "We encountered this gentleman traveling with the lady, her mother, and about three other men. The women were frightful sick with a terrible fever, and the men were about to fall ill with it too." He bounced an exaggerated nod. "That ague they had was so fearsome, I come down with it the verra next day. There is no way these fine folks couldha had anything to do with the robbery of Lord Wattston."

The justice pursed his lips and shifted his focus back to Lord Wattston. "The court thanks ye for attempting to do what was right. It appears someone gravely misled ye. Ye may go."

Jamison tried to shout through the gag while stomping and kicking.

"The black cap," the justice said to the official at his right.

Jamison fought harder. Tears streamed down his face as the official gently placed a square of black cloth on top of the justice's wig, making certain one of the corners faced the front and pointed downward toward the justice's forehead.

"Get him on his feet," the justice said.

It took both the sheriffs with their arms looped through Jamison's to keep him from sagging to the floor.

"Jamison Risk," the lord justice general said. "For the attempted murder of His Grace, Prince William Augustus, Duke of Cumberland, by poisoning, this court finds ye guilty. The law is that thou shalt hang by the neck till yer body be dead, tomorrow at dawn, September seventh, year of our Lord 1760. May the Lord have mercy upon thy soul." With a flick of his hand, he motioned for the sheriffs to remove Jamison from the courtroom.

Heart pounding, Jovianna wanted to laugh, shout, and sob in relief, but held steady and remained calm. Even once they were back in the carriage, she held herself stiffly, staring straight ahead with her fists clutched in her lap, fearing someone might see her celebrating and question it. Not until they stood in their front hallway and Ferguson had closed the door behind them did she clasp her hands to her chest and unleash a keening cry as if mourning at a funeral.

"Lore a'mighty." Tobias caught hold of her shoulders. "Jovianna. Jovianna?"

"I am so very relieved." She laughed as her tears streamed.

Amaranth and Cade came running. Their steps slowed and horror registered on their faces when they saw her tears.

"No! It's fine." Jovianna waved them closer. "Jamison hangs at dawn."

"But Tellerston," Cade said. "Did the man not show?"

"His witness couldna identify the Devil of the Highlands," Tobias said with a lopsided grin.

"And the judge had him tossed out of court for causing a disruption." Jovianna hugged her mother, then grew still as a terrifying thought hit her. She turned to Tobias. "Could Tellerston still head to Risk Manor for revenge?"

"The lads will be ready," Tobias said. "They knew to expect the worst no matter the outcome of the trial."

"And Tellerston may discover that his men dinna grant him as much loyalty when he canna pay them," Cade said.

"I still won't feel like I can finally breathe until we get back home and I see everyone is safe." A spell of lightheadedness made Jovianna drop to a nearby bench before she sagged to the floor.

"And that is why I kept nagging you to eat," Amaranth scolded before turning to Ferguson. "Might we get some tea and biscuits in the library, please? Maybe now the lady of the house will eat."

"Right away, ma'am." Ferguson hurried to fetch it.

Tobias took a seat beside her with a scolding look in his eye. "Yer mother is right. Ye must start listening to both of us, ye ken? I've half a mind to carry ye upstairs, put ye to bed, and lock ye in there. *Alone.*"

"What a terrible thing to say." She scowled back at him. "And when I get as big and round as this house, you won't be able to sweep me up into your arms and tote me wherever you wish. What will you do then?"

Tobias scooped her up and cradled her against his chest. "I shall always tote ye wherever I wish, no matter yer size. What say ye now, wife?"

She wrapped her arms around his neck and pulled him in for a kiss. "I say I am a very lucky woman."

"Aye, well, 'tis about time ye realized it."

TOBIAS LAY THERE, staring up at the shadows dancing across the ceiling, listening to Jovianna as she slept. With each of her long, deep snores, his smile grew broader. The day had spent her as much or more than it had exhausted him. But it was over now. His brother would hang in the morning, and the duke had made it known that he felt himself strong enough to start for London in a few days. With fall well in place and winter close behind, the man needed to make the trip as soon as possible. And if they intended to return to Risk Manor, as Jovianna wished, they needed to do so soon as well, for her and the bairn's safety and well-being.

Safety. The word brought Matthew Tellerston to mind. If the man had not gone to Risk Manor to seek his revenge, then he could still very well be lurking in the shadows of Edinburgh. But Tobias had no doubt that they'd not seen the last of the man. Not when they had cost him so much.

Jovianna shifted with a huffing snort, then pushed herself upright.

"What is it, m'love?" Tobias rose beside her.

"I bloody well need to use the loo again," she grumbled through a yawn.

"What?" Tobias helped her clamber over him and get out of bed.

She blinked hard, as though finally fully awake. "What?" she repeated as she disappeared behind the privacy screen hiding the cabinet holding the chamber pot.

"What is a *loo?*" he asked. She didn't do it often, but now and then, she used words he'd never heard before. Cade had once said that Amaranth did the same.

After a moment of silence and the sound of water hitting porcelain, she answered, "Sorry. *Loo* is what I've always called the chamber pot. Amaranth said I've done it since I was little." When she emerged from behind the screen, the moonlight setting her nakedness aglow made him forget all else. She gave him a wicked smile as she sauntered back to the bed. "You're staring again."

"I will always stare when ye display such bounty before me." He pulled her into his arms and rolled until she lay stretched beneath him.

"When I get big and round, I really should wear a shift to bed." She drew up her legs and rubbed the silkiness of her inner thighs across his flanks. The feel of her skin sliding against his made him ache for her even more.

"When ye get big and round, there'll be even more of your beauty for me to feast my eyes upon. Daren't ye ever hide it from me." He nuzzled kisses along her jaw line while running a hand downward and cupping a cheek of her arse in his hand. "I canna wait to see ye swollen with our wee one."

She went still, her hands on his shoulders. "There was a time when you didn't want me to ever have children. Remember?"

"Aye." He closed his eyes and pressed his forehead to hers. "The fear of what could happen still plagues me." He rose and stared down at her. "Swear that ye willna leave me, nor let death take the bairn." He knew his request was futile, because such a thing was in God's hands and not hers. But it didn't matter. His heart needed to hear it.

"I swear I will never leave you willingly," she said, "and will protect our baby with every ounce of strength and fury I possess." Her eyes glistened with love and devotion. "Make love to me, Tobias. Chase away the demons in the dark."

"Gladly, my own." He sank into her with a soft groan. "I swear I will always chase away yer demons."

Chapter Eighteen

"Keep beside me, aye?" Tobias told Jovianna yet again as they approached Finnich Glen and the Devil's Pulpit. He didn't like her on her own mount. If she had ridden with him, he could better protect her during the journey back to the manor.

"The only way I could be any more beside you is if you stuffed me into your saddlebag." She shot a teasing smile his way. "The weather is lovely, and Cade and Amaranth are way ahead of us. I do not like losing a race to my mother."

"This is not a race, and a woman with a bairn on the way shouldna ride at a hard gallop, ye ken? Especially not my beloved wife." He added a hard scowl to the scolding, and she laughed, making it impossible not to smile back at her. The brisk touch of autumn in the air had her eyes sparkling and her cheeks rosy. He couldn't deny it was indeed a beautiful day, and after years of trials and unhappiness, the future looked a great deal brighter.

"Isn't that the spot where we camped after you rescued me?" She pointed at a break in an overgrowth of trees ablaze with brilliant shades of crimson, orange, and yellow. "Shall we stop and let the horses rest a bit? Get all of us a drink from the spring?"

"Have ye forgotten the steep sides of that gully?" That was the first time he had ever swept her up into his arms and carried her. He had fallen in love with the feel of her against his chest at that very moment.

"What about up ahead? Could the horses reach the water if we ride on a bit farther?"

"Aye, veer to the northeast a bit and we can water them and ourselves."

"Look!" Jovianna pointed in that direction. "Cade and Amaranth had the same idea."

Tobias eyed the pair of horses meandering where the burn he had in mind should be. "Jovianna, wait." Relief flooded him when she immediately pulled her mount to a halt, then urged it closer to him.

"What is it?" She squinted at the riderless horses in the distance. "Aren't those Cade and Amaranth's mounts? They're the same color."

"Aye, but they're smaller. Those are not Amaranth and Cade's beasts." After a subtle tip of his head toward the trees to their left, he waited until Jovianna headed that way, then urged his horse to follow. When they reached cover, he dismounted and helped her down from the saddle, keeping himself between her and the horses that looked too much like the pair from his own stable to comfort him. Instinct warned it was a trap. And he'd bet his favorite dagger it was Tellerston, his men, or both.

"They knew we'd come this way," Jovianna whispered while peeping around him. Then she stepped out from behind him. "But what about Cade and Amaranth? Do you think they allowed them to pass safely?"

"I dinna ken, m'love." He had wondered the same.

"They couldn't have known that we all wouldn't ride together. Or that we wouldn't be in the lead instead of Amaranth and Cade."

"Aye, but all they needed were horses to draw our attention," Tobias explained. "The coloring of that pair resembles our mounts as well. Their intent was to get us to stop for whatever reason we chose."

"We can't ride on without knowing Amaranth and Cade are safe for sure." She moved deeper into the woods, forlornly peering over the edge of the much shallower bank.

"We canna know for certain until we reach the manor and see them." If Jovianna wasn't with him, Tobias would spring the trap and take care of the bastards in short order. But with her with him, he daren't risk it, and with so much cover, so many places for the wretches to hide and spring even more wickedness upon them, he couldn't leave her side while he forced them into the open. There was but one choice—retreat and take another route home. "We must go back, Jovianna, and take another way."

"But what about Cade and Amaranth?" The pleading in her eyes squeezed his heart near to bursting. "We can't leave them."

"We dinna even know if they are here, m'love." He held out his hand. "Come. Trust them to God until we reach home and know for certain. If we discover then that they never arrived, I'll take a host of men with me to find them. I swear it."

"But it's my mother."

"And if Tellerston and his men do indeed hold them, what can the two of us do to save them? What, Jovianna?" He hated to be so cruel, but there was no other way. "I have but one pistol, a sword, and a trio of daggers. I willna risk yer life. Please try to understand."

Tears welled in her eyes, but to his immense relief, she nodded. But rather than take his hand, she pulled herself into his arms and pressed her cheek to his chest. "I understand, but I am so afraid for them."

"I know, m'love," he whispered into her hair. "I know."

The sharp click of a pair of pistols being cocked made him go motionless, then unleashed an uncontrollable rage within him. Tobias lifted his head and bared his teeth at Matthew Tellerston. "Leave her be. This is betwixt ourselves. Not her."

"Oh no." Tellerston spat to one side while keeping his flint-locks trained upon them. "It's 'twixt all of us, by my reckoning. When I visited Jamison afore the trial, he told me about that cunning bitch of yers. The both of ye cost me more coin and land than I cared to lose."

Tobias slowly turned, shoving Jovianna behind him. As he pushed her back, he subtly yanked downward and prayed she would take the hint to drop to the ground. She did.

He lunged at Tellerston, fueling the leap with every ounce of hatred and rage he had ever possessed for the despicable man.

Eyes flaring wide and instinctively swaying back a step, Tellerston fired both pistols and missed. Tobias hit him with enough force to send the man onto his back. Before the fiend recovered, Tobias was on him, driving his knee into the devil's gut as he closed his hands around Tellerston's neck until the satisfying crackle of bones snapping filled the air. Dazed by bloodlust, Tobias took a moment to pick up on the sound of sobbing. Jovianna. Had one shot found her?

He jumped to his feet and ran to her, sliding to his knees beside her. Blood. There was blood. "God in heaven, no. Where, Jovianna? Where are ye hurt?"

Her right hand bloodied, she dove into his arms, either laughing or crying hysterically. He couldn't tell which.

"You're all right," she sobbed. "The other bullet didn't hit you?"

He peeled her away, frantic to discover her welfare. Then he noticed a wetness in his hand where he clutched her left shoulder. Without hesitating, he ripped her jacket and the sleeve of her shift away from her side. There on her upper arm, close to her shoulder, was a bloody furrow the shot had left behind.

"A deep grazing, but a grazing just the same," he said. "Praise God Almighty. Are ye hurt anywhere else? The bairn. Is the bairn all right?"

"I feel a little woozy." She swiped a hand across her eyes, then hooked a hand around his neck and pulled him into a hug. "Just hold me so I know you're all right. Just hold me. I can't believe he missed you. I can't believe it."

Cradling her in one arm, he wadded up the part of her shift

he'd torn away and pressed it to her wound. "I am all right, m'love. Even better now that I know ye're safe."

"Do you think he acted alone?" she asked between pulling in and blowing out deep breaths.

"I feel sure he did. If not, they all wouldha been upon us rather than just him. They probably left him back in Edinburgh when they realized he could no longer pay them." He kissed her forehead as he carefully lifted the cloth to check the bleeding. The tear was deep. She'd be needing some of Mrs. Gibb's stitchery. "Are ye strong enough to make it to the water's edge where we can rinse this and get ye a cool cloth to ease ye?" Her pallor concerned him.

"I'm a little queasy at the moment." She swallowed hard as though trying not to retch, then lunged away from him and vomited. "Blood doesn't usually bother me," she said between heaves.

"Aye, well, when it's yer own, it can sometimes be different." He held her steady, cringing in sympathy with each of her gagging retches.

She straightened and swiped the back of her hand across her mouth. "I feel so much better now."

"It eases my heart to hear it." He cast a glance toward the water. "Shall I carry ye down there so ye can rinse yer mouth while I tend to yer shoulder?"

She smiled and allowed him to steady her as she got to her feet. "No. I'll let you off easy this time—but stay close. I'm still a bit wobbly."

"Ye couldna beat me away with a stick, woman." Slowly, he helped her down to the water's edge and helped her sit on the trunk of an uprooted tree wedged between the banks by a passing storm. He filled his cupped hands with water and helped her drink before rinsing out the piece of her shift and using it to clean her wound.

"It can't be." She pushed away his hands as she rose and made her way to the tree's gnarl of roots. Then she crouched and pulled on something deep within them.

"What is it? Jovianna?"

When she straightened, she held a middling-sized bundle in one hand and an indescribable oddity in the other. Whatever it was, it had a black strap attached to a strange box encrusted with moss and mud.

Tobias went to her, catching her when she stumbled to one side. He guided her back to the trunk and helped her sit, since she seemed unable to take her gaze from the things she had found. "Jovianna."

She looked up at him and blinked as if suddenly realizing he was still there.

"My love." He leaned closer and spoke slowly. "What are these?"

"My things," she said in a tone that worried him. "I found my things." Leeriness filled her eyes as she hugged the bundle and oddity with the straps close without taking her gaze from his. "Tobias…"

"Aye?"

"Are you absolutely certain that you love me no matter what?" Fear replaced the leeriness in her eyes, and her tears broke free and cascaded down.

"My precious love, why would ye ask me such a thing?"

"Because what I am about to show you will not make any sense." She managed a weak shrug with her uninjured arm. "I don't even understand how it can be, and neither does my mother, and she's the smartest person I've ever known."

Perhaps the day had taken its toll on his sweet woman. He knelt beside her. "I love ye, Jovianna. I swear it, my own."

After a hesitant nod, she struggled with the strange, muddy bundle for a moment, then peeled open one of its flaps and reached inside. She rummaged in its depths, chewing her bottom lip all the while. "There. This should have a legible date." She held out a colorful metal cylinder sealed at both ends. After turning it in her hands, she offered him the end that had swelled out like a wee drum. "Can you make out what it says there? It's a little faded from all it has been through."

"Sealed on…" He stared at the dark blue script, then wiped his thumb across it and stared closer. A heart-stopping chill washed across him. Those numbers could not possibly be so. "What is that printed after *May*?"

"The date." Jovianna dug into the bag again. "Here is another with a different month and day, but the same year."

He swiveled around off his knees and plopped down onto his arse. "2023?" He stared up at her. "How is that possible?"

"Because I was born on July 31, 1991," she said. "I was a professor of history at the University of Glasgow, and Amaranth was a successful and noted archeologist in 2023. She and I took a Saturday outing to Finnich Glen and somehow traveled back in time during a flash flood. It washed us to the Devil's Pulpit. Where you found us." She picked up the muddy little box with the straps and made it click. An unholy beam of light, brighter than a thousand candle flames, shot out of its center. She smiled. "I guess the automatic shut-off still works." She stared at him, silently pleading for understanding.

"Ye come from the future?" He stared back down at the strange, waterlogged cylinder. What she just said could not possibly be true, and yet—she had the evidence. The dates on the metal. The box possessing the light of the sun itself. "The future," he repeated.

"That's how I knew about the potatoes," she said. "And that on October twenty-fifth of this year, King George II will die."

"I remember ye saying the king dies."

She nodded. "Lord George Murray dies in the Netherlands on October eleventh. I'm sure Cade will remember him, since he was one of Bonnie Prince Charlie's commanders. But as I told you before, Cumberland doesn't die until 1765. The Old Pretender dies in 1766."

He swallowed hard, staring into the eyes of this woman he loved more than life itself. This woman who could be a witch, an angel, or a demon. But he didn't care. She still owned him, heart and soul. "When do I die?"

She offered him a cringing shrug. "That, I do not know. Thankfully, I can't remember reading anything about Tobias Risk. Or his brother. Or the earls of Grampian."

"Yet Jamison died by hanging," he whispered. "And I live on with an heir on the way."

"I'm sure when Amaranth and I came to the past, we changed history." She fumbled with the end of another cylinder, made it pop, then sniffed at the small, round opening she'd just revealed. "Would you like a drink of canned water?" She offered him a sad smile. "Single-use plastics pollute our oceans in the future, so I never use them if I can help it."

"What the hell are *single-use plastics*?" The words felt strange on his tongue.

"An invention that is both a blessing and a curse." She rose from her seat, moved to the muddy edge of the bank, dropped to her knees, and started digging.

"What are ye doing now?" he asked.

"Burying these things," she said without looking back. "If I don't, someone might find them. It might change the future for the worse."

"Ye're making yer arm bleed more. Stop, m'love." He hurried to her side and pulled her away. "Here. Hold the rag on yer wound. I'll bury the things for ye." He didn't fully understand why he needed to do so, but if she needed it done, it would be done. Once he had everything covered over and hidden with stones, he turned back to where she knelt at the water's edge. As he had dug, the realization hit that it all made sense. Her strange words. Her prophetic dreams. She and her mother traveling through the Highlands unescorted. No murdered cousin's body. "Why have ye never told me this before?"

"Because I didn't want you to think me crazed or a witch." She dampened the bloody rag again and pressed it back against her arm.

He stared at her. A terrible dread churned in his gut. Might she someday leave him and go back to the future? "Do ye ken how to return to yer time?"

"No. And I wouldn't go even if I could."

"Why?"

She rose from the water and went to him, resting her hand on his chest with a gentleness that threatened to take him to his knees. "Because I love you more than I ever thought I could love anyone. I can't imagine living without you."

He caught her close and buried his face in her hair. "I am glad, my own, because I would hate to have to come after ye and drag ye back here."

She hugged him tighter. "I love you, Tobias."

"And I love ye more, my own."

EPILOGUE

Late May 1761
Risk Lands northeast of Loch Lomond
Scotland

BAREFOOT AND WEARING nothing but his oldest léine and a grubby pair of trews rolled up above his knees, Tobias set his shoulder against the crossbar between the curved wooden handles of the mired-up plow. He had thought Pag had better sense than to try working a muddy field. After one last hard shove from him and a long, steady pull from Pag's weary beast, the plow was free. Tobias rubbed his shoulder, glaring at Pag as the lad coaxed the shaggy Highland cow into dragging the farm tool to more solid ground.

"Master Tobias! I mean...Lord Tobias! Lord Tobias!" Tildy Grace's piercing shouts came to him before he ever spotted her. He turned toward the call and shielded his eyes from the sun. The wee lassie topped the hill, running hard, her arms churning at her sides. "Bairn's a coming! Lord Tobias, the bairn's a coming!"

Tobias's heart leaped. He wallowed free of the field as fast as he could. "Tildy Grace, fetch my boots over there." He soused his hands and then his feet in the water trough, sloughing off layers of mud.

Tildy handed him his boots, then clapped her hands. "Hurry—Lady Jovianna's scared. She sent me to fetch ye. She's afeared the bairn will come while she's alone."

Tobias hopped sideways while yanking on his boots, unable to believe what the child had just said. "Alone? Where are Mrs. Gibb and Amaranth? Have Telfa and Maudie been fetched?"

The wee one wrung her hands in her apron, her troubled expression pleading for mercy. "Lady Jovianna and me was bringing ye some of the bread we fried. She wanted to walk here from the manor to help the bairn decide to come. And it did."

More terror than he had ever known filled him. Tobias grabbed the child by the shoulders and struggled not to shout. "Where is she?"

"At the mossy oaks, and she bade me tell ye to hurry. Said to tell ye her water's done come out."

"Dear God in heaven protect them." Tobias crossed himself, then cupped his hands around his mouth and bellowed, "Pag! Find a wagon! Now!" He crouched back to Tildy's level. "Run to the manor house. Fetch the women, aye?"

The child took off again at a hard run.

Thankfully, or perhaps not, the mossy oaks weren't far. What in heaven's name had possessed Jovianna to walk so far from the manor house, when she knew damn good and well the bairn could come at any time, was beyond him. Tobias leaped into the saddle and rode hard toward the trio of mighty oaks growing in a secluded dip in the rolling hillside. Some said the place was sacred and that druids once chanted their mysteries to the powers in ancient times at the spot. Three magnificent oak trees, their gnarled root systems intertwined like clasping hands, forming a circle. Within that circle of exposed roots grew moss that was a deeper green than the finest emerald.

Jovianna was inside it, bent double and holding tight to a knobby root. "Please wait," she groaned down at her belly. "You're the first and not supposed to come so fast."

"Jovianna!" Tobias jumped from the saddle before his mount fully stopped. He ran to her side and suddenly felt more useless and helpless than he ever had in his life. "Jovianna."

"You keep saying that." With her eyes closed, she panted and gripped the root so tightly that her nails dug into it. "Do not scold me. Now is not the time."

"I willna scold ye, m'love." He wiped the sweat from her forehead and swept her hair back out of her eyes. "Hold fast, aye? Pag's finding a wagon, and Tildy's gone to fetch the women."

"Hold fast?" She shot him a murderous glare and bared her teeth like an enraged beast. "Tell your child to hold fast. I have no control over this situation." Then her face crumpled and she let out a pitiful wail. "I don't know what I'm doing. I can't have this baby here. Alone." She flipped a dismissive wave his way. "You don't know what to do any more than I do."

"I ken what to do," he lied. "I've helped when the mares foal, and during the lambing too."

She cut him another narrow-eyed look. "Really? You're comparing me to horses and sheep at a time like this?"

Thank the Lord in heaven he hadn't mentioned working with the sows when the piglets came. Panic filled him as she tensed with another pain, bending double and swaying as she bore it.

"Scream it out, love. Bellow at the pain ripping through ye." He wasn't sure if that helped or not. Wounded men had done it during the war when the healers came. It seemed to help them.

Instead, she panted and blew as she went down into a deeper squat while still clinging to the sturdy tree root for support. "I don't know for sure, but I don't think it's going to be much longer. Everything feels…a lot…lower."

Tobias ripped off his léine and turned it the wrong side out so the cleanest part would be against his child. "Tell me when ye're ready. I'll move yer skirts out the way and catch the wee one."

She nodded, this time gasping to catch her breath as she rested her forehead on her arm. "Everyone said the first one would take forever. Days of labor, even." She huffed a weary snort.

"This one has decided today is the day, and they're bloody well running for it." She lifted her head, pulled in a deep breath through her nose, and blew it out her mouth. "Get ready."

Tobias shoved her skirts up out of the way and tucked the ends into the back of her neckline to keep them from falling back down. The sight of his dear one's pale, wet legs trembling with traces of blood filled him with guilt for putting her through this. Sweat ran into his eyes and burned as Jovianna groaned and squatted lower. A wee head crowned with hair as black as coal.

"I see the babe, my love. Ye're doing it. Ye're nearly there." He moved closer, ready to support the child as it emerged.

"Now," she roared as she squatted deeper and groaned.

The tiny, squirming miracle slid into his hands. He gently turned the wonder and laughed. "We have a fine son, dear wife!"

"He should be crying. Is he all right?" Gasping for breath, she slowly turned and leaned back against the monstrous knot of roots.

As Tobias dried the wee one's red face, his new son growled with indignation and filled the air with his angry cries. "Listen to him," he said as he placed the baby in her arms. "Strong and fierce."

Jovianna smiled down at the babe, then hitched forward and frowned. "Take him. Something's wrong."

With his son cradled in one arm, Tobias knelt beside her as she slid farther down onto the moss. "Jovianna? Jovianna, daren't ye leave me. Hold on until the others get here."

"I'm having another pain," she groaned while pushing herself back up to the roots. "Why?"

"I dinna ken, m'love." Tobias gently laid his son safely on the moss, then turned back to her and held her hand.

"We're here!" Tildy shouted over the rattling of wagons.

"Thanks be to God." Tobias wiped the sweat from Jovianna's forehead as she squatted and rocked in place.

"Take the baby to them," she gasped, rocking faster. "Keep the baby safe."

"I willna leave yer side."

"Do it!" She squeezed his hand as though trying to hurt him. "Take care of our son!"

His heart torn, Tobias scooped up his child and hurried to the women climbing out of the wagon. "Go to her! Something is wrong."

Amaranth ran to her daughter's side. Mrs. Gibb and Telfa, the midwife, followed.

Pag and Fitch flanked him, turning him so his back was to the terrible scene below.

"Son or daughter?" Fitch asked, keeping his arm around Tobias's shoulders.

"My son." Tobias tucked the linens closer around the fretting babe.

Another strong wail from the circle of oaks made him lift his head and turn. He strode back to the mossy cradle just as Jovianna sagged back, smiling. She gave him a weary smile and held up two fingers.

"Two?" He drew closer as Amaranth rose into view with another squirming bundle.

"Congratulations, Papa." She angled the wee one so he could peer into its little face. "Two sons."

"Two sons," he repeated in an awe-filled whisper.

Telfa took the other babe from him and gave him a stern scowl. "That isna how ye wrap a new bairn." Then she smiled. "Go to yer braw wife while I straighten this wee laddie's swaddling."

"Two sons," he said yet again as he knelt beside Jovianna. His heart threatened to burst, and emotions tied themselves into a choking knot in his throat.

"I'm as surprised as you." Jovianna wearily reached out and took his hand. "Good job delivering the first one. I guess we both kind of panicked with the second."

"Horses and sheep are nothing compared to this." He kissed her hand, aching to scoop her up into his arms and hold her against his chest but afraid to do so. "I love ye, my own."

"I love you." She offered a sheepish look. "And I'm sorry I got a bit snarly."

"Ye were hard at work, my own. Ye had every right, and I beg yer forgiveness for being such an unhelpful fool."

She barely shook her head. "You weren't unhelpful. You were perfect."

"And what shall we call these two fine young lads?" Amaranth asked. She held them both, one in each arm, and divided adoring smiles between them.

Jovianna squeezed his hand. "What are their names, husband?"

Tobias shook his head. Never again would he consider a woman weak. Not after what he had just witnessed. "I dinna have the right to name this blessed pair. That honor belongs to their courageous mother who brought them into this world."

"Alec and Alistair, then," Jovianna said, without hesitation. "Their names mean defenders of mankind. We'll raise them to care for and protect their people just as their father always has."

"Perfect." Tobias leaned forward, tenderly kissed her forehead, then scooped her up into his arms and cradled her against his chest. "Now to get my precious family home."

Jovianna smiled and leaned her head against his shoulder. "Are you going to carry me the whole way, or are we riding in the wagon?"

He kissed her again. "I havena decided yet. Ye feel quite nice in my arms."

"It is nice," she said while snuggling closer. "And there is nowhere else I would rather be."

About the Author

If you enjoyed DELIGHTING HER HIGHLAND DEVIL, please consider leaving a review on the site where you purchased your copy, or a reader site such as Goodreads, or BookBub.

If you'd like to receive my newsletter, here's the link to sign up:
maevegreyson.com/contact.html#newsletter

I love to hear from readers! Drop me a line at
maevegreyson@gmail.com

Or visit me on Facebook:
facebook.com/AuthorMaeveGreyson

Join my Facebook Group – Maeve's Corner:
facebook.com/groups/MaevesCorner

I'm also on Instagram:
maevegreyson

My website:
https://maevegreyson.com

Feel free to ask questions or leave some Reader Buzz on
bingebooks.com/author/maeve-greyson

Goodreads:
goodreads.com/maevegreyson

Follow me on these sites to get notifications about new releases, sales, and special deals:

Amazon:
amazon.com/Maeve-Greyson/e/B004PE9T9U

BookBub:
bookbub.com/authors/maeve-greyson

Many thanks and may your life always be filled with good books!
Maeve

Ingram Content Group UK Ltd.
Milton Keynes UK
UKHW020708120723
424996UK00015B/363